Age of Shadows: The story of Timothy Jay Green

Table of Contents

By placeholder
Copyright page

First edition August 2024
Published by Draft 2 Digital from Placeholder
Ageofshadowsbusiness@gmail.com

Dedication page

First and foremost, I dedicate this story to the reader in hopes that I will entertain and that I will inspire.

I would like to give thanks to my editor Olivia, who pushed me into making my dreams a reality.

I would like to thank my dear wife, who gives me hope that my writings might touch the hearts of those who read them.

I would like to thank my mother; the foundation for which inspires me to work as hard as I can to fulfill my dreams.

And finally, in loving memory of my grandfather whose words I will truly never forget: "You made this Hijo? Keep at it... keep writing, and you will go far." -Manuel

Prologue: Descent

Have you ever wondered of our universe? Have you ever pondered the expansive infinite possibility that lies beyond our reach? Imagine if you could. Calculate if you can. Fathom all that there would be past our universe. Into the furthest reaches of our multiverse. Into a multiplied Infinity, repetitively stacking tremendously in all directions. I would like to tell you a story of a single universe within our vast multiverse. in the sprawling expanse of our multiverse is one so close to ours yet with an unfolding reality far different.

In our universe in the year 2012 it was but a changing of the calendar. Marked only by a mass hysteria and an annotation of the end of the world. In this mirrored universe, however, it in fact did have warnings of cataclysmic events on the horizon. And much like our universe there's would be far too unprepared for the things to come. In this alternate universe it was during the first month of the year 2012 that their world would nearly meet its end. Half of mankind overnight would be slaughtered in a ruthless planetary invasion by a coalition named: The War Council, which consisted of four alien species, them being: the Gharials, the Sedgebulls, the Cubozoans, and the Canis-mambas.

A collective that would travel from planet to planet taking anything they would see as valuable and decimating their populations. Invisible to the naked eye, they would bombard the earth with inconceivable weaponry destroying large portions of Russia and the United States overnight. Surreptitiously, producing two enormous craters where there were once strong militaristic forces present.

Immediately following the aftermath of the explosions, the world stood at a standstill unaware of our extraterrestrial invasion. With the world's leaders quickly placing the blame on one another, each side eagerly prepared to go into a hellish war.

Amidst the chaos, certain government agencies discovered abnormalities in areas above northern Africa as well as southern Asia. Undergoing various detection methods, these government agencies discovered cloaked bombs levitating above similarly important military bases, in China as well as India, and what appeared to be a gargantuan flying object in a northern trajectory toward Europe.

Once notified and without hesitation, Russian and Chinese military forces unleashed a barrage of ballistic missiles at the yet-to-be-identified aircraft, while the U.S. government was still contemplating a method to either communicate with or attack the invading UFO.

Russian missiles struck with a direct hit to the located aircraft first, with a sizable nuclear warhead. Yet it remained unmoved from its point of origin. The only known damage was that of a disruption in the cloaking device that surrounded the ship.

On the second impact, China's warheads also landed a direct blow, in-turn, the aircraft shook and spat out clouds of black smoke. They hadn't destroyed it, but they did affect a part of it causing it to crash down to earth in Egypt. United Nations military forces and surrounding militaries then created a perimeter around the aircraft. Demands were spoken for the invading force to surrender, which were made in various languages and symbolic sequences. Silence, however, was the only thing to quickly fill the air.

Hours had passed and there was still no response from the mysterious vessel. All attempts to see inside the ship failed. Some believed it to be nothing but an unmanned spaceship, due to its bizarre, unearthly design. Onlooker's beliefs turned out to be sorely mistaken as soon as the spacecraft opened a multitude of large doors. As the doors eerily unbolted the desert came alive, erupting with ravenous guttural croaks and hissing that ground against the ears of the waiting soldiers. The sky went black with millions of flying aliens vomiting down blistering acid that dissolved anything in sight into a green gelatinous slosh.

Their army was brutal and relentless, with numbers that showed them as never-ending waves, raging onto humanity, crushing earth's forces as if they were dealing with mere insects. Their towering bodies and monstrous appearances paralyzing even the most experienced of soldiers. Outnumbered, even on the home front of earth, humanity was increasingly outmatched by the power, numbers, and technology of these new enemies. In the first weeks of their invasion, the casualties ranged in the billions. Families were torn apart, and the world was thrust into utter calamity as mankind tried desperately to ensure its survival.

Throughout the struggles, a spark of hope was lit, which gave way to humanity's turn of the invasion. Rising from the shadows of their battered world what few resistances remained, fought off the invading forces exploiting their weaknesses of greed and brashness which would topple their bravado and helped the survivors save what was left of humanity. Only a few smaller vessels of the “Mudlurks” were able to evade and make it off the earth. "Mudlurks" being the slur the survivors of the invasion would begin to call them, because of their habits of digging through waste in an insatiable urge to collect what they sought as treasurable. After the invasion retreated it took 30 long years of rebuilding.

Through the grueling years, humanity grew closer to a unified government and purpose. Using the remains of the Mudlurks devices and spacecraft they advanced their technology and understanding of space travel. With that, their thirst for revenge shot them outward to the vast emptiness of space that was followed by earth's largest reconnaissance mission a force of 6.5 million troops, with a plan to find out as much as they could and hopefully gather the perfect strategy to overpower their world.

However, Upon the arrival of their solar system, those on the reconnaissance mission realized how overwhelming the Mudlurks truly were. Not only was their planet ten times the size of earth but the initial invasion on earth was by a single ship. Their planet had billions, which were even reported to block out the sun. All of them were ready for what was reported to be a second invasion of the earth. What followed suit was a near massacre as in the first ten hours their outnumbered fleet was down to the last 2 million troops. And although they had bested a number of the Mudlurks fleet, their onslaught was too insurmountable.

They had jammed all signals, leaving seemingly no hope of reinforcements, let alone warning to be sent to earth of the coming doom. Until, coming from behind the remaining reconnaissance fleet, blazing in-between humanity's fleet and the Mudlurks was a gigantic Galactic cruiser. Followed swiftly by an armada of 12 different species that would call themselves the Alliance. In the coming months an enormous battle transpired and although humanity's fleet had sustained heavy losses, humans along with the help of the Alliance were able to not only detour the secondary invasion, but also force the remaining Mudlurks off-world.

What little forces remained helped the Alliance in several critical dog fights that were necessary wins. With this, the Alliance offered a place in their ranks and societies, and in two years humanity unanimously agreed and became the 13th species to join the Alliance. What followed was a time of growth and expansion never seen before in human history. The Intergalactic Renaissance had begun. Not only had humans avenged the invasion of earth, but they had joined with completely new species and ways of life and because of this humanity began to travel throughout the stars, with themselves no longer earthbound.

However, not everyone ventured into the stars, many stayed with the earth to grow what had been damaged. One of these families would grow the Nie Fallen Corporation focusing on Galactic travel, human cultural expansion, as well as safe mining in the outer systems. The grandson as well as the successor to the Nie Fallen Corporation is Timothy Jay Green, and this is his story.

| Page

Chapter 1: Anguish

June/9/2046

34 years after the invasion of Earth

They had been shouting for some time now. And Timmy knew better than to interrupt his father while he was working. So, he stayed outside of his office pacing back and forth until the shouting had stopped. He waited a minute, his hand on the door handle, wanting to make sure the arguing had finished. The door creaked slightly as Andrew rubbed his forehead in irritation.

"Dad?" Timmy's timid, soft voice called from behind him. His father turned with a smile; any sign of annoyance gone from his face as he looked at his son.

"Hey bud, thanks for waiting, I'm sorry you had to hear all that..." He answered with a tired sigh. Before saying anything else he noticed the look of fear in his son's eyes. "Oh, Timothy..." Sighing and frowning slightly, he patted the chair beside him. "Come here bud, sit in your chair. I didn't mean for that stuff to scare you. I should know better than to bring my heavier work out of the office." Timmy walked over to his father sitting up on the smaller rolling chair, spinning it side to side still not looking up at his father.

"It wasn't the shouting." He said sniffling. "It- it was the news ... about the war." he said, nearly whispering at the end of his sentence.

"Oh, I see..." Andrew said, rolling his chair closer to Timmy. "Listen, I understand the war can be scary, especially how the news shows it, but you have nothing to fear." He gently reached out, rubbing Timmy's shoulders, giving him a comforting smile. "The war is thousands of light-years away. With millions of Alliance home worlds and defensive fleets between the war and us." He put his arm around Timmy and pulled him in for a hug.

Timmy's face lessened in sadness as he wiped his nose. “Hey, it's okay to be afraid though bud, it's natural.” Timmy looked up at his father for a moment before lowering his head again.

"But Blake said he wasn't afraid..." He said, looking away again, turning himself slightly back and forth in the chair.

"Well..." Andrew started leaning back in his chair giving a slight smirk. "He wouldn't be much of a big brother if he was, now, would he?"

Timmy looked up at his father, thinking about it. "And besides I'm sure he's afraid of some things and I'm also sure he'd never tell you that either." Andrew said with a chuckle before adding. "Think about the soldiers on the frontlines or the people who fought off and survived through the invasion. They had never seen anything like the Mudlurks before."

“I'm sure they were scared. Heck from what I've heard people weren't even sure humanity could come back from the invasion.” He concluded stretching his back and giving a light sigh from exhaustion, Andrew looked at all his blueprints and sketches which were taped and pinned along his walls, models of his creations hanging from strings and propped up on shelves.

He stood up, continuing his gaze around his office until a glimmer shined in his eye, the very thing he wanted to show Timmy. He walked over to the model, picking it up off the shelf and tilting it, examining it and all its features. “Do you know what makes someone overcome their fear?" He asked, not expecting a response. Timmy's father continued. "Some might say it is bravery, others' strength. But do you want to know what I believe? I believe it is hope... Hope gave the soldiers who fought off the invasion the idea that people would survive and that they would thrive and live through the horrors. We have hope that one day the war will be over so that people won't have to fight to survive, it's that hope that makes the soldiers fight on the front lines, it's that hope that gives them the bravery to face their fears head-on..." Andrew said with a captivating infectious passion. "That everlasting natural desire that resides within all of humanity. The desire to seek happiness, safety, and a better tomorrow. It's our hope in those things that drive us forward."

He held the model closely, giving a smile. "So, do you know what you need to do Timothy? You need to find that hope. Use it to build your strength and bravery to stand up to any of your fears. Use it so that you never run away from what you fear, but to run at it, to overcome it." Timmy looked up at his father smiling at his resolve. Andrew turned, smiling back at his son walking over and sitting back down now with the model in hand. "Do you know what makes me hopeful, Timothy? It's you, and your brother, you two prodigies of your mother and me! Our perfect creations. So much smarter and inventive than either of us could ever be." He said holding the model more into view.

Timmy's eyes lit up seeing the model. The model was none other than a Starship created by his father, its silver shimmer glistening excellently. Eyes wide Timmy took in every detail of its sleek shape. Mirrored on both halves of the ship so it could face either direction. Timmy's father called it, Charon.

"You went with Blake's design!" Timmy exclaimed.

"Not only that." His father replied.

Pressing a button on the top opening it horizontally showing off the inside, like a blueprint it clearly outlined that it carried two control rooms, a living quarters, a food production area and finally a power room that was specifically designed by Timmy himself.

"My idea! The one I had to add an entire section of the ship for cooling!" Timmy exclaimed, Andrew smiling at his response. "Thief!" Timmy shouted, snatching the model, and taking a closer look.

"ha-ha I'm sorry, was I not supposed to?" Andrew laughed.

Timmy continued looking over the model as he hummed to himself.

"It comes at a price." Timmy said. Andrew cocked an eyebrow before asking.

"Oh, and what might that be?" Timmy hesitated as he quietly murmured.

"No shot tonight?" looking up at his father with soft pleading eyes.

"Ah, anything else I might have said yes. That on the other hand you shouldn't have reminded me of." He said, as he checked his watch.

"You should go get your brother, it's time for you boys to get your shot." Timmy pouted, getting up and handing the model back to his father before walking off grumbling, "Okay."

"Hurry up now so we can go out to eat tonight, your mother and I wanted to talk to you two about something." His father said as he ushered Timmy out. Timmy's mother meanwhile was already getting ready for tonight's outing, while his brother had been working on another one of his paintings. The day moved on turning quickly to night and all thoughts of the war had once again drifted from Timmy's mind, now only centered on his favorite place to eat.

It was an old-fashioned diner, plucked straight out of the 1950s. Pulling up to the front would show its barrel-vaulted roofline with a dazzling neon pink light seen from blocks away. Before even having a glimpse of the "Josh's Diner" name which was emboldened and showcased right above the glass doors at the front entrance of the local family-owned diner.

Shining checkered floors under bright ruby red leather stools lined across the counter that stood in front of the prepping station. Matching the stools, and red booths that laid vertically against the large windows. The waitresses had their uniforms, black with white collars, cuffs, and aprons with the food being the cherry on top for the Greens.

"Simple, Americana, and delicious." As Andrew always stated. Timmy had always felt comfortable being in a restaurant that wasn't for his family "the normal" extravagant restaurant where he'd have to dress up; Timmy despised that, choosing instead to dress casually and comfortably.

Adding to the day was the fact that his parents were finally talking about putting him and his brother into a public school. His brother was already on a football team, but this was what they had wanted to make them finally out of their private life. His worries of being home-taught and growing up with no friends, and that he'd be treated differently would soon be a thing of the past.

The Greens celebrated by staying a little longer than they normally would, ending their time at the diner with a little dessert. Timmy having a rich chocolate lava cake served with vanilla ice cream on top. Timmy scarfed it down while his brother treated himself to his football team's favorite treat a root beer float. Eventually, after the boys had finished their desserts, the Greens began to make their way to their car. It had been raining for a while, but the rain became a downpour once they began to depart from the diner.

When leaving, Timmy's love for the rain controlled him and in a bit of childish fervor he splashed around in the puddles that had quickly surrounded the front of the diner with the rest of the Greens already by the car. After realizing that Timmy wasn't with them, his mother sent his brother off to go get him. His mother called out to him; her voice slightly muffled by the rain but still Timmy could hear her as she shouted in a loving tone. "Timothy!"

He turned quickly, hearing her as he saw his brother running back across the street to him. In an instant, the sound of falling rain was obliterated and combined with a flaring light that blinded Timmy as he was wrapped in an unbearably uncomfortable warmth. Shutting his eyes reactively, he was suddenly rocketed off his feet and flung back onto the sidewalk.

A wave of pain was shot across his back and arms as he tried to brace for his fall. He rolled back laying on his stomach, his skin peeled where he had slid across the sidewalk. A bitter taste of iron roamed in his mouth which lingered and mixed with the leftover taste of chocolate. He slowly lifted himself, struggling at first but eventually being able to sit up. He turned dazed slowly regaining his composure, looking over to where his family had once been, the area now engulfed in flames with only the outline of the scorched car being visible.

The world trembled, filled with a ringing that pulsed in his ears. Slowly fading until all he could hear was screaming. Panicked, he shifted his head looking for the location of the screaming only to be met with the realization that the world was not shaking, and no one was screaming aside from him. He got to his knees in a struggle as he looked on at the scene before him. Tears rushed down his face faster than the cold rain could hit the ground.

He noticed lying in the street only a few feet away from him was his brother. He tried to stand but stumbled, simply falling back down onto his hands and knees. Pain etched across his face, as he crawled, limping slowly to him, nearly collapsing with anguish as he reached his brother. Unable to speak he only despairingly forced his brother's name to pop into his mind.

He extended his hand to his brothers smoking and blistering back. Touching it and immediately recoiling from the heat. He tried to speak but nothing came other than whimpers and the sound of himself catching his crying. Trying again, his voice whispered out.

"B-Blake ... Blake..." as he tried desperately to raise his trembling voice. "Blake please... we gotta go check on mom and dad, I... maybe they... they need our help." He said through tears.

He tried again to touch his brother but again the heat burned him. This time, however, he endured trying to shake him which brought nothing. Timmy got up his strength coming back as he paced back-and-forth now sopping wet from the still coming rain. His coldness seeped under his skin as he was unprotected, alone now. And he could not shake the feeling of watching eyes, of an oddly inhuman sensation of being, hunted.

He grew anxious and the panic suffocated every step he took. He felt trapped in a box that was shrinking by the second as the weight of his drenched clothes anchored him down, sinking him until a loud alarm that wailed across the town sent him into a full-fledged panic attack. Causing him to burst into a sprint, afraid of what might be after him. He ran faster than he could comprehend as the rain pelted his face and body like sharp knives as he nearly slipped on the now slick surface he was running over.

He looked up, gathering his surroundings and halting immediately his body lunging forward as his momentum tried to yank him onward. Planting his feet still, he managed to stop just short of a cliff edge. There panting and gasping for air he looked out at the valley before him as thunder raged above him. He stood there taking in the valleys seemingly endless expanse making him feel evermore alone. Fierce emotions hammered in his chest, hitting him just as hard as the explosion had.

Lowering himself on the muddy gravel path beneath him. Exhausted, knowing the truth of what his life would be now made him cry again, sadness overtaking his fear as he wept. A sudden yet soft voice came from behind him.

"Sweetheart?" he flinched, startled by the new noise from the stranger behind him. "Hey, hey you okay there hun?" she asked, walking over, taking off her raincoat and wrapping it around Timmy.

Timmy tried inching away, but he was so tired he could barely move. "What are you doing out here all alone?" she asked, looking up from him momentarily as she tried to find who Timmy might have been with.

"T-the diner m-my family." the woman looked back at him with an equally concerned and puzzled look.

"What diner honey?" she asked, to which Timmy looked up and finally noticed his surroundings. He couldn't utter a word as he was completely at a loss as to where he was and how he had got there. He had run to a park and the stranger, who was a nature photographer, noticed him just as she had reached the top of the hill. Her car had been close by, but Timmy panicked, refusing to go near the car.

So, she stood there out in the rain with him as she called the cops and waited for them to show up. They arrived quickly questioning Timmy, but he could barely speak, instead he only cried as he tried to tell them what had happened seemingly minutes ago. Again, Timmy feared for his life as the officers ushered him to their car. Eventually, he reluctantly agreed, but only after one of the cops reassured him.

He was shaking and crying even after the paramedics arrived. The officers questioned Timmy again, this time asking him his age and full name and where he had been last, followed by the officer calling in Timmy's information. After which Timmy noticed that the other officer was also questioning the woman who found him. Chatter from the officers' radio came through making Timmy snap to the sound. He listened hard to the small bits of what seemed to be another officer at the scene of where Timmy's family was.

Hearing the words "dead on arrival." Timmy's heart sank, lowering his head he held his tongue so as not to cry again. The officer in quick thinking silenced his radio, stopping Timmy from hearing anymore. Hurriedly the officer walked Timmy over to the paramedics who checked on him. The EMT's surprised to find nearly no injuries aside from what looked to be slight trauma to his arms and back. Still, they settled him in the ambulance taking him to the nearest hospital.

Hours had passed as Timmy sat in his hospital room; the doctors walked around puzzled as the trauma just recently seen by paramedics was now gone completely as if nothing had happened at all. The staff offered some food and drinks, but Timmy politely refused. Timmy's uncle B.G. would show after being contacted about the news. Taking him in as an investigation went underway while a closed casket funeral for Timmy's family followed quickly.

Timmy refused to speak for the entire process, instead he sat idly by his uncle until the caskets were laid in the ground and buried. There he sat by their graves for hours. Staring off to nothing, simply thinking to himself. He thought for a moment about whether there was something he could have done. Was it because of the people shouting at his father on the phone? Why didn't he die too? Questions he wanted the answers to but was sure he would never get.

Later he would inherit his parents' money and a spot on the board of the company. His age, however, made it so his uncle would oversee all his funds. His spot on the board would be held but only accessible once he turned 18. And so, with his money and uncle's approval, he continued to own his family's home and even renovated it slightly to what his family had wanted to change it to.

There he continued his father's work inventing things and improving on his existing projects all while keeping up to date on his family's case in a discreet manner. The shots his father gave him, replaced with antidepressants as he watched the case hit dead ends over and over until the investigators inevitably closed the case. Timmy's hope, crushed by the news, he laid in his parents' room as he wore his brother's oversized hoodie, he had felt at his lowest. Walking around his family's home he went into his father's office.

A place he had avoided entering even when trying to improve upon his father's creations. It still sat the way his father had left it that night. Looking in his father's office he noticed his computer was still plugged in. Curiosity got the best of him as he decided to look at what was on his father's computer. His eyes were immediately fixed on the flashing call log icon. He hesitated for a second before clicking on the app. Almost feeling someone would walk in and yell at him for being on it. It opened showing around ten missed calls from his uncle and a few other family friends.

He kept scrolling down until he reached something different; a contact labeled: 'Business.' Timmy stopped and his heart felt like it was being crumpled up as if it were a paper ball. The time was before they had gone to eat. *This was it. This was the last person or people who his father talked to. Could this have been what decided their deaths?* He sat pondering this, unable to move from his father's chair, unable to look away from the screen as he continued to look at the log.

"30 minutes. That's all it took. "

Anger rose and boiled its way to the surface erupting into fury as he slammed his fists onto his father's desk, shaking it, his mind whirled in rage until he heard the sound of something tumbling off his father's desk and hitting the floor. He looked down, noticing his father's model. It shined in its polished silver finish which caught Timmy's eyes just like his father before him. His eyes filled with tears as he clenched his teeth. He held back his cries looking at it, it being just as still as him and he remembered his loneliness, his depression, and his...anger.

He focused his gaze as his gritting teeth and quivering face changed to that of determination. He reached down and picked it up and held it to his chest. With this new wave of determination, he rose to his feet, as tears fled from his eyes. He would no longer cower in fear. No. His resolve would be to find who had taken his family so prematurely from him and bring them to justice.

With this new determination Timmy got to work starting with the contact he found. With his knowledge of different technologies used by his family's company, he was able to hack through using a type of spyware to find the location of the contact which luckily for him happened to be in the city. Staking out the location began with days turning into weeks until he noticed a pattern, which was that the contact lived alone and would only ever travel to two locations: a store and a church.

He followed the man as he went through his daily route going shopping and delivering groceries and other items to the church. He seemed like an average person simply helping his community. Timmy had begun to feel discouraged in his research. However, under further examination of the church, he noticed multiple Inconsistencies compared to other churches. For example, there were no depictions of Jesus, no crosses to be seen anywhere and the mentions of God sounded different, almost menacing. And that any who wasn't a part of the church's congregation were "Heretics.'

Timmy eventually through the months decided to investigate less of the original contact and more on the church, its parishioners, and their supposed pastor who even went by a different name of Noble. By eavesdropping conversations, the Noble had with a select group, he was able to determine that their organization was not under the Pope or any bishops. Instead, they worked for "The Lords of the new Messiah" and called themselves "The True Final Crusade."

As years passed, Timmy trained himself in defensive martial arts in case he was ever caught. He spent long nights learning new techniques and growing stronger until he was confident in his own abilities. Holding on to his father's aspirations, he worked tirelessly on his father's creations. Praying to live up to the potential his father saw in him. He spent his days singeing his fingertips improving his father's creations, knowing his father would have loved to see him now. along with his research of the True Final Crusade. Alas he was barely able to ascertain what he had gathered. Things seemed to go endlessly in no discernible direction, that is until they mentioned the name "Escalero Martí ". A supposed high-ranking Noble within their organization. A man who would frequently oversee high-tier assassinations was whispered about being ordered to come to oversee and protect a shipment planned by the True Final Crusade.

This was Timmy's shot, his best lead yet. And as nightfall came down on a solid black night, he snuck into the church and past the guards who stayed on watch, going into the Noble's office, and taking pictures of where Escalero would go first and what time. Finally, Timmy's patience would pay off and now all that was left was to confront Escalero.

| Page

Chapter 2: Convergence

May 21, 2057

He couldn't sleep, pacing all night as he went over his plan in sketches that littered his father's room along with all the devices, he believed would be of use to him. A camera for capturing evidence, homemade smoke bombs, miniature robots that would make a loud noise to distract people if he would get caught, A sequence tapper that would cycle through passwords unlocking things for him, his "X-board" an unfolding levitating board that his father made specifically for him, a memory chip and a knife.

The last of which he was most hesitant about. He had been training for years now on trying to protect himself but the thought of him actively stabbing someone or possibly killing another person disturbed him. He looked over at the knife as he adjusted the X-board. His anxiety shook him. There were so many years of planning that was put into him getting this far and it all rode on Escalero being the person who killed his family. And yet Timmy wasn't quite sure what he would do once he confronted him. The phone next to him suddenly rang causing him to jump which made him shock himself with the X-boards wiring.

"Shoot!" He yelped, sucking his injured finger, as he set aside his tools. He turned to the phone and rolled his chair over to it. He stopped looking at the caller ID and read: Uncle B.G.

Timmy stopped in his tracks looking at the name as he thought about what his uncle would say about all this. He remembered back when he had just heard about the case for his family being closed and how his uncle was so accepting and even when Timmy mentioned what he found he simply told him not to get into any trouble. *"He wouldn't understand."* Timmy said in his mind as the phone continued to ring.

For a moment Timmy turned to it, thinking he should at least say something. Just in case the worst were to happen. But before he could press the answer button the ringing stopped. So, Timmy hung his head slightly and went back to adjusting his equipment when the phone A.I. spoke aloud.

"You have. One missed call. With voicemail attached. Would you like to listen?" It asked.

Timmy answered quickly with a "Sure." And the message from his uncle began to play as he worked.

"Hey Timo- um I mean Timmy it's your Uncle Greg I was just calling to check on you. It's...uh been a while since I saw you... I thought maybe you could stop by the bar. It's just me for now but there's someone I'd like you to meet." His voice was hesitant with every word and each one was so pleading in its tone.

"Well come by if you can or call it's up to you... love you bud." He said, and the voicemail ended with the A.I. asking: "Would you like to send a reply?"

"No..." Timmy said softly as he got off his chair and shoved all his equipment in a backpack. He had only until about 6 am to get to the outskirts of town where an old supposedly abandoned chemical factory was.

Which through his investigation was the first location Escalero would stop on the shipping route. And so, heading out into the dark early morning streets, he unfolded his X-board hopping on, as he used the dial on the X-boards controller sleeve. Which accelerated the X-boards speed as he levitated his way down back alleys and past sleeping neighborhoods. The chilling bite of the early morning oceanside breeze being that much more noticeable as Timmy reached the outskirts of the city. To which he thanked his past self for deciding to keep his brother's hoodie during his ride out of town. Dialing down his speed only after he encroached on the factory.

The sun was still down as he slowly walked up to a barbed-wire-topped chain link fence that wrapped fully around the factory. He crouched beside it, before reaching down to his side and unsheathing his knife, looking at it before pressing the blade against the fence. It sliced effortlessly as if he was moving it through the air. Putting away the knife he took off his bag, sliding it under the hole having made it as small as he could to not draw any unwanted attention. He then crawled through himself before picking up and sliding on his bag.

Looking back at his handy work he patted the now sheathed knife that hung on his belt loop. "Say what you will about the Mudlurks, their Hak-Ya-Guh metal ([illegible] or God metal) really is something." He whispered as he bent down, having the tall grass cover him as he drifted closer to the warehouse. As he got in range he rose slightly just barely above the grass where he could see a back entrance.

Darting his eyes, he looked to see if any guards lingered by but all that was around was a single jeep that was turning a corner. Looking up, however, he noticed a security camera. He thought for a moment as he felt around in his bag looking for his phone. "Gotcha." He whispered using the spyware on it to tap into the plant's security system. As he navigated their system, he found the cameras which were facing where he was.

His heart stopped at the thought that all it took was for him to stand up and they could see him. He held his breath as a chill from a breeze brushed up his exposed neck and arms. He exhorted a slight shiver and a sigh as he took control of the camera's movements, slowly diverting its view to hide his approach to the back entrance.

He pressed his back tightly against the wall as he looked again through their system looking for access to the door before him when suddenly a light peered into the corner of his vision. His heart spiked as he whipped back to look behind himself. "Shoot, shoot, shoot!"

He exclaimed as the headlights grew in the distance. His fingers darted across the screen trying to unlock the door as he had begun to hear the crunching of the tires on the old rocky asphalt. The sound grew louder with each passing second until...*C***lick***

A metallic mechanism within the door unlatched, unlocking the door. Without wasting a second Timmy quickly yanked the door open, swinging himself to the other side trying quietly to close it. The light was gone, and he could barely see his arms as he turned. He was lucky as most of the light was focused on the center of the plant, which illuminated a large, draped object that barely touched the building's ceiling standing at about 20 feet tall.

Curiosity ushered him ahead until he bumped into a crate. He stopped, trying not to topple over as he looked down. Kneeling he looked for an opening on the crate before spotting a crowbar. Using it, he slowly pried open the crate with the creaks and snaps of wood making him cringe. He felt lucky that the sound of moving machines drowned out the noise he made as a final...****Snap****echoed as the crate popped open. "G-guns?" He stammered as he delicately set down the crowbar. His hand grazing across it as he felt its metallic frame. "These ... these are U.M.E. guns." He whispered to himself. "How do they have that kind of equipment? Not even regular people of the U.A. (Unions of America) are allowed to keep Alliance grade arms, who are these people?" He questioned. " First the church and now this?"

His eyes scanned the room cautiously as he looked for any guards that roamed nearby. Timmy's breath halting as he started to count in his head several people that roamed around in the dimly lit plant. A counting process that ended as footsteps appeared from behind him. Panicking, he jolted from a crouch pulling up the spyware and acquiring access to their lighting systems, having seen the option beforehand, now pulling it back up and disabling it.

The entire building went into a panic, with shouting and loud boots rushing all around Timmy as he slid to where he recalled the large tarp was. His hands extended as he desperately reached for a proper grip as he connected with the tarp, rolling under it. *"What am I doing... this isn't gonna work ...am I really doing this?"* He thought to himself.

Slumping back against the structure within the tarp, he buried his face in his knees as tears filled his eyes. Timmy muffled his cries, still worried about the guards who roamed around in the distance. "What am I even doing here? I don't even have a plan. Escalero is on his way, and I don't even-" the shine of flashlights startled Timmy as he shot upwards still against the structure. The footsteps grew louder as the weight of the boots clanged against the metal flooring of the plant; the light creeping its way further under the tarp until Timmy could hear the tarp folding and wrinkling from being grabbed. Timmy's breathing stopped as he grasped his knife so tightly that it stung.

"What the hell do you think you're doing David?" A voice shouted. The tarp folded and wrinkled back as the grip on it loosened. "What? Come on aren't you curious? You had to have heard all the crazy rumors about this shit." A shiver went up Timmy's spine as he heard how close the other person was. "Don't be a dumbass, this job is a hire-in, we ain't getting paid to be nosey and R.J. isn't in charge this time meaning if we aren't at our post by the time lights are back, we're both fired."

A moment of silence passed as Timmy's heart raced in his chest. "***Tsk***, fuck it I don't even wanna see it that bad anyway." The closer voice said, the footsteps gradually dampening in sound as the men walked away. Timmy breathed a sigh of relief as he sheathed his knife, with his hand slightly pulsing from the constrictive grip he had on it. Gradually he laid down on the cold metal floor placing his ear to the surface as he peeked under the open slit of the tarp.

He could hear the faint clanking of footsteps reverberating through the floor. Taking this window of opportunity, he slipped out of the tarp. Ahead of him was the faint outline of stairs from a glow that came from an office window that was off to the left of the stairs. Without a moment of hesitation, he darted up them he making his way into the office locking the door behind him. Holding his breath in anticipation, he turned around surveying the area. Relief flooded through him, and he felt the air rush from his chest as he realized he was alone. The light source he had seen was a computer left on. All around it stacks upon stacks of paper and files like that of a maze.

Grabbing a nearby chair he sat down in front of the computer, his ears tuned cautiously listening for any guards that might come by. "Maybe there's some info I can take to the police, and they can come and shut them down ... " he whispered to himself as he connected his phone to the computer gaining access to it. "Dang It! I should have taken pictures of the guns!" he exclaimed, still trying to whisper as he smacked the side of his head in disdain.

Sighing, he continued to go through the computer, going through its history, files, pictures, and everything that could be of use. Which is when he stumbled across "Trading Routes Proposition." He clicked over the files and using the spyware disabled its password. He opened the file, and his eyes widened with fearful interest as he looked throughout the file. It was a map of the earth with it highlighted yellow and labeled ACCESSIBLE; TRADING ROUTE ON WORLD: IN TESTING. Timmy moved the mouse and the computer out of the file showing the moon with it having a green highlight and being labeled ACCESSIBLE; TRADING ROUTE: COMPLETED. Timmy held his breath as he used the mouse to scroll out with it showing everything as green-lit Mars, moons of Jupiter, and Saturn, zooming out even more causing a bar to appear labeled: GALACTIC TRADING ROUTES.

Timmy clicked it, with the file zooming out to show the entire Milkyway galaxy, with it highlighted green and a list with a counter at 3,464 SOLAR SYSTEMS ACCESSIBLE FOR TRADING. To the left there were two other galaxies. Canis Major Dwarf and Andromeda. The smallest of the two Canis Major had around 1,600 accessible solar systems, while Andromeda had around 8,400. Timmy sat back his mouth a gape as he looked at the screen stunned. They traded through U.M.E., Alliance, and even War Council territories? "T-that's impossible, h-how can that even-"

Before Timmy could finish a light shined through the window causing Timmy to duck down. He waited a moment in agonizing silence waiting for footsteps or voices. His heart thumped in his chest as the sudden whistle of settling trucks caused Timmy to lift his head peering over the window's border when panic instantly struck his core. "*Escalero ...*" he whispered in his head *"He's here? Now? That's three hours earlier than what they said at the church."* Timmy thought to himself as he jumped back into the chair behind him. Attaching a memory card as he started to download any files he could get from the computer.

Tapping his fingers as he impatiently waited for the download to finish his body suddenly froze by a low groan that echoed around him. He whipped around as his eyes pierced the darkness around him as he tried to find the source of the sound. Arming himself with his knife. He readied himself. Only to see a guard slouched on a chair drooling, his gun barely in his hand as it touched the floor. "Woo, thank god." Timmy whispered in a sigh of relief at the sight.

But the silence was quickly shattered as the door next to Timmy was opened from the outside.

"Ronnie, I swear to god if you're asleep again!" Timmy and the guards' eyes met in unison both in shock at the others' presence. "Who the hell are you? What are you doing here, this is private property!" The guard shouted. In an instance of pure panic, Timmy tossed his knife across the room. The guard's eyes widening as he realized what happened as he followed its path leading toward him. Only for Timmy's knife to hit the wall beside him handle side first with it bouncing off the wall and clattering to the ground.

"You little shit!" the guard snarled as he pulled back the hammer of his rifle. Timmy dashed to the guard smacking the gun out of his hands.

"Nope, none of that please!" Timmy shouted, ducking a swing from the guard, and slipping between his legs, latching onto his back, and wrapping his arms around the guard's neck trying to make him pass out.

"Ron- you piece of shit! Wake up!" the guard gasped as he kicked a random object at the sleeping guard.

The sleeping guard grumbling as he wiped his grimy face. Slowly the guard swayed to his feet as he used the chair, he slept on to help himself up.

"Hey, no Ron go back to bed!" Timmy yelled as he squeezed the first guard's neck tighter causing the guard to jump back slamming himself and Timmy into the wall. Timmy winced in pain as he stopped choking the guard, switching to yanking the man's shirt collar back. Using the leverage of the wall to kick the guard into the sleepy one. Both stumbling over one another. Grumbling in pain, the sleepy guard cocked his gun and squinted his eyes looking for Timmy.

"Nope, you're not allowed to have that either!" Timmy shouted as he jumped across the room smacking the gun out of the sleepy guard's hands with the guard then swinging wildly in Timmy's direction. Timmy swayed back and forth dodging each attack before punching the guard straight in the face causing the guard to reel back in pain holding his nose. "Ouch sorry sorry I didn't know that would hurt that bad!"

"Ahhh!" The first guard screamed as he charged at Timmy.

"Woah!" Timmy shouted, leaping onto the chair the sleeping guard was on as the first guard slammed to the ground missing his charge.

Jumping off the chair and barely missing a swing from the other guard, Timmy landed on the first guard's back and tumbled forward. "Sorry." Timmy said, as the other guard charged him with a swing going right over Timmy's head as he ducked. Timmy punching back as he, slammed his fists into the guard's gut repeatedly. The guard leaned forward, grunting in pain as Timmy slid behind him. Sweeping his legs out from under him, causing the guard to fall back hard and slam his head on the ground knocking him out.

"Stay down! Please ... wait you're not dead, are you?" Timmy said in a panic as he leaned in and put his head on the guard's chest. "Okay sweet you're still alive." Timmy said, sighing in relief.

"Little bastard." The first guard muttered as he aimed a gun he managed to grab at Timmy. Timmy swiped the chair behind him spinning back at the guard as fast as he could, whacking him across the face with the metal chair knocking the guard out instantly.

"Oh, shoot dang it! Why'd you scare me like that! I said no guns!" He shrieked.

Timmy stood there looking at what he did, the silence filling back into the room, his breathing slowly settling. With no time to rest, Timmy unplugged the data transfer from the computer when seemingly out of nowhere alarms started echoing throughout the plant. "No no no shoot! They must have heard the fighting!" Timmy said. The lights suddenly turned on in the plant blinding Timmy for a second. "Ah! What the?"

Timmy stopped himself as he rushed out the door where the first guard originally came from. Stepping out onto a catwalk the guards below immediately spotted him, aiming their lights in his direction. Covering his face, Timmy ran along the catwalk as the guards below shouted and began to climb ladders to get to him. Following the bend, Timmy made his way to the other side of the building which led to where he entered.

Now, however, there were semi-trucks and gun mounted vehicles all on the previously empty road. In front of him, guards rushed down from the far end of the catwalk charging at Timmy. With only a second to think Timmy leaped over the railing and onto the bed of one of the semi-trucks. Nearly tumbling off it before catching the edge of the truck and pulling himself back up. Standing back onto the roof of the semi-truck, he ran to the back of it, hopping down onto the hood of the other semi-truck with a loud metallic bang as his feet slammed onto the hood.

As he made his way down another guard ran at him, with a baton in hand, swinging it at Timmy's legs. Leaping into the air Timmy used the grill of one of the semi-trucks and the back of the other as leverage dodging the guard's baton, before kicking him in the face. The guard recoiled, coming back with another swing at Timmy. Ducking just in time Timmy lugged back at the guard grabbing the man's hands, squeezing them tightly as he whipped the guard back and forth slamming the man into both trucks before kicking him to the ground.

Running past the guard, Timmy reached into his bag and desperately yanked out his X-board, tossing it out in front of himself. With the X-board uniformly unfolding, the levitation engine kicking on with a wobbly base, as the X-board pushed the dust around it. Timmy ran forward chasing the board before leaping forward and landing atop it. The board reeling in response, nearly tapping the ground before re-stabilizing, and locking it to his feet while Timmy fastened the board's controller onto his hand and forearm. Turning the speed dial to four the back turbines revved loudly before boosting Timmy forward.

Guards were now running from every corner of the plant as they all ran after Timmy trying to catch him. One guard even yelling for the entrance guard to close the gate. Hearing this, Timmy eyed the gate and sucked in his gut as he dialed the board's speed up to five, narrowly gliding past the screeching gate, as it slammed shut behind him. Looking behind himself Timmy watched as the plant now fully lit back up with power, when out from the side of the plant two motorcycles darted out with people riding along with them on their back seats.

"Oh jeez!" Timmy yelped as he dialed the board up to seven vaulting off the side road and across the grass as he hovered onto the highway dashing past other vehicles. Looking over his shoulder, Timmy gasped seeing the two motorcyclists had also veered onto the highway and were now right behind him. "Crap, crap, crap!" He shouted as he swerved past more traffic, as his heart pounded in his chest.

Looking down at the dial he held his hand over it, contemplating setting the dial to eight, but remembered his father's warnings about going past even six and that 7 to 11 were only for testing the prototype's limits. Time to decide was up however as one of the motorcyclists had caught up to him grabbing Timmy's arm amidst his lack of focus.

"Gotcha!" The guard snarled, yanking his arm slightly.

"Let go! " Timmy screamed back, punching the guard's helmet rapidly. The guard waved his arm back and forth trying desperately to block Timmy's fist when suddenly from the other side of Timmy the other motorcyclist group appeared with its passenger reaching over the driver to snatch Timmy's free hand. Looking back in shock he tried to yell at the guard to stop but was too late as he yanked Timmy's arm back causing his body to turn. With the thrusters from the X-board now pointed at the first motorcycle. Burning the passenger and melting the wheel popping it. The force from the thrusters against the motorcycle propelled the X- board against the second motorcycle with both passengers promptly letting go of Timmy. As the first motorcycle halted instantly, their rear wheel melted to the road, flinging the riders off.

The levitation mechanism then pushed the board up the second motorcycle where it collided with the driver cracking his helmet, causing them to swerve away. The X-board now briefly angled upward, jettisoned twenty feet into the air as Timmy held onto the front of the board. Looking back at the road, Timmy saw the distance he was from the ground.

His breathing quickened as he turned the dial down to zero. Yelping out in panic screaming. "Oh god, oh god, oh god!" As he back flipped, holding his arm as he altered the X-board's levitation, enhancing its output with it, slowing the speed at which he fell until he was only a few feet above a car. The board's levitation pressing down onto the roof of the car making it bend and pop as Timmy glided down it.

Back on the road Timmy hardly had a moment to think of what he just did. Dialing down the levitation and turning back on the turbines, he dialed the speed up to 7, as he rocketed past the other vehicles on the interstate. Looking back in a panic, Timmy watched the traffic jam that had been created by the motorcyclist group that crashed. Gratefully, Timmy breathed a sigh of relief for a moment as he saw both guards slowly sit up from their accident. When to everyone's horror, the two cars behind them abruptly skid out of the way, as two pitch black SUVs barrel through traffic. The first of which brutally colliding with the slumped over riders, rolling over them as it sped up. The engine squealing, as the SUVs tore across traffic as they drove straight towards Timmy.

Shock and fear rocketed into Timmy's face as he looked forward, switching to an off-ramp to see if he could lose them in the city. Turning sharp as he made a hasty dash in and out of oncoming traffic. Horns honked at him which mixed with the sound of screeching tires as he peeled right, into a construction zone.

Timmy's maneuver turned futile however with the SUVs catching up to him with them now directly on his heels. Turning back, he could see the vehicle pushing up, nearly bumping the X-boards turbine. The vehicle showed no warping or melting due to its armored plating. The second motorcycle group had caught up as well and even sped up past Timmy. Grabbing the speed dial Timmy readied himself, about to turn up the speed, but before he could the sound of a large metallic object whisking through the air forced his attention in front of him, where he could see a giant support beam careening towards him.

Holding his breath Timmy turned off the levitation mechanism completely as he slid forward, bending backward as the beam grazed over his body. Swinging himself around and out from under the beam's path before sitting back up and turning the levitation back on. Whipping his head back just in time to see the beam crash into the SUV vaulting it back into the following SUV with it bouncing backward, stalling it with the engine smoking.

The steel cable tying the metal beam to the crane snapping from the force of the collision. It echoed around the construction site as a part of the cable collapsed beside Timmy. With him narrowly swerving out of the way. Breathing a sigh of relief, he looked forward and started to dial down the speed. "Ack!" Was all Timmy could cough out as he was flung onto his back. The now rough gravelly path beneath him tearing into his back sending piercing shots of pain throughout his back all while he gagged and gasped for air.

The X-board pulled at Timmy's legs as it tried to move his now stationary body. Holding his feet down, he dialed down the X-boards speed and levitation as he looked around with him now noticing the rope that had been tied in front of him and the people who were manning both ends of it. It was the second motorcycle group that drove ahead of him. The two of them sprung up after seeing Timmy fall back. Quickly thinking, Timmy unlatched the X-board from his feet, sending it flying into the stomach of one of his assailants. The man groaning in pain as he knelt on the ground holding his gut. The X-board folding back into its square dormant state after getting too far out of range from Timmy. Still gasping for air, Timmy saw the other man walk towards him. All Timmy could see other than his clenched fists was one of his eyes only slightly visible from the cracked visor on his helmet. Fuming with rage was the only expression Timmy could make out as he watched the man stomp closer and closer to him.

Timmy kicked at the ground scooting himself away as much as he could. But it was too late as the man was now upon him gripping the collar of his hoodie, as he lifted him off the ground. His hateful eyes piercing straight through Timmy, and in one quick motion, he pulled back his arm before swinging it back at Timmy punching him in his face. Timmy winced but only a pathetic whimper could be heard as he still struggled to breathe the sharp blistering pain racking the left side of his face. Feeling tears swell up into his eyes, with grunts of pain being all he could mutter as he held his hand over his eye, his other hand still on his throat.

"Piece of shit. Good for nothing baby Mudlurk is what you remind me of." The man scoffed as he tossed Timmy back to the ground. "Stay shithead or I can show you how I took care of ugly Mudlurks back in the day." He snapped, as he turned his back to Timmy. The man reached down and grabbed a radio from his belt, clicking it on. "I got the little bastard." The man grumbled into the radio.

His conversation was slightly muffled to Timmy's ears as he tried to deal with his pain. Something, however, was changing as the pain and ache of his wounds seemingly faded without any reason that Timmy could understand. He held his throat confused as the air began to fill his lungs once again. And even now his face that once felt crushed from the blow of the man now only felt slightly tender.

Timmy turned to see the other man finally getting to his feet and in a quick flurry, Timmy grabbed a nearby rock and chucked it at the man with it cracking across his helmet as he rushed the other one who was still on the radio. Tackling the man to the ground before he could even turn around. Timmy repeatedly thrashed at the man's neck turning it red before yanking off his helmet and tossing it aside before rearing back his fist and slamming it into the man's eye.

"How. Do. You. Like it!" Timmy shouted with spiteful tears in his eyes punching the man every time he spoke, until he knocked the man unconscious.

"Hey, you little shithead get off of him! " Yelled a voice from behind Timmy. He turned to look, seeing the armed group from the SUVs running over to him. Timmy jumped up darting over to his X-board and scooped it up, nearly tripping as he ran to the sound of traffic where he hoped the exit would be.

Running along the wall and passing shouting construction workers who yelled for him to get out of the property as the armed men shouted to stop Timmy. Luckily the exit finally showed itself. Timmy dashed into the road without a care for the cars honking and screeching their tires, one even bumping him as he rolled onto the hood.

"Sorry... sorry!" he shouted at the driver before leaping off.

Looking back, he could see the armed men waving their guns, one even shooting in the air with cars scattering in every direction. Timmy profusely rummaged through his thoughts trying to figure out how to get away and there it was just in front of him. The busiest place in all of Ultimo city. ***Last Salvation Plaza.***

Chapter 3: Captivated

Bewildered strangers gasped and whispered in confusion, as Timmy stumbled brazenly through the large crowds huddled about in the bustling high-end shopping center. His eyes feverishly roaming for an exit when abruptly, like a moth to flame solely drawn to its source. He was struck, by a view that gave him such a jittery sensation of utter jubilation, as he held his mouth a gape. He was stunned, almost forgetting the purpose of his hasty sprint throughout the city, caused by only one. By only her.

Her eyes were the first that his own had gazed upon. They were gentle and had a curious interest, that shared the look of soft milk chocolate. Her dress was next, for the shimmer sparkled in his eyes from its shining velvety red silk. Which laid against her skin in such a manner as to perfectly complement her breathtaking physique. A moment of pure guilt rushed him as he violently turned his head up in innocence, nearly giving himself whiplash, and lastly. Her voice, which played across the strings of his heart like a harp that played a delicately sweet melody in his ear.

"Excuse me." She spoke harshly in her tone. "Hello?" She spoke louder. Timmy broke from his trance; his mind was gone but his legs were still in motion. With his path driving him directly into the stunning stranger before him. Waving his arms as he skipped forward, he could do nothing, as he tumbled onto the woman causing her to yelp as the two of them plummeted backwards. Afraid of hurting the girl, Timmy spun the two of them around with him smacking the ground first.

The back of his head crashing hard against the tile beneath them.

"Ahh!" Timmy yelled, grasping his head, and wincing as he groaned in pain. Curling in a ball, Timmy scrunched his face as he tried to endure the pulsing pain, as the girl slowly shifted to her knees.

"Jeez kid what the hell are you running from? Fuckin... Idio-." She stopped herself as she watched Timmy writhe in pain. "Damn I... are you okay? Here let me see your head dumbass... Are you bleeding?" She spoke lightly, the harsh demeanor vanishing.

Reaching her hand out to him, Timmy looked up at her with a single teardrop in his eye as he sat up slightly, still holding his head.

"I'm sorry I um ... are you okay? ...I didn't mean to." He muttered in a low whisper.

"Gotcha!" A loud angry voice boomed from behind, as Timmy turned around to see a man with a scar across his eye, reach out and grip his arm tightly, before lifting him to his feet. Timmy's eyes widened as he looked around him and the girl.

They were surrounded by three other men, one on the left of him in a heavy vest that had tons of rifle magazines strapped to it, another across from him with a gold chain and excessively greasy slicked back hair, and the third guy on the right of him looking exactly like the other vested man except for his egregious smell, each of them armed with rifles.

"Let me go!" Timmy shouted. Swinging at the scarred man that held onto him. The man shouting back as he got struck by Timmy saying.

"Ouch you little shit knock it off!" Before pressing both Timmy's arms behind his back and handcuffing him.

"Hey, whoa, whoa is that necessary he's just a kid. What did he even do?" The girl stammered, putting her hand out.

"None of your damn business girly now fuck off." Barked the musty one of the group.

"Excuse you?" She hissed back. "Are you even fuckin police? The hell with this?" She said as she pulled out her phone backing away from the group.

"Oh, don't you start some shit like that little missy." The greasy man said, gripping her hand and yanking her to him. "A cute little thing like you, don't wanna end up broken do yah?"

The others laughing as the greasy man pressed his head against hers and sniffed her.

"Hey!" Timmy shouted at the group. "Let her go, I was the one in the plant not her, she's not a part of this!"

The vested man swung hard into Timmy's gut barking out. "Shut it brat. You in enough shit as is." Timmy coughed aggressively panting as he took the hit. The girl starting to kick and scream, as she shouted for help. The crowd behind them starting to gather. The vested man turning around and proceeded to walk over to the crowd waving his gun around and firing off a few rounds shouting, "Mind ya fuckin business nosey asses!" The people beginning to scream and run off. Turning back to the girl, the greasy man gripped her face growling at her

"Shut those lips before I shut them for you." She groaned in disgust as she tried to yank herself away, before spitting in the greasy man's face. "Oh, ho ho you bitch!" The man scoffed, tossing her to the ground, as he wiped his face.

"I said leave her alone!"

Timmy screamed lifting himself in the scarred man's arms as he kicked back hitting the man in his privates before charging the greasy man, knocking him to the ground as he tackled him. Lifting himself off the man only to jump back on him, jabbing his knee into the man's face, slamming his head against the ground so hard that the tile cracked beneath him.

"Fucker!" The musty one yelled as he began to reach for Timmy. Quickly, Timmy twirled over the greasy man jumping up to his feet before kicking the musty one in the face. Aiming at his wrist, Timmy kicked the man's gun out of his hands, as the man fell back into the wall beside him.

The vested one then ran up from behind Timmy grabbing his handcuffs. Timmy bent down and hopped onto his own hands as well as the vested man's pulling them both down, as Timmy pinched their hand between his feet and the tile floor. The man winced, gritting his teeth, as he swung his gun at Timmy. Dodging quickly, Timmy rolled forward off both their hands now moving his arms in front of him before turning around and lunging back, slamming his fists down onto the vested man's head before kicking at his hand holding the gun.

Turning quickly, Timmy snatched the gun from the man and tossed it behind him, hitting the scarred man's face with a loud whack. The man yelling out in pain, as he collapsed backwards holding his head. Timmy then climbed onto the vested man's back, wrapping his cuffs around the man's neck before swinging the man's head against the wall knocking him out. Panting heavily Timmy slumped back against a wall taking a moment to calm himself. Hesitantly the girl slowly got up, still holding her assaulted face, as she looked at all the men knocked out or grumbling in pain. All while Timmy now laid back controlling his breathing as he shook with adrenaline.

"W-what the fuck just happened?" she asked, walking slowly over to Timmy.

"R-run..." Timmy shakenly worded between deep breaths

"Ah yes and leave you here for when they get up, don't be fuckin stupid. Come on." she said, grabbing his hand and helping him get to his feet. The two of them heading towards an exit. Stopping for a moment as she kicked the greasy man in his privates. "Asshole." She growled. As they got to the stairway door leading to the lower half of the plaza Timmy started to hear shuffling. Right as he looked back the man with the scar weakly aimed his gun and a loud bang was all Timmy heard as he pushed himself and the girl into the stairway. The girl screamed, looking at Timmy as he fell beside the wall holding his side. Timmy's eyes grew wide as he gasped.

Torn flesh jutted from his wound as Timmy rushed his hand to the side of his stomach. His warm blood wetted his shirt as well as his brother's beloved hoodie.

"N-no no" He gasped and winced at the sear pain as he held his side. Feverishly yanking off his brother's hoodie so as not to stain it any further.

"Oh, my fuckin god! Oh my god! Shit, Shit, Shit, it's okay Saph, it's okay Saph." The girl began to ramble, pacing back and forth. "H-hey look at me it'll be okay uh uh um." She said, staring at the wound then looking at Timmy. Hearing the men shuffling more outside the door she shouted out "Fuck!" before noticing a dry standpipe quickly grabbing it and grunting as she slammed it down next to the door blocking it.

"Ok hey hey... um imma pick you up, okay? I'm so sorry but we gotta go now." She said wrapping her arm around Timmy as he yelped.

"Ahhh I-I'm sorry." he said.

"Shhh not now come on I got you." She replied as she slowly limped down the stairway making it to the bottom level. Timmy breathed sharply as he started to tear up. "Hey now, it's okay... you saved me back there okay...I'm making sure you get out of here in one piece. Trust me I-I've watched like five good spy movies." She said, giving a slight smile to Timmy.

"I... I like spy movies." Timmy said weakly, giving a small smile back. Timmy and the girl made it further down the hall with Timmy having an odd sense of Deja vu.

"Here I think I got someone who can help us." She said as they made their way to the door at the farthest end of the hallway knocking on its old heavy metallic exterior, the sound echoing through the hall. Suddenly it clicked as to where the girl had taken them.

"Greg !?" Timmy shouted out with wide eyes, before another wave of pain washed over him making him wince again, before curling into a ball.

A small window slid open as eyes peered into the hallway.

"Oh? Saph? What are you doing? I thought you had that business meeting soon; did you forget something?" A voice asked from behind the metal door as the locking mechanism began to turn, the door slowly sliding open. "Heck for a second there I thought I heard my nephew Ti-" The man trailed off as his face turned white looking at Timmy's dirty and bloodied body.

"H-hey BG." Timmy weakly smiled before looking down shamefully.

"Good God!" Timmy's uncle shouted, dropping to his knees passing the girl and scooping Timmy up off the ground and rushing him into his uncle's small restaurant kitchen. “Sapphire, please clear off that table, and get me that first aid kit in the corner! " BG ordered as he nodded his head in the direction of the kit.

Sapphire quickly pushed everything off the table in front of them before running over to the first aid kit hanging from the wall "Oh Timmy, oh god ... if your parents could see you right now..." BG said as he held Timmy's wound.

"I'm sorry I had to see him..." Timmy said as he winced with another jolt of pain pouring throughout his body in worsening pulses.

"No, no this is my fault... I knew I should have paid more attention. I should have been there more... him?" BG asked, realizing what Timmy said.

"Is this about who killed them? Timmy, I told you to stay away from that kind of stuff why-"

"Because I had to!" Timmy shouted, interrupting BG with tears filling his eyes. "I-I had to see what monster would... would take them from me." Timmy winced as tears dripped from his face as he clenched his brother's hoodie tightly. BG sighed looking away from Timmy unsure of what to say.

"Um... hey look, let's not get off track here." Peeped Sapphire lightly. "We have a bigger, more immediate problem on our hands here... he's bleeding badly, and the nearest hospital is 30 minutes away." She continued instinctively tapping her foot anxiously, as she leaned on the table.

"You're right. I'll shut off all the lights and lock up the bar, you call us an ambulance. They'll be quicker than we would be." BG said as he ran off to the front of the bar. With the lights off and the ambulance on its way they sat cautiously in the dark and in near silence. Aside from the occasional back and forth between BG and Sapphire, as BG tried his best to tend to Timmy's wound. Sapphire hovering close by while she worriedly twiddled with her thumbs.

“You know you don't have to stay hun” BG spoke softly, not fully turning to meet Sapphire's gaze as he held pressure on Timmy's wound. "I have him now and I can’t thank you enough for bringing him to me." He continued.

"It's no problem. I didn't wanna go to that stupid thing anyway. Plus, those people, they ... I think this is the safest place for me right now." She replied shivering, disgusted by the man who assaulted her face.

“Alright then, that's no issue with me” BG responded along with a nod.

Before too long the place was surrounded by police. With the paramedics rushing Timmy from the bar. "We'll meet you at the hospital Timmy! Don't worry, you'll be okay bud! We're right behind you, and I got your hoodie too bud!" BG shouted, as he and Sapphire made their way to her car after Timmy had been ushered into the back of the ambulance. Timmy's eyes moved sporadically, cautiously watching the medic with groggy and dazed vision. The medic cutting off his shirt and checked over his wound, when a sudden look of confusion flashed over the medic's face.

"What the..." he trailed off before quickly wrapping Timmy in gauze and moving to the window towards the front of the ambulance. "Hey, we're gonna need to get a hold of the hospitals telemetry, something weird is going on here." Timmy tilted his head back to look at the medic but before he could ask what was going on Timmy succumbed to the pain and loss of blood, fainting in the back of the ambulance.

Meanwhile moving achingly slow through traffic, Sapphire along with BG made their way to the hospital Timmy was being transported to.

"I can't thank you enough." BG spoke up, breaking the silence.

"Oh, please don't even go there. With how much you've helped my mom and dad you're like family. Not to mention I'm not gonna just let some dude bleed out in front of me, I just find it odd I never met Timmy before all this." Sapphire replied.

"Believe it or not I tried to get you two to meet." He said with a chuckle. "I wanted him to be around people more but ... he locked himself away..." BG said his smile quickly fading to a frown. "I should have done something; I should have tried harder I just-" He said choking up on the last word, as he pressed his hand to his face. Using his thumb to wipe a tear from his eye, before shaking his head.

"Hey, come on now I'm sure you did more than enough." Sapphire said, taking a hand off the steering wheel and reassuringly patting B.G. on the shoulder. "I'm sure he'll be fine, heck he's already at the hospital I'm sur-" Sapphire froze in sheer terror as her eyes stared agonizingly, locking in a perpetual gaze.

"Hun are you okay?" BG asked, baffled by the sudden shift in expression from Sapphire.

"It's them." She spoke in a harsh whisper as her hands gripped the steering wheel tight, her eyes darting back to face the road before her, as goosebumps riddled her arms.

"Them?" BG asked.

But before he could turn his head Sapphire shrieked "Don't look!" BG jumped slightly before holding his sight to the road as well. "Why are they in a cop van?" Sapphire whispered in a panic.

"Did they get caught?" BG asked as he slightly turned to her.

"That'd be great... if only he wasn't the one driving the van!" she shouted, panic only festering more in her body. Curiosity took over BG as he spun his head to where Sapphire was looking. And indeed, a greasy man wearing all black was driving the loaded van filled with other matching individuals. The van suddenly blared its sirens, with its light flashing on. Quickly the van pulled off into the safety lane and sped far off out of view. "This is bad, BG, call Timmy." She snapped, looking to her side, as she desperately tried to maneuver farther down the highway.

At the hospital, slowly opening his eyes, Timmy looked around his hospital room. He started to sit up when he winced still in pain from the gunshot wound. Holding his side, his ears perked up listening for anything that might be nearby before looking at the table beside him and spotting his phone. Picking it up he noticed ten missed calls, all, from BG.

"What the heck?" He muttered as he scrolled through his phone to his voicemail.

"Timmy, get to security, or get out of there! Those guys are on their way!" BG shouted in a frenzy before the voicemail could end.

Timmy looked around thinking of where to hide or if he should escape. Looking over at the door as he slid out of bed, he breathed a sigh of relief as he noticed he was by himself, and that the door was locked. A monitoring robot then rolled over to him asking.

"Is everything okay dearie?" in a soft calm tone.

"I-I don't-" Timmy stammered as he dashed around the room looking for his belongings.

"You seem distressed. Do you want me to contact your nurse, or would you like me to do something else?" The monitoring bot asked as it tilted its head, following Timmy to the closet, as he rummaged through it. With Timmy happily finding his clothes and picking them up before taking note of the fact the monitoring bot was scanning him from behind.

"It appears you're in peak health conditions from my scan, with your consent to continue I would like to do a quick physical to check for any other traumas." Almost on cue, a breeze chilled Timmy's exposed backside to which Timmy snatched the hospital gown shut exclaiming

"No!" As he inched his way into the bathroom "I gotta get the heck outta here!" He shouted while fumbling with his clothes.

"Would you like me to contact your nurse or doctor to check when you can be discharged, and bring up related treatment options?" The monitoring bot asked as it rolled to the front of the bathroom door.

"Actually, what you can do is forget I'm here." Timmy said as he walked out of the bathroom now a bit more dressed, using his spyware to turn the monitoring bot into "vacant room" mode. Loud heavy footsteps then became apparent, Timmy focusing on where they were coming from and possibly going too. They were down the hall slowly becoming quieter with a new noise of a rattling cart making its way matched with the pace of the person stepping closer to Timmy's room. In a panic, and not taking any chances. Timmy dove across the room, folding himself into the cramped closet where his clothes were kept. Listening more intently it became suddenly harder to hear the now silent footsteps.

Even the carts rattling vanished with instead the heavy beating of Timmy's heart and the slow mechanical rolling of the monitoring bot taking up most of the audible noise for him. The door eerily creaked open as Timmy held his breath. His body strained trying to hold himself still. Thoughts of a man tearing open the small closet and attacking him played over and over driving him insane as he began to shake nervously.

"I'm sorry but this room is currently vacant and undergoing cleaning for the next patient." The soft feminine voice from the monitoring bot spoke.

A moment of silence slowly passed as time stood still until a disgruntled scoff came from beyond the doors of the closet, the man who entered Timmy's room shoved the monitoring bot aside pushing things around and sliding open curtains before grumbling

"Those dumbasses, how did they get me the wrong room!" before violently rolling the cart out of the room and slamming the door behind him.

The rattling cart and his heavy footsteps slowly dissipating down the hall. Slowly peeking out of the closet, and noticing the coast was clear, Timmy gradually slipped out of the closet. He slowly walked past the monitoring bot patting its simplistic yet humanoid head as it repeated its statement that was said to the stranger who came into Timmy's room. Taking note of his belongings he felt around in his pockets double checking he had his phone. However soon he remembered the memory card that he shoved in his pocket.

“Wait what? no, no, no!” Timmy shouted double checking his pockets. “Where is it?” looking around in the closet again and yet he couldn't find anything. “Ugh, I don't have time for this!” He yelled out in frustration. Peering his head out into the emergency room hallway he noticed the cart he had heard earlier and froze before noticing the man was nowhere to be seen. Looking back, he noticed a stairwell exit and slowly Tip toed backward to it looking back and forth hoping not to see the man at the other end of the hall.

At the entrance of the stairwell, Timmy took a glance at a map on the wall which had a simple layout of the hospital. He turned his head back down the hallway checking to see if anyone had spotted him then looked back at the map looking for an exit until the words "Security/ Lost and Found" were spotted. "Hmm first floor I'm... on the 6th... quite a walk but ... it's right by the stairs!" he said to himself as he rushed to the stairwell opening the door and quietly making his way down the steps.

Even the quiet steps made slight echoes as he made his way down the stairwell. Peaking back up from where he came as he eventually reached the first floor. Nearly stepping out of the stairwell, Timmy stopped himself as he began to see 4 brooding men walk away from where the security room was located.

"Stay down here. Make sure no one comes into the security room until we get back." One armed man said, looking back at the security room, before moving with the other three beside him to an elevator that dinged as it opened its doors.

Trying to wait, hoping to hear the elevator door close. Timmy looked back, hopping up to see through the window of the stairwell door noticing that the door to the security room was now starting to shut. Jumping out of the stairwell Timmy rammed into it as hard as he could. The armed man inside falling back into an empty chair. Timmy lunged at the man's hand which held a gun and bit down viciously trying to make the man drop his gun.

After a moment or two, however, Timmy gradually looked up at the man and saw he had knocked the guy out when he rammed into the door. Still latched onto the man's wrist, Timmy slowly opened his mouth releasing his wrist.

"Oh ... uh...sorry." He whispered, getting up as he looked around the room, lifting and moving boxes until he found one with a baggy holding his knife and the memory card. "Yes..." he whispered, shoving them both in his pocket.

Taking a step back Timmy's leg slid forward for a moment sending him back slightly with him flailing his arms before regaining his composure. Looking down, horror suddenly filled him as he noticed the dark red pool slowly forming beneath him. Kneeling he followed the path of blood under a desk. Gasping harshly as his gaze fell on a hospital security guard's still lifeless body. "No..." he whispered in an almost regretful tone thinking somehow, he could have prevented this. Whipping his head back looking at the slumped over armed man still out cold. Emotions of burning, furious anger boiled inside him.

"I take back my sorry!" He snapped childishly as his temper cooled slowly, turning his head back to the body. Sadness wrapped him completely as he lowered his head. He didn't know the dead man before him, didn't know his name or hear his voice. And yet still Timmy mourned him. "I hope you didn't have a wife... or kids." Timmy said softly. "But weather you did or not...for them, for you." Timmy stopped and held the memory card in his pocket. "I will bring them to justice, I promise. "

Rising to his feet and giving one more dirty look at the armed man contemplating attacking him out of rage. Timmy sighed and walked out of the security room and ran as fast as he could out of the hospital. Continuously looking back, fearful of being chased out by the other armed men. Desperately he swiped through his contacts looking for his uncle when screeching tires sped down the road to his left with a shining chrome car skidding to a halt right in front of him.

Cautiously taking a step back, Timmy stared at the vehicle blankly, shocked by its brash immediate entrance. When suddenly to his surprise, his uncle flung open the door rushing to him. Taking him in his arms as he held him tightly.

"Thank god..." BG whispered, as he squeezed Timmy more with his hug. "Are you okay? I... I thought we were gonna be too late." He said holding Timmy's head tilting it and looking for any injuries.

"I ... I'm okay... t-they we're in there like you said in your message they ... they murdered someone...I..." Timmy stammered over his words, his voice turned sharp and hoarse as he looked back. "It was because of me." He whimpered, tears filling his eyes, a slight feeling of embarrassment making him turn his head, as he noticed Sapphire staring at the two of them.

"No! Hey...you don't start with that; Those people don't care who they hurt. You're a kid, and they were gonna kill you!" BG said, wiping the tears from Timmy's eyes. "What matters now is your safety. And I'm gonna make sure it stays that way." Determinate he ushered Timmy into Sapphire's car saying. "Look, I know you don't trust people or like being with people. But the Prices have always been good to me. And right now, I think your safest bet is to stay with them in the hills." BG said, shutting the door behind him.

"I- wait! I can't! And she's already done enough I can't-" Timmy said, grabbing the door handle and trying to open the door with his uncle pushing back, keeping the door shut.

“No Timmy...please! For me, stay with Sapphire. I'm gonna head into the hospital, see if I can have it locked down, maybe get the police to come to get these assholes." Sapphire grabbed Timmy's hand softly as she lightly tugged him back into the seat. He looked back at her, and he blushed slightly as she began to speak.

“Your uncle’s right Timmy, they’ll be looking for you not him, he’ll be okay. If you stay, they’ll go back for you and your uncle. I’m sure you don’t want the latter option.” Timmy paused for a moment looking back into Sapphires gentle pleading eyes, eventually giving in and sitting back in the seat. BG then gave a big sigh as he lowered his head, turning to look at the hospital before looking back at Timmy and Sapphire and whispering.

"This really was not a part of my plan for hooking the two of you up." Both Timmy and Sapphire exasperating asking one after the other. "what?" Ignoring both of their puzzled looks, BG continued saying. "Look... I made a promise to your parents the day they were lowered in their graves. I said I'd raise you as best I could... I said I'd keep you safe..." His eyes began to water as he held Timmy's arm. "Let me keep those promises, please." Timmy sunk in his seat looking away from his uncle knowing nothing he could say would stop him.

"Okay..." He whispered, in a heavy-hearted tone with his uncle nodding his head then looking past Timmy and at Sapphire. "Do you still live down Quarter Avenue?" Sapphire perked up nodding her head, saying.

"Yeah, uh yeah same place." BG patted the roof of the car.

"Good. Take care of each other. I'll try to make my way up there as soon as I can." And with that, he turned around and made his way into the hospital as Sapphire began to drive off.

Silence permeated throughout the entire car ride as Timmy sulked gazing out the window, his mind mainly swirling elsewhere. More focused on what if his uncle were to get hurt, what if they knew where he was heading or what he could even do to change anything?

He had the evidence but nothing else. He had nowhere to take it. No one to blame. An organization that didn't exist, a serial killer presumed to be dead. All his leads would simply lead nowhere and then he would be back at the same spot he was at with his family's case. The police not being able to do anything, leaving him alone and helpless once again.

Before long they arrived at Sapphire's home in the hills, a gated lavish mansion with a lush floral garden in the front, busts lined the driveway showing depictions of war heroes and innovators belonging to the Price family.

"'Woah this is all yours?" Timmy said, aghast and entranced by the scenery around him.

"Oh please, I know your family. Your father's company has been a competitor since our grandparents' early days when they founded the companies." She said with a Tsk and a roll of her eyes.

"Well, my parents never really cared about profit, he preferred smaller homes and didn't really care for fancy things." Timmy replied, still viewing the garden, cocking his head as they drove past. “My dad always mentioned paying workers more, providing more for them, giving to the community." Timmy smiled for a moment, reminiscing on his father's words and actions hoping he could one day fill the shoes his father and mother left for him.

"I wish my parents did that more. They're too busy with profit and building relationships with Alliance companies." She frowned, tapping the steering wheel with her thumbs as she pulled the car into the large garage next to an assortment of other sports cars.

"Actually, I was heading to a meeting when we bumped into each other. I know they're gonna be pissed when they find out I missed that." She sighed, turning off the car. Timmy apologized for dragging her into this, but she just shook her head instead, chuckling as she said, "Heck it's nothing, besides this is the most excitement I've had in years." Sapphire gave Timmy a wink as they both hopped out of the car. Timmy turned his head away from her as his face became shyly flushed.

The both of them making their way into Sapphire's home. "Top floor is all the bedrooms, there are a few guest rooms if you wanna relax until your uncle gets here...uh." She swayed back and forth; her arms folded as she thought of other things in her home. "Uh, there's a lot, I don't know. What I do know though is that these fucking heels are killing me." lifting her leg she began to slip off her heel which inadvertently revealed more of her other leg.

Timmy blushed and turned his head away to the side, as Sapphire slipped off the other heel before holding them both up saying, "Heels can be cute... sometimes... sometimes, but god do I hate them." She said, as she shook them in her hand, turning to Timmy, finally noticing him looking away. "Oh, cute and respectful I'm beginning to like you already." She smiled, patting his cheek only to make him blush more as the two of them separated.

Slowly, Timmy passed through all the halls and rooms. With two luxury pools, bar rooms, home theaters, and marble kitchens, Timmy was completely in awe of everything. Far too nervous to touch anything, afraid that he'd break something. Continuing his exploration throughout the house, Timmy discovered the final room, a trophy room filled with awards for sales and medals of military victories. Walking about the room, Timmy eventually made his way to a painting showing a large depiction of the battle at Fort Salvation. What it had showed was massive silhouetted Mudlurks slain about the blood-drenched battlefield, buildings and land turned to corrosive slosh, the sky's dark and orange hue, not from sunset but distant burning cities illuminating the horizon.

Wounded soldiers and civilians alike helped up and treated from wounds and a group of well-armed resistance fighters stood triumphantly above a mound of dead Mudlurks having retaken the center of the city. Looking down from the painting Timmy noticed a metal plaque that read. "This depiction recognizes the bravery and will of the human race, as Hero of the Resistance and our own Captain Johnathan Price, along with many others. Take humanity's first major victory in pushing back and later eliminating most of the iniquitous invaders of earth. Memorial Commissioned by the Never Forgotten Association."

Timmy placed his hand upon the painting, feeling its rigid detailed surface. Not made of just paint but materials that matched the scenery and things inside said scenery. From the unearthed ground feeling like soil to the clothes on the soldiers feeling like cloth, everything was so meticulously crafted with such detail. His eyes strained as he stood back in admiration examining every detail of the unique piece of art. Doing so, he noticed a particular constant that appeared on a number of the different soldiers in the painting, being that of a medallion that leisurely laid across their chest.

Looking closer at the medallions Timmy realized that each of them were the same in style. Brown leather looking straps that hung around the soldiers' neck and connected to the center of the medallion; The center of which being a triangle and in the middle of it a symbol of an eye.

Leaving from each median of the triangle would extend a deltoid, towards the tip of which would be a unique glyph in the same style as the one in the triangle. Lastly there would be a ring that connected just past the middle of each deltoid. On the ring would be several glyphs that appeared to be from various ancient human races.

As Timmy inched closer to the piece of art his hand felt beckoned to touch the medallion. He raised his hand and hesitation crawled over him. Something in him pleaded to stop and yet he could not comprehend why he was so compelled and terrified to perform such a simple action. Cautiously he stretched out his hand and gently brushed his fingers across the cold metallic surface of the medallion.

Then with his breath bated, his vision was enveloped by absolute darkness. His body ran cold, constricted by unyielding pressure. With a sensation of liquid suffocating his lungs. His very mind dazed in a blurry shock completely overwhelmed until finally a deep red blood-soaked fog filled the empty void in front of him.

Timmy screamed and thrashed around and yet nothing. His very soul would not heed to his instinctive reactions. Tears fled his eyes as a raw primal fear rose inside him with a lurking presence now rumbling in the distance. Shadowed and hidden just out of view before bursting across in a cacophony of rattling, infinitely spanning, inconceivably gargantuan, chains; that traversed like lightning in all directions. The burst of sound pounded at Timmy's core as he wailed. Suddenly the chains went taut and with this, they became clearer in their appearance as his swollen bloodshot eyes gazed upon this eldritch visage before him. It burned his eyes to look too long, and yet closed the fear he felt only solidified.

"Timmy." A soft voice echoed across the scarlet fogged void. His eyes tore open as they shifted hesitantly in all directions and yet all he could see were cracked and rusted chains. "Timmy." Growled another much gravellier resounding voice. This time the chains shook and shifted, and a new shadow filled the fog, undulating masses of various shapes and sizes writhed in a mixture of aggression and restraint.

"Timmy." He heard again only this time the voice sounded like his own only heavier and distorted. His vision filled with absolute blackness before a falling sensation met with him flailing his arms, closing his eyes only to open them to the art piece still before him. Stunned and gasping for air, Timmy's fingers and toes curled as he tried to peel himself from the tiled flooring beneath him. Staring off completely deadpanned Timmy shook his head and smacked his face a bit.

"Yeah, uh okay no." He said in a stutter as he rushed out of the room.

"Did I just have a trip? I know dad said to be careful with other rich people but ... do the Prices do drugs? Was that Ambrosia crystal?" he whispered to himself as he held his dizzying head.

"Timmy?" called out Sapphire from across the hall startling him. Sitting on a toilet with a needle in her hand, she popped a blister on her foot and sat up squinting her eyes looking curiously at Timmy. Frozen and still reeling from his experience with the painting he hardly moved an inch. "Yeah?" He asked in a very dazed and spaced-out response.

"You look pale dude; you've been through a lot" she said stopping for only a moment to lean down and check her foot again before turning back to Timmy. "How about you go lay down in my room I'll chill in my parent's room after I'm done with this." He stammered taking a step back as he said

"Okay." responding to Sapphire.

"It's just down the hall on the right! I'll come get you when your Uncle comes by!" She shouted to him as he made his way to her room.

There he laid, eyes closed tossing and turning unable to rest, instead haunted by nightmares of Escalero's men sieging upon the house. Of Escalero himself hiding in the shadows waiting as he did for Timmy's family, for the perfect time to strike. And so, he never slept; he barely wished to close his eyes. His mind was unyielding in thought until he got up, too stirred about, finding himself now pacing back and forth in silence. Waiting, and yet Sapphire never came, his Uncle never came.

A migraine began to form, making him hold his head along with him noticing the dryness in his mouth. He hadn't eaten or drank anything all day. And almost on queue his stomach growled. With a frown he left Sapphire's room and headed down the stairs. Meandering through the dark halls he finally made his way to one of the kitchens present in the vast mansion. Looking out the window beside him, he noticed how dark it was outside and could clearly make out a thick fog that pressed casually against the window.

Entering the marble kitchen, he fumbled about through various cabinets until he found a cup for him to pour some tap water. Finding the faucet, he hung the glass under its automated sensor filling the glass before guzzling it down and giving out a loud sigh. Looking across from him he noticed the LED red glow of a clock which read 2:58am. Taken aback, Timmy quickly took out his phone and indeed as the clock had stated it was 2:58am.

24 hours prior he was preparing for his encounter with Escalero and yet his mind now was on his Uncle. It had been hours, and he hadn't shown up from the hospital, nor had he called or sent a text. Thoughts of what might have happened to his Uncle ran through his mind and now in addition a foreboding feeling of déjà vu swept him. Escalero, BG, and now this spontaneous feeling of being watched but by something that he had already noticed.

Was he still under the influence of whatever he might have touched earlier. Why was he feeling like this? Why could he not figure out what was making him feel this Déjà vu. Peering over at the clocks glowing red. His eyes suddenly widened as he began to realize what had made him feel so unnerved. Immediately he dropped to the ground.

"Crap!" He hissed with his knees hitting the cold rough tile as he narrowly avoided slamming his drinking glass on the floor.

Thinking back to the previous day and looking at the red glow of the kitchen clock he quickly deduced as to why he had felt such an imposing presence. Remembering back when he mindlessly looked out the side view mirror of Sapphires car. Remembering what he had seen in the corner of his eyes for only a passing moment. Remembering red, piercing eyes, that stabbed through the tinted windows of a pitch-black van that had seemingly followed behind them. Now just seconds ago, the same piercing red eyes, drove like daggers through the thick fog beyond the large living room window. His heart raced in his chest as he slowly shakenly set the glass in his hand down on the tile floor before sliding it aside.

Inching his way out of the kitchen trying to crawl beneath the view of the living room window. He fearfully brought himself to his feet after dragging himself out of view. He then dashed up the stairs and down the hall trying to remember the dark layout of the halls and where Sapphire stated she would be. Peaking in, he whispered her name louder and louder before she finally shifted in bed waving her arm in Timmy's direction.

"I'll be up just a minute chill." She groaned half muffled by her pillow.

"It's those men Sapphire! I think they're here." He whispered louder.

She sprung up, one eye still closed, and her hair mashed to one side.

"Shit! I uh... yeah ...Wait outside, gimme a sec, so I can get dressed." Timmy nodded his head, checking his pockets again and breathing a sigh of relief having felt both his pocketknife and the memory chip still pressed together. Swinging open the door Sapphire grabbed Timmy's hand, and with a groggy tone, half-heartedly ushered him back down the hall "Come on my parents made a safe house if we can get there fast enough, we can avoid getting in another fight with those bastards!" She said as she and Timmy bolted out the back door of her house.

Chapter 4: Clandestine

Stepping out into the gauzy fog, Timmy felt as all others would in said environment; that iota of unease due to the uncanny nature at which it was created and used by Mudlurks during the invasion of earth. How they would pounce their prey with malicious methods, without tactic or strategy. Simply rampaging in a blinding whirlwind of brutality and callousness.

The horrific stories of those who managed to survive said attacks, let alone the genocidal invasion of earth itself traumatizing even Timmy's later generation. In this moment he was unsure of what to be more fearful of, the possibility of Mudlurks still around on earth or Escalero s men undoubtedly closing in behind him.

Looking back quickly he could barely make out the outline of the door they left, and with looking forward all he could see was Sapphire, but in the corner of his eyes a foreboding shadow etched from beyond the mist as a figure easily towering over Timmy loomed only inches away. Timmy jerked back from Sapphire as his heart harshly tensed from the sudden appearance. Reactively, Timmy crouched as low as he possibly could, before kicking up into the shadowed figure. The shadowed figure jolted back holding their gut and yet no noise had exerted from their mouth.

"Saph run!" Timmy shouted before barreling into the blurry shadow. Sapphire gasped taking off in an in-discernable direction. Gravel grinded against itself as the person's boots dug firmly in place holding Timmy back. The stranger then began to speak in a withered rustic unfamiliar voice.

"Mr. Green wait! I am not here to hurt you." Regardless of the man's words Timmy resonated only on hearing his family's name causing him to grit his teeth with scolding resentment.

"Don't say that name!" He shouted trying to push himself away from the man. Unable to move, however, due to the man's tight grip, Timmy then bent forward biting down into the stranger's forearm.

The man only grunting, his face not changing from its stern cold fixed looking. Freeing one of his hands the man struck Timmy hitting him squarely in the nose causing Timmy to lurch back holding his face.

"Please Mr. Green, I am not wanting a fight. All I want is the memory card." The man said correcting his posture and holding out his hand. Timmy staggered, caressing his nose and wincing as the sharp immediate pain gave a taste of metallic blood. Gritting his teeth he growled out in his retort.

"You hurt Sapphire, killed that man at the hospital! You murdered my family! The only thing you're getting out of me is a fight!" In a flash Timmy closed the space between himself and the stranger and with rapid secession he began to bash his fists into the stranger's chest pushing them back. Fury fueled his body with endless amounts of endurance, as he relentlessly advanced on the stranger blow after blow. Continuously outpacing the man jabbing just under each of his blocking maneuvers.

As each strike continued though the stranger began to match Timmy's attacks, with his own deflections quickening in their pace. Until in an unforeseen opening the man momentarily peaked behind himself. Glancing back at Timmy showing a startling pair of glowing eyes as he redirected Timmy's fists upward, snatching one of Timmy's wrist. Shock and fear washed over his face, as Timmy looked back into the man's luminescent red eyes before the man twisted Timmy's wrist behind his back and slammed him into a nearby tree.

"Enough!" the man shouted over Timmy's grunting as he pressed him harder into the tree. "This is pointless, and you could not beat me if you tried. You are fast, but predictable." Timmy huffed, leveraging himself away from the tree making just enough room to swing his leg back hitting the man in his privates. The man dropped to one knee loosening his grip giving Timmy the leeway needed to yank free.

The man groaned, balling one of his fists and hitting the ground in frustration as he rose to his feet. Timmy stepped back from the man, his unnerving unmistakably gleaming eyes locking again with Timmy. He gasped as he took in what he had seen. Not a mask, not eyewear, but human eyes. Eyes that looked tired and strained with a mountain of annoyance, cold rich dark blue irises hugged his pupils that radiated a burning crimson light. Timmy recoiled at the sight but did not waver.

Slowly the red hue in the man's eyes dissipated causing him to nearly vanish as the fog enveloped him, once more turning into a shadowed blur. Looking behind himself Timmy saw the faint view of the tree he was pushed into, quickly he thought of a plan to take out the mysterious stranger while silence left them both cautious with anticipation. Until at last Timmy heard the sudden gentle crunching of gravel against the man's boots, panic shooting through Timmy motivating his movements as he ran full speed to and then up the tree with the man following closely behind him.

Leaping over top the man as he reached the tree. Timmy, in the middle of the air, then turned his body, flipping himself and kicking at the man's head, connecting to it with a loud whack as the man's head was lunged face first into the tree. Landing successfully Timmy watched hesitantly, squinting his eyes until he made out the man's silhouette slumped against the tree, causing Timmy to smirk to himself, even giving a chuckle of self-admiration.

The man held himself up and shifted himself checking his head before turning to face Timmy. Straightening upright and giving a sigh, he spoke adamantly. "Two things are going to happen, one: you are going to give me that memory card. And two: Now, you are coming with me."

Timmy scoffed, giggling slightly before shaking his head.

"Actually, you got that wrong." Getting to his feet he held up three fingers and continued. "Three things are gonna happen, one: I am not givin you the memory card, two: I'm not goin anywhere with you, And Three: I'm gonna knock your head into that tree again." He smiled as he lowered his hand.

The man stood there looking back at Timmy, not moving nor saying a word. It put off Timmy and sent chills down the back of his neck, but he held his head high and readied himself.

"Boy, listen. I have fought things ten times your size and twenty times stronger. Do not get ahead of yourself."

Timmy scoffed again at the man.

"And? Am I supposed to be impressed? All I'm saying is you might not wanna tell your buddies that you're getting your butt handed to you by a seventeen-year-old." Appearing dimly at first, the glow in the man's eyes quickly grew easily bleeding through the fog ahead of them as the distant sunrise began to shine across Sapphires back yard.

The man easily became clearer with the fading of the fog, him being entirely equipped head to toe with tactical gear. It was then that he saw the man's hand reaching for his side holster.

"You should not have forced my hand like this boy." His holster clicked as he grasped his weapons grip. Timmy's eyes widened as a phantom pain brushed his side.

"Uh yeah, no thanks I've already been shot and that's not something I plan on rehearsing with you for a second take." Timmy said, grabbing his side.

The man's eyes looked downward practically examining where Timmy's wound had been when confusion inexplicitly took him.

"I see, then you know all too well. That what is coming ... you cannot run away from." Like a blaring siren it had struck Timmy as he replayed the man's words. He took a step back, fear rattling his bones with him unable to move at first. Shaking his head, he retraced his step and whispered.

"Try me." With that the man un-holstered his weapon aiming it perfectly at Timmy.

Time began to slow as the projectiles fired out of the weapon and Timmy watched their approach as he perceived every inch of ground being gained, holding his breath he pushed himself away from the path of the two barbs as they seamlessly passed where he stood before casually landing on the ground beside him. Turning his head to face the man he simply blinked and in said short time not only did he advance completely on the man but went as far as to get partially behind him. The man's body and eyes were still stuck in their original position of firing the stun gun.

Timmy exhaled and time continued its normal speed, as it did, The man looked around, and for once even showed a bit of surprise. Honing this advantage Timmy kicked at the back of the man's leg knocking him down. Bolting in front of the man after holding his breath. Time again slowed, and in an inconceivable motion Timmy swung five swift punches straight across the man's face.

Exhausting all his body could muster, however, Timmy began to pant uncontrollably as his spontaneous ability disappeared. Time returned to normal with the man being thrust to the ground from the sheer force of Timmy's assault. Holding his face, the man quickly looked about firmly gripping his stun gun and replacing a cartridge.

As the man turned to his side, he looked at Timmy, and watched him as he hyperventilated whilst grabbing at his chest. Without saying a word, the man rushed Timmy lifting him over his head before driving him down into the gravel beneath him.

Blisteringly white pain shocked Timmy's back as the wind was knocked out of him. He tried to move to speak but he could barely breathe as the man climbed over top of him and jabbed at Timmy with his stun gun. For only a snapping second, time slowed, and in that moment, Timmy grasped the man's hand holding it back with all his strength, at the same time he fumbled about in his pocket snatching out his blade and thrusting it at the man's throat.

With time quickly returning to normal, the mans red eyes diverted from Timmy's eyes to the blade as he narrowly grabbed it mere inches from his throat. They both glared at the knife determinately before switching their focus to each other grunting and growling with gnashed teeth as both fought inflexibly in their power struggle. Barely visible in each budge, as they excruciatingly continued their deadlock.

Timmy's muscles began to give and slowly his fatigue piled up as the man's stun gun drew closer. Timmy tried to hold his breath to somehow summon the time slow until, finally breaking their stalemate, a brilliant light blinded both Timmy and the man completely. The man leaped off Timmy and shouted out.

"What the hell!" Standing up Timmy looked for the source of the flare shot, only to see Sapphire staring back fearfully and pale. Whipping around Timmy kicked the man knocking him unconscious.

"Timmy!" Sapphire shouted.

"What? I had to; he could have killed us! Besides, he's not dead...I don't think I can kick that hard." he said, scratching his head.

Timmy looked at the man hesitating thinking about what to do. “I have some questions... can you help me with him?” Kneeling Timmy wrapped one of the man’s arms around his shoulder.

“I uh... okay.” She said doing the same as Timmy as they dragged the man into Sapphires bunker and closed the door. Dragging the man to the back of the bunker, Timmy persuaded Sapphire to help in tying the man to a chair. Hesitantly she agreed, considering her own nerves on the stranger that attacked Timmy. “I... can’t believe I’m doing this.” Sapphire murmured as she tied the man’s hands behind his back.

“Alright that should be good, I think.” She said after returning to Timmy's side. Standing there, Timmy watched silently as he constructed questions for the strange man. As he did, he turned to check on Sapphire. Taking note of her standoffishness. Timmy began to apologize for the situation saying.

“I’m sorry I got you into this ...” she turned her head to face him shrugging her shoulders and responded saying.

“It’s fine he was attacking you after all.”

“Hmm.” Is all he could mutter as he pondered the statement. Questioning the validity of what sapphire said. He didn’t use anything lethal despite the other attackers shooting him, he didn’t swing at Timmy first merely reaching for him. If this was truly Escalero or one of his men. Why was the man so passive? Why was he alone? Timmy replayed what the man had said and the fact that the man did appear to be separated somewhat from the others.

“So how long should he be out? I mean in movies they usually just cut to them being awake.” Sapphire said abruptly switching Timmy's attention.

“Well, I’m not really sure, in the training and research I did they would sometimes be out for a few seconds to hours depending.” Timmy said, folding his arms.

"He isn't dead ... is he?" Sapphire asked tilting her head as she slowly made her way to the man sitting limply in the chair. Looking at the man she outstretched one of her fingers nearly poking the man's face until without warning he spoke.

"Not even close." The man grumbled. Both Sapphire and Timmy's eyes shot wide open watching the man as he rose his head with no hesitation.

"What !?" Timmy said drawn a back.

"Ah! Shit!" Sapphire exclaimed snatching her hand away from the man. Stumbling backwards as she slipped onto her rear, before crawling backwards until she reached Timmy. Shakily she stood up next to him, both frozen in place by the man's sudden resurgence.

"I would not go that easily." The man said as his eyes slowly drifted open. He coldly glared back at Timmy unblinking in his steely gaze. Shivers ran across Timmy's body as he straightened himself and cleared his throat.

"I-I would hope not. Cause I got a lot of questions." Timmy said with a stutter. The man nodded his head simply replying with

"Okay."

"Okay?" Timmy asked inquisitively.

"You have questions, I may have answers." The man replied as he sat back in the chair.

"And you're just going to give them to me?" Timmy asked, tilting his head.

"There is no alternative to me getting out of this is there?" The man said cocking an eyebrow.

"Uh no, no there isn't." Timmy mumbled worriedly.

The man looked back at Timmy deadpanned.

"Alright then. Ask your questions." The man said. Cautiously Timmy looked away from the man, meeting eyes with Sapphire pausing for a moment trying to gauge her view on what was happening which was met with only a shrug of her shoulders and a wave of her hand to continue.

Nodding his head Timmy lightly spoke saying.

"Okay... are you Escalero? If not..., where would he go? Would he stay at the plant, or would he be somewhere else?" The man frowned before asking.

"Escalero who?" Annoyed by his response Timmy barked out.

"Escalero Martí!" The man's eyes went red, but his face showed no anger, only that he was thinking. The unnatural and effortless way the man turned his eyes to that glowing red sent chills down Sapphire and Timmy with Sapphire even looking away as to not make eye contact with the man as he began to say.

"Do you mean the serial killer from Spain?" Again, the man frowned before saying plainly "Dead. Irrelevant."

"What? Your lying, you can act however you want but I spent months spying on your men. Finding out about your fake church and hearing all about your Crusader people. So don't lie! Cause I already know that Escalero is tied into it...and you're gonna tell me where I can find him!" Timmy said slamming his hands on either side of the chair the man was tied to. The man however, immovable like a stone wall, continued to stare down Timmy impassively.

"Say my sources are wrong, and Escalero is alive. You must realize that The Final Crusade as a whole is a more urgent matter to attend to." The man said. Timmy huffed walking away from the man as he continued. "You said you were gathering information and, in that time, did you even find out their true intentions?" he asked. Timmy turned back to him puzzled at what the man said.

"Their intentions?" Timmy asked.

"Yes, to put it in other terms what they believe in." The man's inflection grew steep and heavy Shining a light on the severity at which the man saw The Final Crusade. Timmy couldn't reply only listening as the man kept on with his rant.

"You must have heard of the first Crusade, a march to the holy land, the conquest that killed thousands upon thousands of people? All in the name of God. That is what The Final Crusade is rooted in, only this time it is more than just 'reclamation of land'. They are a cult that spans throughout the galaxy believing God is unsatisfied with humanity, that our world, that we all have been consumed by sin. That everything must be cleansed. A new Ark, A new flood, only this time more of blood than water."

Struck with fear, Sapphire nervously chuckled.

"You've gotta be kidding us, right?" The man turned his head to Sapphire.

"Aside from their simplistic adopted moniker and beliefs, The Final Crusade is not a joke, and should be taken very seriously." The man said before turning back to Timmy. "Tell me, your 17, right? A kid, doing this on his own." The man stopped himself and nodded his head to Sapphire saying "Respectively." before continuing. "Do you understand how ill prepared you are? The Final Crusade have armies listing in the trillions on and off world. Defectors from the Alliance and the War Council lying in wait for their signal to purge."

The man inched forward leaning to Timmy as he hissed out. "Your hunt for Escalero is futile. If you even manage to eliminate him, they will put someone in his place in mere moments. Tell me boy, how would you do what so many others have failed to. How would you save the universe from another civil war? You have speed and tenacity but your helplessly predictable!" The man began to practically shout as Timmy could hardly stutter out any words in defense simply staring back dumbstruck.

"You think it is so easy? Defeat Escalero! Save the day! be a hero ?!" The man yelled. Timmy gritted his teeth and screamed back at the top of his lungs his voice crackling as he yelled out

"No!" Before muttering quietly to himself. "I I don't know...I." stepping forward anger flew across Sapphires still shaking body as she yelled at the man.

"Hey, fuck off alright! You have no fuckin clue what this dude has been through in even the past 24 hours alone!" She stepped in front of Timmy, closing the distance between herself and the man.

"He's in pain, his family was stolen from him, and no one was helping. He took that weight on his own regardless of him being a kid." She stopped for a moment admiring the young man's bravery despite the odds he already endured. "He's a brave guy just trying to get justice for his family! Heck, he's probably acting more of a man than you were at that age!" The man giving a notable cock of his eyebrow at the last statement as Sapphire continued. "So, fuck you okay! He kicked the guy's asses who were at the plaza, took a bullet like a champ, He escaped the hospital with them hunting him down. And he kicked your ass too!" She yelled, getting in the man's face.

The man sat unblinking easily disturbing Sapphire as a shiver ran down her spine and still, she carried on. "As far as I'm concerned you and your little Crusader buddies should be watching yourselves." She snapped in a huff before stepping back to Timmy's side. Awestruck Timmy's eyes couldn't be prayed away from her, he was completely stunned by her defensiveness to his endeavor.

"Sapphire..." Timmy said softly before being interrupted by the man.

"Well, she seems confident, but you look distraught and on the edge of abstaining from this whole mission you have found yourself in." the man said coldly as he turned attention from Sapphire to Timmy. Hesitantly Timmy stepped forward raising his head and slouched shoulders.

"I won't run away from this. I'm gonna go at them with everything I got." Timmy said Determinately.

"You could die." The man said. His voice this time held a hint of remorse and hesitation that confused Timmy.

Holding true to his words Timmy replied with no resentment in his voice saying.

"Then I'll take Escalero out with me. And if I can't even do that ... then at least I'll be with my family again." Timmy said, lowering his head. Silence stained the dimly lit room as minutes passed with nothing more than what Timmy had said on the minds of everyone in the shelter.

Finally, the man started to speak.

"How about I do you one better." He said relaxing his body in the chair "You do have skill and something else ... something I have never seen before. Something that should not be physically possible, and I cannot quite put together what I even saw but, I think what I have researched before coming here was an understatement to say the least." Timmy tilted his head and looked at Sapphire before looking back to the man saying.

"What are you on about?"

The man gave a sigh.

"Let me be more direct. I will help you eliminate Escalero. If you help me take on the Final Crusade." Timmy shook his head dumbfounded.

"You're not making any sense." Timmy replied. The man sighed again and leaned back in the chair.

"You do not catch on well do you." The man sighed shaking his head. "Hmm, I was too rash, and I apologize for that, but I felt we did not have the time. Now I just need to get you on my side. I am not with the Final Crusade if that's not abundantly clear yet.

You can call me Rivers. I am the squad leader of a special forces group for a division within the U.M.E." The man said.

Sapphire's eyes went wide as she looked at Timmy lunging at him and smacking his arm.

"Timmy, you beat up a U.M.E soldier!" she shouted as Timmy covered himself with his arms as he repeatedly muttered the letter I. Rivers shook his head as he chimed in.

"I wouldn't say that as I stated I felt the only way I could communicate with him was to make him feel comfortable. I allowed myself to be subdued."

Timmy looked at Rivers in disbelief.

"I could have killed you." Timmy worriedly said. Rivers gave an unenthusiastic chuckle.

"Not possible. Even if my back up was not with me." He said giving an oddly stiff attempt at a smirk. Timmy's head jerked back as he asked.

"Back-up?" Rivers softly leaned his head back, before calling out.

"Reaper, turn on your laser." Instantly a red line shined visibly fixed on Timmy.

"What the!?" Timmy screeched as he covered the area at which the focus point of the laser was.

Sapphire looked for a moment before noticing the focus point was Timmy's privates to which she immediately blushed and looked away.

"Do not worry, from what I have heard that means she likes you." Rivers said with his odd smirk returning.

"How long has she been there?" Timmy asked, still covering himself.

"As long as I have been here." Rivers replied before continuing. "So, no need for pleasantries." Finally regaining composure, Sapphire turned back to Rivers saying.

"Oh here... let me untie you." Sheepishly embarrassed, she walked over to Rivers only for him to abruptly stand up from the chair, with the rope casually slipping off his wrists.

Timmy snapped his head to Sapphire.

"I thought you tied him up good!" he asked, his voice slightly cracking. Sapphire's face puckered as she glared at Timmy.

"Don't mood at me, I never said I was a part of the boy scouts." She said shrugging her shoulders.

"It would not have mattered. I have gotten out of much worse." Rivers said before stepping to Timmy. "So, then Mr. Green." Rivers started until he was interrupted

"Call me Timmy." Timmy said.

"Very well Timmy. If you would, I would like you and Sapphire to come with us to our base of operations." Rivers said holding his hand towards the shelter's entrance.

As they all emerged from the shelter Rivers continued to give out an explanation of his mission. "That memory card I was trying to obtain from you was just the beginning of my intel to be gathered on The Final Crusade." Rivers rambled on. As they reached a tinted unmarked black van Rivers eyes turned red, and the doors began to open. Both Sapphire and Timmy cautiously entered the vehicle followed closely by Rivers and Reaper.

As they all sat down Rivers' eyes shifted and an automated voice from the front of the vehicle echoed as it stated it had confirmed their destination and the time at which it would take to get there. Gradually Rivers eyes reverted to normal as he faced everyone. Looking at the van it appeared to be retrofitted to hold more passengers as well as turning seats which allowed the passengers to look around in multiple directions as the vehicle used self-driving.

"I was able to scan the memory card momentarily, but I could not get a proper connection to the files, there was too much distance. Along with the scuffle we had things became...difficult." Rivers said a little disgruntled. "What I had managed to collect though shows my intel so far was right." He confirmed.

"And that is?" Timmy asked, twirling around in his chair.

"I will explain more once we have reached our M.O.B." Rivers answered before gesturing to Timmy and Sapphire to put on their seatbelts. They turned and looked quizzically at him.

"M.O.B.? What the heck does that stand for?" Sapphire asked.

"Main Operating Base. Now enough questions we have a long drive." Rivers roughly replied.

An hour later, they had now driven well past the city limits, out to the arid, desolate, expansive desert that laid beyond the city's reach. In the distance after a great bit of time Timmy began to observe a silhouette beginning to expand. Gradually it showed itself as a rustic and withered shack. Feeling uneasy with the sight, both him and Sapphire began to squirm anxiously in their seats.

Settling to a stop, the sound of roaring cicadas and thrashing panels against the shack became abundant in their windy ambiance. Timmy turned looking out the van windshield. When from behind the shack two armed men began making their way to the van. Timmy got up from the seat quickly, ready to throw himself and Sapphire out of the van, until Rivers reached back grabbing his shoulder. "Steady, they are with us." He said as his eyes turned red.

Timmy watched the men eyeing them cautiously. Nodding their heads, the two of them stepped away from the shack training their guns outward in the direction Timmy and the others came from. As loud mechanisms bellowed from under the ground itself. Trembling the van and its passengers as it swayed side to side. Dust and rock beginning to kick up around both the shack and the van. Suddenly the shack and some of the ground around it lifted from the surrounding earth. Timmy and Sapphire watched in awe as the hydraulics of the base's entrance were extended fully holding the shack back at a 60-degree angle revealing a steeped ramp that peeled into a lit underground hanger.

Steadily the van descended deep into their base of operations with the men outside of the entrance following suit. Pulling into a parking spot alongside various other vehicles, the two men stepped up to the van opening the doors, welcoming back both Rivers and Reaper.

"What is this place? It's got so much stuff, looks more like a warehouse." Sapphire said as she stepped out before Timmy.

She looked around walking up to and touching a ship as Rivers began to explain.

"This, as I said, is our current base of operations. But it was a precautionary shelter in the late 2030s in case of another War Council invasion." Rivers said as he walked up to the ship Sapphire was touching. "Ever since 2051 it has just been storage for U.M.E armaments and Alliance Star-Fighters. That one there is a two seated fighter made for Raffinierts or Adjustable for a single human pilot." Rivers said before ushering the group further through the base.

As they made their way through Timmy and Sapphire noted a number of different living quarters, shooting ranges, training rooms, and cafeterias. It was endless, with Sapphire even joking saying.

"I'm glad my old man's not here he'd have a few ideas for additions to the house." She said with her and Timmy laughing at the thought.

Finally arriving to the very back of the facility, they came to a large room with the two men, who had met them at the shack entrance, opening the doors to show eight other individuals scattered around the room. Timmy looked at everyone, taking in each person's appearance as those who were closest looked back at him and the rest of the group he had entered with.

Starting from the back were two people, a man and a woman, who turned hearing the group enter. The both of them quickly snapping to attention, standing straighter as they saluted Rivers, the woman shouting out.

"Attention!" causing the rest of the room to stand and face Rivers to salute him.

"At ease." Rivers said allowing the soldiers to continue what each of them were doing.

The woman in the far back however watched closely spotting Timmy and Sapphire. Scowling with a very harsh demeanor as she walked up to Rivers exuding with purpose, stopping only an inch away from him before hissing out.

"Sir, may I speak with you for a moment." Rivers simply cocked his head and the two of them stepped off to the side.

Stepping past Timmy, both of the men who entered the base with them sat by the other soldiers and began to clean their weapons. To the left corner of the room, was another woman reading a book and kicking her feet as she leaned back in a chair.

Off to the right corner was a man lifting weights with a skull imprinted mask over his face and a woman behind him. She sat on the table behind the man with her legs dangling on either side of him as she playfully tried to peel his mask from his face. To which he would delicately smack at her hands shooing her away.

Beside those two was a man imbedded in a mountain of paperwork his hand scribing rampantly as he simultaneously sorted a number of medical supplies. Across from the man we're the last of the soldiers. One of which was woman drawing with the other closely watching and criticizing every stroke of the woman's pen.

Timmy watched the woman as she pushed the man's head away snapping at him, yelling.

"Fuck off X-ray." The man smiled back at the woman.

"Oh, I'm teasin Queenie you know that, but seriously...is it spose ta look like an ass crack?" He said smiling an even bigger grin. With her flicking her pen at him, closing her sketch book, and smacking him with it as she yelled at him.

"shut the hell up".

Suddenly a loud clang from the back of the room pulled Timmy's attention away from the pair. He stared curiously as he saw the largest man in the room set his gun down on the table beside him. It was one of the men who had entered the base with Timmy and the others.

Pulling up a chair the man sat in front of the masked man and smiled to the woman behind him before looking back at the masked man.

"Hey Shining." He said leaning towards the man.

"What's up Apollo?" The masked man asked.

"How's about you go look for food today in the cafeteria." Apollo asked. The man named Shining shook his head.

"Oh no, I don't think so you're on-cook duty this time." He snappily replied.

"Oh, come on Shining I was out in that desert for the past three days eating that crap Maci brought with him." The other man who Timmy came in with scoffing, rolling his eyes as he took apart his gun cleaning it.

"And we all know who the best cook is huh." Apollo said with a smirk nudging Shining's shoulder.

"Nope, not doin it, I ain't. I gotta do a few curls anyway and shit." Shining said grabbing a weight beside him.

"Oh, okay well how's about this then, we do a little bet who can do the most reps in two minutes." Timmy watched seeing that Apollo Must have already known of Shining's vice. As even saying the word bet caused Shining to twitch. Which made the large man smile big.

Shining turned his head more directly to Apollo and set his weight down.

"Okay, okay, but if I win your buying me a new vest." Apollos eyes widened hearing Shining say that.

"Buddy that's a bit pricey don't you think?" Apollo asked giving a chuckle.

"Well, I have very fine taste, no?" Shining said smiling under his mask.

Apollo scratched his head for a second before holding his stomach. Grumbling, he rolled his eyes as the woman behind Shining gave an impish smile.

"Ugh fine but you better go cook right after this if I win." Apollo said as he stepped over to a weight rack grabbing the two of the second heaviest weights and handing one to Shining.

Grunting Shining quickly grabbed the weight with two hands. Turning back to the woman behind him he breathily asked her.

"He isn't cheating... is he Kilo?" To which she smiled leaning into him saying.

"No honey, he isn't." Giving a sigh, Shining nodded his head.

"On your go." He said with Apollo giving a three second countdown with the two men beginning their reps.

Stepping past Apollo and Shining was the man who was one of the first two that saluted when seeing Rivers. Taking a seat, he sat by the table in the middle of the room and began to tinker with a number of different robotic, animal-looking devices.

Each animal looked uniquely different. From color, design, and even species. All of them appeared to be personalized. The man grabbed one that happened to be an elephant, before taking a seat as he adjusted its parts. Timmy quickly becoming infatuated with the devices.

Leaning in, all Timmy could do was take in the detail of the intricate little devices.

"Uh, so Rivers... what's up with the kid?" The voice snared Timmy's attention. Darting to the origin of the voice, Timmy noticed it to be the woman that was leaning back in a chair, rocking it back and forth.

Her eyes glared at Timmy before altering to an oddly flirtatious smirk and wink as she peaked over her book. Baffled and blushing Timmy was speechless, looking behind himself, as if to check if the woman was truly referring to him. He was met with only Sapphire standing quietly, and observing as he was, now looking past him. Curiously he could swear Sapphire gave an almost territorial look back at the woman in the chair, but before anyone else could say anything, the woman who had taken Rivers aside spoke up.

"Yeah, Rivers. Wonderland has a point, what are these damn kids doing here?"

The room became immediately divided half looking to Rivers, whilst the remaining half looked curiously at Timmy. With a spotlight cast over him, Timmy began to squirm, and a feeling of him being trapped in a pool of sweat started to form. His hands shook as he darted his head about the room anxiously. Timmy attempted to secretively shrivel up in his brother's hoodie. Trying desperately to create an answer when unexpectedly, and coming to life ecstatically, one of the animal styled robots marched forward. Particularly an elephant, which trumpeted towards the table edge causing the tinkerer to leap to it trying to grab it.

Missing his catch, the creation tumbled off the table only to be caught by the woman who called out Timmy, correspondingly named Wonderland. Who held out her book just in time as the creation flopped off the table and onto it. Softly smiling the woman pulled the book to her chest where she scooped up the creation setting it on her shoulder. Doing so it started to morph, fitting onto her shoulder as if it were a plate of armor, leaving only the elephant's head sticking upright.

Subsequently, each of the other animatronics awakened, crawling, running, and flying. Making their way to what was presumably their owner. The first of which was the tinkerers animatronic that looked like a cheetah that purred as it turned to its owner curling up in front of him. To the man called Shining, a huntsman spider crept up to his shoulder similarly morphing itself into a plate of armor with only its head showing.

Swooping down behind Shining, to the woman he called Kilo was a Peregrine Falcon which also morphed into an armor plate until it was just the head of the falcon. Stomping on its way to Apollo was a silverback gorilla. Smiling at the creation Apollo lowered his hand and stuck out one of his fingers allowing the Creation to grasp on to it as he raised his hand to his shoulder with the creation swinging off morphing to his shoulder.

Trekking over to the man sitting by the towering pile of paperwork was a German Shepherd that nuzzled its head against the man's palm as it reached him. The man lifted his head from his work and petted the creation before hastily resuming his work picking up the creation and a syringe as he moved across the room to the other man who had met Timmy and the others at the base entrance.

"Okay Macedonia you're the last to receive their shot." The busy man with the dog creation said to the other man as his own creation, a hyena, stepped onto his hand cackling as it laid happily on his hand.

"I told you call me Maci, just Maci, Doc and hurry it up you know I hate fuckin needles." He said, already wincing, with 'Doc' placing his Shepard creation onto his shoulder. Shaking his head, Doc lifted Maci's sleeve, injecting the needle he had into Maci's shoulder. Maci letting out a yelp, causing both his creation and Doc's creation to begin growling and howling at one another.

Behind Doc and Maci were two more creations slowly moving with one another, a King Cobra and an alligator snapping turtle. Both of which came to face their respective owners the cobra going to the man called X-ray and the snapping turtle going to the drawing woman who X-ray had called Queenie.

"He better be adjusted right this time!" both X-ray and Queenie said to the tinkerer before looking at each other and giving the other a side eye.

Lastly were the three at the entrance of the room, Reaper, Rivers, and the woman that confronted him. Timmy Believing that theirs were the most creative of the squadron. Floating to Reaper was a transparent box jellyfish that pushed itself to its owner landing delicately on her shoulder as it morphed to its armor-plated form, the tendrils creating a unique design.

Crawling up the woman who confronted Rivers was specifically an enlarged bullet ant that clearly showed its features being simulated by the detailed hair on its abdomen, large mandibles, and antenna. Coldly she stared down the tinkerer, as she stretched out her hand allowing the ant to further its stride up her arm, and too her shoulder.

"Pitiful Rook, keep a better watch on the damn War Companions next time!" She snapped at the tinkerer. His face went flush as he lowered his head again.

"Yes, ma'am." He spoke softly. Proudly stepping to Rivers, with its head held high, was a lion that roared as it faced him.

Rivers looked at his companion blankly as he casually extended his hand. It roared before leaping off the table and up his arm then to his shoulder where it morphed into his shoulder plate. With a sigh, he too looked at Rook with disappointment before meeting eyes with the sharp-tongued woman again. Pointing her finger at Timmy, she seethed as she scowled at Rivers.

"Answer me, why is this boy here Rivers!" she shouted, "You said it was simple, grab the intel and get out!" Her anger steamed to a boil as she shouted again at Rivers.

Even with her stature being close to Timmy's she still stood boldly before her obvious superior. She held her imposing presence powerfully. Like with Timmy, however, Rivers was undeterred by the woman's show of brazen distain. "Well, are you going to answer me Rivers?" She shouted.

"Enough Nimitz." Rivers barked out. The whole room now returning their attention to the pair. Nimitz huffed rolling her eyes looking back at the group before turning back to Rivers.

"So that's what gets you all worked up huh? Playing 50 questions?" she said slyly.

"No. I just refuse to cooperate with you when you choose to berate your superiors." he said back sternly.

"I was your superior." she replied coldly. Rivers looked down at Nimitz lowering his head to be but an inch from her face growling out in his rustic voice.

"You were."

Rivers eyes turned red, and the room found ways to be even quieter than before. Nimitz's face visibly became unsettled from Rivers eyes, her resolve almost completely shattered.

"You think you can scare me with your little light show?" she asked an audible tremble in her voice. Rivers didn't say a word, and for a moment the tension choked the air to suffocation, until finally Rivers turned from her to look at the group.

"If you believe I am trying to scare you...then you have mistakenly misinterpreted how I operate." He scowled as he disappointingly sighed. River's voice suddenly boomed in everyone's chest as he said aloud. "Nomads face the war table!" In unison the soldiers all switched attention and no one, not even Nimitz dared defy his order. Out of fear or respect Timmy could not yet gather how they listened to Rivers, but he did not question it instead looking nervously to Sapphire who had already followed shakenly along with the others.

Looking at the war table it beamed with a blue hue, as a holographical pattern appeared before everyone. With everyone's attention finally to the war table, Rivers then reached out to Timmy saying. "The memory card please if you will." Timmy jolted at first, shocked to hear Rivers speak his name as he had still been focused on the back and forth between Rivers and Nimitz. Reluctantly at first Timmy stepped over to Rivers and slowly began to rummage through his pockets.

Staggering for a moment, Timmy became slack jawed, his eyes opening wide as he now a bit more franticly rummaged through his pockets tossing everything out, realizing he did not have the drive.

"Rivers I-" He started to say his voice almost ready to quiver, as he looked distressingly at Rivers. Noticing quickly, that between River's fingertips was the memory card itself.

"I do not mean to be deceitful, but we had hardly the time to wait." Rivers said.

Timmy questioning when he had even snatched the memory card. "If you did not join us. I still would have needed to complete my mission." he said, as he continued. "On our way here, I managed to transfer the documents to my chip." Holding out his hand Blue holographic folders began sliding across the war table.

Timmy held his tongue, far too nervous to question Rivers further. “To answer your questions Nimitz, it was simple. All that happened was that the number of objectives changed.” Rivers said flipping through folders before reaching the one he wanted and clicking on it. Opening the file showed schematics, map layouts, and photos of various individuals.

An Intel network of leads: Possible Final Crusader informant in Rivers Division, deals between the war council and the Final Crusade, motives of the Final Crusade, the emerald knight, whereabouts of the Messiah, and names of lead generals within the Final Crusade.

Timmy read each name as it circled the other pieces in the holographic file. Alexander Kovach, Phoenix, and finally it stopped at Escalero Martí. A shiver ran up Timmy's back as he thought about recent events. Instinctively grabbing his phone to still see no service as well as no calls from his Uncle. He sighed, still worried ever since he separated from him.

Returning Timmy's attention was Rivers as he spoke. “Confirming intel from previous missions was my main objective, which is now complete. Taking into account the reconnaissance myself and Reaper went on, intel from informants on previous missions, and this memory card given to us by Timmy here.” Rivers said pointing to Timmy before continuing “We can ascertain that this...” Rivers paused for a moment, as his red eyes flickered, causing a schematic to appear on the war table.

Examining the schematic showed an image of a 3D design, a piloted mech-suit. It read that it stood 12 feet tall, made of the recently discovered Istellium metal and needed only one pilot. It came equipped with a high-density laser and a belt fed grenade launcher capable of firing 40x53mm high velocity rounds. Timmy stared stunned by such an instrument of death. "This is Project David." Rivers said, causing the room to show a multitude of shocked faces.

"Project David? That can't be right Ja- I mean Crimson and Omega 1 were supposed to be in charge of testing that." Wonderland said sitting up in her chair as she set aside her book.

"Wasn't it supposed to be labeled ineffective?" X-ray asked as he flung his hand in the air in confusion.

Queenie leaned into him calling him stupid as she interjected.

"It was very effective, but exorbitant 'big money' and kinda overkill from what Crimson said." Queenie said mockingly with X-ray smacking his lips in response.

"That's right, this is what Nezumi was trying to tell us before the Final Crusade confronted us." Rivers said. Shining stood up slamming his weight on the ground clenching his fist.

"So, they were fuckin workin together!" He shouted out before sitting back with Kilo hitting the chair he sat on. "Dirty fuckin Mudlurks!" He Hissed.

"Shining, temper." River snapped at him sternly.

"Sorry sir, force of habit." Shining said with a sigh.

Maci sat forward pointing at one of the intel points as he looked at Rivers asking.

"Aye Rivers, is this supply route right on its intel? 50 plus units?" he asked worriedly as he continued. "If so, I don't know if we can handle this even with Omega 1 as back up." He said before yelping again. "Ouch Doc what the hell!" He shouted. Doc scoffed, rolling his eyes.

"That was the last one you big baby."

"Fortunately, it seems this is only one, a test either to see how well they can smuggle it or for other means." Rivers said.

“Even with that being the case, one unit from Project David is enough to change an entire battlefields outcome in minute’s, we shouldn’t underestimate this.” Nimitz pointed out to the group.

“Another question I have is I thought the power wasn’t sustainable, I thought that part of the expense would be too much?” Maci asked.

“Seems that was another part that might have been fixed with the dealings between the Final Crusade and the War Council.” Rivers replied.

“They probably traded that Intel on the Alliance for the Mudlurks to give them a viable power source.” Shining added. Nimitz stepped back from the war table.

“Which might I say, speaking of the Final Crusade, what's our game plan, seriously? We got our asses handed to us the last time we fought against them?” Nimitz began to say.

The room shared a similar look of disappointment at the statement with none of the soldiers speaking up in defense. "Well come on... anyone? We need a strategy here. We can't just go in and expect to hold our own against the Final Crusades numbers even with back up.” Nimitz said looking around the room. Timidly raising his hand, Timmy looked over to Nimitz.

“I might have an option.” He stutteringly spoke nearly cowering as her fierce eyes fell onto Timmy before barking out at him.

“Well, speak boy.”

“I ah... well when I was gathering Intel on the Final Crusade regarding Escalero, I found a church that they primarily work out of. I imagine that might be a good place to start.” He watched patiently expecting a bit of discourse but was surprised to see that instead everyone was quietly listening to him. Coercing himself to continue, he briefly gulped before going on. “If you guys... I don’t know, take it out maybe that would disrupt their... organization. Maybe leave them in the dark somehow?" Feeling a bit braver from their consistent silence he began again. "Not to mention as far as I've seen and heard Escalero doesn't like working with the Crusade. Everyone who's been working with him on this smuggling thing is hired in."

Timmy took a step closer to the war table. A calmer, more deliberately confident tone holding his posture upright. "Now, I didn't realize this at first. From the church I gathered bits and pieces when I was hearing things, but I found out more when I was at the plant. People were saying that they were hired not as part of the 'religious cult'. They seemed less united in things, less devoted, unlike the people in the church. Maybe that's something that will help."

Snapping his fingers, Shining stepped closer to the war table adjusting his mask as he looked from Timmy to Rivers.

"Captain this kid's got something here. If what he's saying is true, this is perfect for us. If Escalero is on his own aside from the small amount of Crusade at the church, that is helping them. And if we're just dealing with second rate mercenaries, then we might have a better chance." Shining said.

"Hmm, alright then good work Timmy." Rivers said, getting closer to the war table himself.

"We still don't have enough evidence though. I want to be more secure before I make this mission final." Nimitz said with Rivers now looking across the table as he pointed out two of his soldiers.

"Wonderland and Macedonia, you two will go out, regroup with Omega one, catch them up. From there I want accurate whereabouts on Escalero and who he's with." Nimitz said, with Wonderland and Maci nodding and replying with; 'Yes, sir.' Followed by them immediately grabbing their things and leaving the room.

"The rest of you, get ready for our green light weather it's in 10 minutes or 10 hours we need to be primed for taking on the Final Crusade just in case Escalero has Nobles on hand." Rivers said with nearly all of Nomad filing out of the room gathering their things as they left.

Watching everyone leave Sapphire and Timmy stood patiently. The latter half praised Timmy for his quick thinking and bravery needed to speak up even with Nimitz's imposing presence.

"Timmy." Rivers said calling the two over while looking through files on the war table. "Listen, you have helped us more than enough. The whole reason I brought you here was to present you with a choice." Rivers said now turning to face the young man. "If you want, you can back out now, I do not want to ask too much from you. Let the professionals take care of this, you can stay here where you will be safe. The both of you...Or you can join us." Rivers said.

"I've seen your abilities first-hand. And in this war with the number of missions I've endured, the trials I had to face... After discovering the Final Crusade and coming up against them." He paused on his words almost reliving every event, experiencing the pain and torment that resulted during said events. Finally returning to Timmy. "I've not seen anything quite like yourself. You're something different. Not every kid off the street nor soldier I have faced human or non-human is capable of the feats you've displayed. Not just against the Final Crusade but also against myself." Rivers said.

Timmy held a deep contemplation. For once he would finally have help in taking on the Crusade. But he could not help but think whether or not he could truly live up to River's standards and expectations. "Well, what do you say?" Rivers asked. Timmy looked up to him still locked with hesitation, and inconsistent dedication. "I. I'm not..." He stuttered. "Could you give him some time to think?" Sapphire defensively chimed, nearly stepping between them yet again coming to Timmy's aid.

"What if me and him go back to my place? Think it over." She deliberated.

"We don't really have the time to think things over like this." Rivers replied now, turning his attention to Sapphire.

"But you did just send out people to look for things. Like you said that could take a long time." She countered. His eyes were unnaturally unblinking which sent a shiver up both their spines. Fully trusting Captain Rivers but still unsettled as he sustained that unnerving uncanny machine-like expression. Relief comforted them both as he finally retained his humanity. Blinking after his brief period of thought before saying.

"I suppose Macedonia and Wonderland heading into the city itself would take a bit of time..."

Turning to the war table, his eyes glowed red as the table's hologram changed from the files to a layout of the city. "And if they go with you, they could leave from your residence instead of entering into the city in an unmarked vehicle which might draw more attention to them." Rivers said zooming in on Sapphires family home.

"Exactly, and last I checked. They didn't follow us from the hospital otherwise I assume you guys would have taken care of them." Sapphire noted.

Rivers retraced the route they took from the hospital thinking back on it.

"True with Reaper and I tailing you, we didn't see anybody leave the hospital. And as we scouted the house nobody tried to converge on you either." Rivers confirmed.

The topic only refilled the sensation of guilt that lurked within the pit of Timmy's stomach.

"Speaking of the hospital, my Uncle...he stayed behind, he wanted to make sure they wouldn't follow." Timmy managed to say, looking from the war table, his eyes already begging for Rivers to do something.

"Could Maci and Wonderland look for him?" He pleaded.

"They have a tall order as is and finding one person knowing how the Final Crusade take care of things..." Rivers contested before truly taking in Timmy's despondent plea for help. Giving a sigh Rivers nodded his head shutting off the war table. "I will send two of my best Nimitz and Apollo. They will go with you." Rivers said. Appreciatively Timmy smiled, as he softly thanked the grizzled man. "Thank you, Rivers."

Waving Timmy to follow, Rivers took him to the other side of the war table to a 3D printing machine. Standing to the side of it, Rivers eyes turned red, and the piece of equipment whistled and whined as it began to spit out a precise sequence for a rather small device. Timmy watched curiously with sapphire, both unsure of what Rivers was partaking in. Until with a final high-pitched chime the machine had finished assembling the quaint blockish shape that left a center button protruding from the top.

"This is an intergalactic communications device, used primarily within the U.M.E and the Alliance." Rivers said tilting the small red and black detailed device.

Handing it off to Timmy, Rivers continued. "I or another member of Nomadic squad can alert you when we have substantial intel for adequately taking on Escalero and the Final Crusade." Timmy looked over the surprisingly simplistic device. Marveled by how such a small and basic looking thing could allow communications throughout space.

"Until then you can go home. Press the button if Escalero's men or the Final Crusade show up, and we can be there to protect you." Rivers said hesitantly seemingly wishing to take back his statement. "You have a finite time to make your decision. Weather you will be ready to face the Final Crusade and Escalero, or not. The choice is yours." Timmy froze, not wanting to give up everything he worked for. Yet his nerves would hardly let him look Rivers in the eyes.

With that as Rivers final words, Timmy and Sapphire were escorted back to Sapphires house. Hardly anyone talked through the entire ride, and the stale tension that was glimpsed within the war room between Nimitz and Timmy, showed more prominently during the ride. Her directing distasteful glances at him from the front passenger seat. Finally, hours later the group pulled slowly into Sapphires large garage. Wonderland commenting.

"If I don't find a man living in a place like this then I aint tryin hard enough." Maci rolled his eyes as he slid open the van door.

"Ha, you getting a man." He said leaping out already anticipating her swipe at his head.

"Oh, I hate you!" Wonderland hissed. Both of them tucking tail as Nimitz barked out from the driver's side shouting.

"Objectives!"

Apollo sighed deeply heading into sapphires house checking the area. After a few minutes passed he called on the radio telling Nimitz the area was secure. Hearing Apollo's words from Nimitz's radio, Sapphire took her leave from the car, telling Timmy.

"I'll see you inside." As Timmy reached for his bag from the back. Just about to leave the car, the doors suddenly locked from the inside a parental lock stopping Timmy from even opening it manually. Curiously and with a pinch of fear, Timmy turned to Nimitz, who looked away from him blankly.

Emotionlessly staring off into space before turning to face him.

"Listen, kid. I saw from the moment you walked in the war room. You're scared. I can smell it off you like a stench. And it reeks... I don't know what you've read off comics, what you've seen in movies." She sneered, gritting her teeth. "But war is death. What we deal in is death. There are no heroes. There are only caskets, and people who tell stories about the ones who lie in them. So cut the act. Before you or someone else gets hurt!" She solemnly spat. The leather from the steering wheel loudly creaking from how tightly she gripped it. Fighting back his tears. Timmy hugged the inside of his brother's hoodie. Until the doors unlocked, with Nimitz shoeing him out.

Flipping his hood over his head he quietly rushed into the house running directly into Apollo.

"Woah killer slow slow I said its clear haha." Apollo boisterously chuckled patting Timmy on the back. Hearing a sniffle however Apollo knelt down holding Timmy shoulders as he looked at the boy. "Oh, hell Nimitz not again...Hey Timmy, look don't mind Nimitz okay, she may be rough, but she means well. She doesn't wanna see a kid get hurt in the middle of this." He said softly. Timmy looked away hurtfully. Apollo gave a frown grumbling for a moment. "How's this sound huh?" He said beating his chest. "Whatever you choose I got your back okay, whether it be me flying back here on a Scorpion gunship to knock down a few Final Crusaders or if you fight alongside us. If my Captain trusts you, I trust you." He proudly pledged. Puffing out his chest he stood statuette with a widely gaining smile as in a near shout he proclaimed. "And in case you do choose to join us allow me to be the first to welcome you to the family, to the 5th squadron of Division 180! Nomadic 5!"

Chapter 5: Trauma

Hours passed since Timmy and Sapphire waved off Nimitz and Apollo. Timmy sat soberly still looking at his phone. Realizing that even out of the dead zone he still hadn't gotten even a call from his uncle. Horrible intrusive thoughts of his uncle's body being swapped with the guards' body that Timmy discovered at the hospital. It haunted him as he shook his head trying to wrestle those thoughts away.

Slowly stepping out onto the porch, Sapphire sat beside Timmy patting his shoulder. It startled him at first as he tried to wipe away the tears that formed in his eyes.

"He'll be okay Timmy; your uncle BG is a smart guy he wouldn't do anything stupid." Sapphire said softly, looking gingerly into his eyes. "At least nothing that would keep him from you. You mean the world to him, your all he ever talks about." She said, giving a smile.

Timmy's heart ached hearing her. He couldn't lose him too. '*Hadn't I lost enough already*?' He thought as he curled himself in a ball hiding his face between his legs. Sapphire sighed, frowning, she pondered what might cheer up Timmy. Lost, without a solution, she sat up holding Timmy's hand. "How about you go get some sleep, it'd be for the best. You've been through a lot." She reasoned, trying to sound as comforting as possible.

Begrudgingly Timmy stepped to his feet nodding his head.

"Maybe your right, I haven't slept in the past 2 days." He said, feeling the heavy bags under his eyes more prominently as she walked him to her room, stopping at the door as he slid into bed.

"I'll keep my ear out in case anything happens so seriously get some sleep. Heck I might need a bit of shut eye too but don't worry I'm a light sleeper." She smiled waving goodbye as she stepped away from the doorway.

With Sapphire leaving, Timmy closed his eyes and whether it be from sheer exhaustion or Sapphire's comforting bed he drifted to sleep. His mind was at peace, his body becoming weightless, there was nothing. As lucidity reached him, he began to see the gentle glow of moonlight and feel a gentle breeze, breathing calmly, he felt content as his body floated in nothingness. Until he heard it, metallic and foreboding.

It shook even the nothingness and the moonlight that surrounded him. His eyes shot open as he fell through the night sky. Darting his eyes, he desperately looked for the red fog, the chains, or that abhorrent amalgamation of disorienting shadows. Instead, he found an absolute absence of anything other than that moonlit sky above him. He flung out his arms, reaching for anything to stop his fall as the wind picked up increasing the momentum of his descent.

Again, the chains roared in the sky above him, only this time it gave a careening screech as their rattling became louder. Timmy looked forward and he braced himself believing the chains to be falling straight down from the sky onto him. He braced himself, knowing it was useless, but still he instinctively recoiled at the thought of the gargantuan chains eviscerating him.

Instead, he was met with shock encompassing his body, as he was embraced by a dark abyssal ocean that proceeded to ignore his buoyancy as he sunk further and further into its cold flowing current until even his view of the moonlit sky faded from his sight. Hitting the bottom of this mysterious ocean he laid motionless.

Spontaneously Timmy's arms and back began to burn and itch. Panicked, he felt his arms trying to look at them through the now pitch-black water. Just as he squinted his eyes to adjust to the dark, a warm orange glow cascaded over Timmy's arms. Looking ahead at the source of the glow. His eyes peered through the blurry water when suddenly he froze. His body tensed, and his heart halted, aching, feeling as if it were a foreign object that needed to be retched out of his body.

Forcefully he began to rise from the ground as the ocean current pulled him upward. The ocean rushing up his body with enough force to easily cast Timmy away. Remarkably, he remained in the place where he stood until the entire ocean was lifted above him. Now seeing more clearly, he could visually confirm that the outline he saw was the burned wreckage from all those years ago.

He stood motionless, still reeling from the sight until he was assaulted by an audible impression that clawed at his ears.

"Timothy." The apparition hauntingly cooed. Timmy's heart shattered, looking onward he could now clearly see the orange hue was from a blazing inferno. Inside of which stretched out a hand that extended from the flaming car before tearing its body from the driver's window.

Timmy held his breath, a chill running up his spine. Struck with fear, he trembled before such a frightful view. It was chard, black as the night, with embers dusting off the living corpse of Timmy's late mother. Tears rushed down his face as he dropped to his knees wanting to cover his face only to be overtaken by a compulsive revulsion of morbid fixation as she called out once again. "Timothy."

Her voice was breathy this time and it sounded strained, as if speaking alone was a near impossible task. The flames barreled out of the car as his mother stepped toward her son with outstretched arms. "Why Timothy?" She asked the crackling fire distorting her voice. Timmy couldn't move as he shook uncontrollably. "Why couldn't you have just died with us!" She screamed louder and angrier than he had ever heard her as the fire grew larger.

It rose and lashed about as his mother took another step, before bursting across the distance between them, as she let out a blood curdling scream. Timmy met it with a scream of his own as he fell back pushing away as she reached for him. The unbearable heat battering him as his mother scratched and tore at his face and arms. "Why did you run away!" She screamed over his sobbing.

"Mom, please!" Timmy screamed panting gushing sweat and tears as he awoke in Sapphires bedroom. Loud steps closed in on the room met with Sapphire bursting into the room.

"Timmy!" Sapphire yelled out wielding a bat in hand as she barged in. Timmy jumped for a moment startled by Sapphire as she scanned the room.

"It's just me..." Timmy sighed as he sat up out of bed.

He wiped the sweat off his forehead as Sapphire lowered the bat. "It was just a dream... I thought I'd be done with dreams like that." Timmy said softly crying. Sapphire set aside the bat before sitting beside Timmy on the bed.

"Healing takes time Timmy; it doesn't go away easily. Especially if you don't have things to distract you from your pain." She said putting her hand on his shoulder. "Or if you let it consume your life."

Timmy sighed, nodding his head, agreeing with her as he sat up. Jumping from the bed as well Sapphire headed out of the room waving Timmy to follow. "Come on when's the last time you ate? I know a good place." Sapphire said with both of them making their way out of her house. Driving around town Sapphire started to reminisce on old times saying "I used to love this place. It was one of the few places my family would go to just relax." Her voice suddenly grew sadder as she spoke pausing as she reminisced.

"Then the place closed for some kinda remodeling and in that time my parents got busier with work. 'Competitors got more vicious' they said." The red light from the stop light shined in her eye illuminating her face from the surrounding night. "Still wish I could have gone back before now." she said slightly pouting.

"Well, I'm glad you'd wanna take me." Timmy said smiling at Sapphire.

She smiled back at him before facing the road again. Timmy also looking out enjoying the calm drive through town. It gave him an almost nostalgic feeling as they made their way further into town. Turn after turn Timmy grew uneasy however, feeling a confusing notion of discomfort and yet he couldn't understand why.

He cocked an eyebrow as he read the distant street sign. Looking back, it was almost edging to the forefront of his mind as he asked Sapphire. "So, what's the name of this place again?" he asked.

"Oh, I forgot to mention it, it's Mr. Kelly's." She replied as they turned the corner to the view of the restaurant.

Timmy became paralyzed as he could once again feel all those old sensations. Scraped arms, an unbearable warmth, and the dread of loss all roaming his body as Sapphire continued. "I will say though I prefer the old name for the place. 'Josh's diner'" Timmy was in shock, unable to react as they pulled in front up to the restaurant.

Diving into the back of the car Timmy screamed. Tears swelled in his eyes as he shook his head in disbelief. The memories of that night flooding back in his mind. Visions of his mother from his recent nightmare, still fresh in his mind. "Timmy! What what's going on!" Sapphire exclaimed slamming on her brakes looking back at Timmy then darting her head around to look for what might be setting Timmy off.

Finally, Sapphires mouth hung a gape as she realized what she had done. “Fuck, Fuck, Fuck!” she screamed, peeling away from the street and down several roads. “God Timmy forgive me, I’m a fucking idiot, shit!” She said smacking her head, pulling into a random parking lot. Unbuckling herself she climbed into the back seat alongside Timmy.

He stood stiff in a vacant stare while Sapphire gently grasped his shaking hands. “Hey, Timmy it’s okay we’re away from there you’re okay Timmy, I-I’m so sorry.” She whispered as she conscientiously moved his body to face her. Pulling their hands to her chest, as Timmy's panting went into heavy bursts. Sapphire hushed him compassionately and slowly began to calm him, his eyes hesitantly meeting hers.

“I’m okay.” Timmy whispered weakly to Sapphire. He looked about their surroundings cautiously, giving a shiver before slumping back against the car door. “Is it bad that I’m still hungry.” Timmy whispered before giving a sniffle, still staring off in space. Sapphire chuckled shaking her head no.

They stayed there sitting together, holding each other’s hands for some time. Eventually Sapphire as well as Timmy made their way back to the front seats. After driving to a random fast-food location at which Timmy ordered five different meals, stuffing his face as he apologized to Sapphire. “I didn’t mean to react that way.” He muttered softly. “It wasn’t the first time I've been back there...” Timmy said soberly pausing from his feast as he continued. “When the case of my family’s murder was still open, I begged B.G. to take me back. I believed I could find something the police missed.”

He lowered his head tilting it to look out the window. “Once they gave up the case I just... I lost hope I guess...” he said softly.

"You have nothing to be sorry about Timmy I should have known better after what BG told me about your parents." Sapphire replied placing a hand on his shoulder. She gave a comforting warm smile to him, and he smiled back as she continued to drive.

Casually Sapphire would reach over grabbing some of Timmy's food and the two would playfully fight Timmy tossing a fry at sapphire only for her to catch it in her mouth. With sapphire quickly retaliating by smacking his nose with her own fry in hand as the both of them giggled like little school children.

"So where are we heading now?" Timmy asked as he stuffed his face with food. "We heading back home?" He asked through bites.

Sapphire rolled her eyes and giggled slightly at his manner-less eating.

"Well actually, I wanted to head to the place that I go when I wanna feel calm." Sapphire said. Timmy quickly gulped down the food in his mouth.

"Saph... I said I was okay, really." he said softly.

"No-no, I believe you, I just thought with everything that's happened we both need some chill time." She replied. Her smile quickly turned, however, to a face of anger. "And listen here you little shit if I bought the food, I should be allowed to have some!"

Timmy jerked his body away hiding his food as he yelled back.

"I'm a growing man! I need all the sustenance I can get!" He gave a weird face at Sapphire with her making one in retaliation.

"Let's be level, nothings helping that, short stuff." She laughed as he stuck his tongue out laughing with her. Eventually after some time had passed, Sapphire head pulled into a parking garage. Timmy was puzzled, questioning if this was really the place that made Sapphire so calm.

Driving all the way to the very top of the parking garage Timmy and Sapphire both exited the vehicle. Timmy wiped himself off giving a big stretch before asking Sapphire.

"So, do you like this place because it's so quiet? I mean it does have kind of a good view of the city... Not the biggest parking garage in the town, but it's a nice view." Timmy said with a smile as he waved his hands in a grandiose fashion.

Sapphire laughed getting out of her car as she waved for Timmy to follow to the parking garages elevator.

"This isn't what I wanted to show you smart ass." Entering the see-through elevator Sapphire smacked the elevators button panel causing it to pop out sideways. Behind the panel hid a small blue button. Timmys eyes widened in surprise. Sapphire pressed the button sitting back as the elevator slowly lowered. "The place I'm taking you is well... I'm kinda bad at describing things it's like... an underground city." She said as she popped the button panel back in place.

"From what I was told it was a pop-up city during the invasion, it held survivors and was later used as a base for the resistance fighters." Descending lower they passed each floor of the parking garage. Going past its foundation and into the ground as darkness suddenly snuffed out any light.

Lightly Sapphire began to speak again in the darkness saying. "Eventually after we fought off the War Council most of the people returned to the surface." She said as Timmy grew slightly anxious of what was to come. "Some however rebuilt beneath in case of a new invasion only to be forgotten by the world above as it moved on with the Alliance." Sapphire said.

She went quiet for a moment and Timmy held his breath with anticipation. The sounds of metal gears straining became abundant as light crept from the doors of the elevator. Stepping forward Timmy suddenly winced from a bright light that beamed through the glass elevator doors at the both of them. Adjusting his eyes he squinted, before opening them wide as he saw the wonder that sprawled out before him. An expansive cavern that dug itself as far as the eye could see.

Timmy looked below barely making out the bustling crowds scattered throughout the underground city. His eyes followed the traverse city scape seeing an abundance of towering buildings made of stone and earth. Lights shined off buildings and streets and the aroma of food could be smelled even from the height Timmy and Sapphire were at.

Off to the very edge of the city was a light so bright and big that it appeared to be a sun itself. Timmy covered his face as he looked at it watching as it slowly started to dim as a cover began to shift in front of it casting the city into night. Successfully highlighting the city's beautifully orchestrated night-time ambiance.

As the elevator reached the floor level, the doors opened to the underground city. Where Sapphire proudly stepped forward joyfully waving her hands about before declaring. "This is my peaceful place. My home away from home!" Smiling at Timmy, she took his hand and outstretched her other arm exclaiming. ***"Welcome to Sanctuary!"***

Stepping out of the elevator Timmy stared stunned at the marvel of human ingenuity. As crowds of people laughed and talked, going about their daily lives in this hidden city below. Before they could make another step however a rather large man standing easily at 6 feet, stomped to Timmy and Sapphire. Glaring at them both, the man shouted out.

"Halt, who enters the tortoise layer!" Rolling her eyes she scolded the man shouting back.

"Raph don't be stupid, first off you got the wrong amphibian, second you know who the hell I am, and lastly nobody calls it that!"

The man grumbled, his hardened attitude almost immediately switching as he began to pout.

"Well not with that kinda talk." He said, folding his arms.

"Oh, you poor thing. Look all I'm saying is maybe don't scream at people when it's their first time down here your gonna scare them." Sapphire said pointing back at a fairly startled and surprised Timmy.

Raphs looked at Timmy in shock.

"New! Welcome to Sanctuary." He excitedly yelled leaping at him picking him and tightly squeezing Timmy in a back cracking hug. Timmy even squeaking from the sudden surprise.

"Hey woah big guy don't kill him either please." Sapphire laughed patting Raphs back.

The man apologized quickly saying.

"Right sorry I'm a bit of a hugger." As he gave a gentle smile. Timmy waved his hand as he took a sharp breath.

"All good haha if anything it reminded me of my brother's bear hugs." Timmy said giving a big grin.

Taking another look at the big man he noted that he was certainly a strong man, with a muscular physique that was strikingly bulky. With casual clothes aside from a red scarf that wrapped around his neck. As Raph turned continuing to talk to Sapphire, Timmy spotted a familiar symbol peaking above the scarf.

It was the same branded design barely visible on the skin. A diamond with wings and a red sword in the center. Timmy's eyes locked to it as he struggled to maintain a still face. While none the wiser Sapphire and Raph continued to laugh reminiscing on old times. Loudly Raph clapped his hands together giving a big smile, scaring Timmy from his trance.

"Whelp, I'm heading on my way. I got a meeting with some of the Sanctuary leaders, and they've been more Sedge-nosed than usual." Raph laughed as he began to walk off with Sapphire waving goodbye.

Unable to address his concerns due to Sapphire quickly pulling him aside Timmy shouldered his suspicions. Pulling her purse to her side Sapphire dug for some cash running up to a local booth with a sugary confectionery smell roaming around it. Timmy sniffed the alluring aroma. The scent so sweet that he could already taste it.

Handing two still warm neatly wrapped pastries. Sapphire smiled gently before saying to Timmy.

"These are legit the best thing to get in the whole city. I know we just ate but I had to get you some." Happily, Timmy took the pastry Sapphire handed him, taking a bite as it warmed his heart. The pastry was a soft pillowy dough with a flaky golden-brown exterior, that came with a rich and creamy peanut chocolate swirl interior. Scattered inside the swirled pastry was also a type of purple alien berry with red dots. The berry tasting closest to a strawberry and leaving the slightest after taste of a tingling snap and pop on the tongue. On the pastries exterior were large red crystal-like rock candies, which tasted mostly like brown sugar. "They're a human take on a Goliathan delicacy, 'Beefer Legs' I believe is what they call them." Sapphire said with a smiled.

In just a few big bites Timmy had practically devoured the entire dessert As he exclaimed just how delicious the uniquely tasting treat was. Finishing it, he smiled back at Sapphire only to notice her amused smirk and the fact that she was intently watching him. his face now beat red as he became accustomed to the mess he made On his face when taking in the gifted treat.

"I'm sorry I can't remember the last time I had dessert... and it was good." Timmy shyly confessed as he wiped his face clean with a napkin.

Rolling her eyes sapphire pointed to her own face motioning for where Timmy had missed a spot.

"It's okay tomato boy...besides you should see me with a slab of ribs, now that's messy eating." She coyly smirked before giving Timmy a wink. To which they both laughed as they continued their walk throughout Sanctuary. the young man none the wiser that he was succumbing to her naturally comforting personality. As the young lady for the first time in years could see and enjoy someone's intoxicating childlike happiness and free-spirited nature.

And for a brief moment the two of them were much more apt to blissfully navigate their way through Sanctuary. Timmy following her compassionate and seemingly kindred spirit. Allowing even the simplest of her actions to dash away any dread that chained his cracked and battered heart. And for once he set his troubled mind a side and he allowed another to calm his beating heart. Letting his wall chip away in this haven of a city underneath the surface.

Finally exiting the towering city scape of Sanctuary Sapphire and Timmy stood before the giant mechanism that once appeared to be a sun. Which now cast a blue-ish white glow across all of Sanctuary. "okay, good we're finally at the city center." Sapphire said as she moved directly under the Moons replica. "We're not too far away from where I wanted to take you." She said with a smile.

Pointing behind them she began to speak again saying. "Where we were was kind of the residential and food district. Now we're kinda in their art district where a lot of people come together and make fancy sculptures, mosaics, or other kind of cool creative things." She said as she joyfully moved through the sculptures that lined the city center.

She put her hands in her pockets walking beside Timmy as she pointed out different art pieces. "When I first came to this place, I was kind of overwhelmed. Eventually I ran into Raph, and he made me feel more comfortable." She said shrugging her shoulders as she waved one of her hands at some of the people who walked by. "He showed me a lot of the area especially the art district. I literally would come here every other day and just create to my heart's content." She said.

Turning down a corner, they walked into an alleyway until Sapphire stopped in her tracks. "One day one of the city higher ups or mayors, I guess... I don't know one of the city people came to me and said they liked my art and wanted me to make one big mural in the center of the city...kind of like an attraction piece for everybody to go to and see, that is where I'm taking you." Sapphire said as she proudly waved Timmy forward.

Stepping out from the alleyway they started to pass in front of shops that displayed numerous works of art. Along the shops were small outdoor cafes where a number of individuals crowded around discussing ideas and crafted artwork unlike anything Timmy had ever seen before. "It took me probably three years to make this entire thing. I will say I didn't do it by myself, I had a lot of the kids who are around the city, and some other people help me craft the whole thing... but I think it turned out just fine. I'm proud to say it's one of my better pieces." Sapphire said giving a prideful yet nervous smile to Timmy.

Stepping onto the street she finally presented in all its glory her hand-painted mural. At the end of this popular city street stood a three storied building which had Sapphire's mural of the universe painted across the entire wall. Floodlights illuminated the mural allowing it to shine brighter than the replica moonlight at the center of Sanctuary.

The mural depicted the interstellar collection of gas and dust called the Pillars of Creation. In its spectacular artistic rendition Sapphire painted the concept of a mirror like reflection that puddled and flowed throughout the galactic visual piece.

"This...is amazing Saph!" Timmy exclaimed breathlessly as they stepped closer to it. Sapphire blushed, nodding her head in response as she too admired her wonderful masterpiece.

Timmy took in the meticulous detail that was put into every part of the hand painted mural. "My mom and brother Blake loved to do art. They would have loved to see this." He said looking poignant at first before gradually pushing down his sorrow as he happily told Sapphire. "I think they'd love your artwork." Sapphire smiled back at Timmy.

"I'd have loved to see theirs. If you still have some maybe you could show me some day." Sapphire said with a smile before looking back proudly at her artwork.

Interested more in Timmy's family's love of art she asked him what had inspired them.

"Well, most of my mom's art was work based, but her favorite drawings were what she said, 'from the heart', and my brother had always agreed with her." Timmy said as he slid his hands into his brother's hoodie pocket smiling as he remembered his mother's comforting personality.

Yet even with such thoughts a chill rushed down his back as visions of his horrendous nightmare flashed briefly in his mind. He winced and recoiled as his body shivered off goosebumps. Shaking his head he fought to hold himself together. For a moment Timmy questioned the dream, specifically why he had heard those foreboding chains again.

To a bit of frustration, he had snapped from his fading train of thought as Sapphire began to speak again.

"I agree fully with your mother." She said, smiling as she took a step closer to Timmy. "I tried with this piece, and so many others to take inspiration straight from the heart." She beamed with pure exuberance that warmed Timmy completely, unable to hide his smile for seeing her happy.

It was at this moment that Timmy came up with an idea to continue her happiness, to make Sapphires vision a reality.

"Would you like to see the Pillars of Creation up close." Timmy asked softly. Sapphire's eyes grew wide as she registered what Timmy had said.

"You can't be serious... how?" Sapphire stammered taking a step back.

"My father before he passed Trying to make a Starship one faster than even The Alliance's Gilleon class cruisers." Timmy said reassuringly.

"After his passing, I started to finish any of his projects, the ship was one of them. It was a way I could keep myself distracted." Timmy said pulling out his phone. "Let me call a few people, it should be towards its final stages of flight testing. My father always had access to fly the ship and I've even flown it a few times." Timmy said with a smile.

Sapphire gave a stunned expression, before berating Timmy with questions about the ship itself, space and how often he flew it. "It's been a while since I've flown but to me it's like riding a bike." Timmy notably mentioned excitedly anxious as he called his contact at his family's company, asking to use the ship stating it was for another flight test to map out areas of interest.

After securing the go-ahead Timmy and Sapphire hurriedly vacated Sanctuary. Excitedly giddy at the prospect of going into space, and in no time at all, due to the company being close by. they arrived at Timmy's family's company: the ***Nie Fallen Corporation***.

Driving up to a security gate Sapphire Rolled her window down. With a stationed guard exiting his booth, before stepping up to her car, as he peered in giving a stark glance at the pair until meeting eyes with Timmy.

"Ah sir I was told you'd be visiting today." The guard said as he gestured to a parking spot.

After moving to their designated parking both Sapphire and Timmy exited the vehicle waving at the security guard as they started to make their way inside the building. Quickly catching up to the two of them the guard spoke quietly to Timmy saying. "Hey, look I know that you were permitted to come here, but I'm just wanting to warn you. The board has been a little more aggressive lately, and I'm certain I'm seeing some smoke...they might be trying to get rid of you."

Timmy took a step back giving a frown as he listened patiently to the guard. "Look I'm not trying to scare you Timmy I'm just saying be careful, okay?" He said with Timmy nodding his head at the guard. Giving a thumbs up the guard whispered "Good luck" as he walked away.

"What was that all about?" Sapphire asked. Walking back to her side Timmy replied shaking his head saying.

"Nothing, nothing, I just... after my family passed the company was starting to go under a little and so to save face, they had sold out to a kind of shady company at least from what I heard."

Waving hello to a few passing researchers. Timmy hushed his tone waiting till they passed before continuing. "I don't know too much about them but everybody around here has always been on edge since they took over. And I guess from what he said now they just don't want me around." Shrugging his shoulders Timmy gave an anxious sigh as he led Sapphire down another corridor.

"Are you kidding me? After all your family did for this company? They practically are the company!" She spat as he harshly eyed the new brazen logos that had been plastered on every door.

Waving his hands to signal Sapphire to quiet down he continued his explanation.

"I know but unfortunately they don't see it that way." Looking around he began to whisper weary that nosey listeners could linger closely. "Which is good that I started stumbling across my father's blueprints... they started to back off a little when that happened, but I guess old habits die hard." Timmy said with a sigh until another beam of energy shot from him as he spotted the entrance to the research wing of the building.

Pride glowed with him as they made their way through research halls. Housing a multitude of researchers walking about testing on numerous things stretching from household appliances to state-of-the-art robotics. Evidently Sapphire became impressed at the magnitude of ingenuity within the complex.

"Well, I guess now it's your turn to show off! Now I know why your family's company is such a stiff competition." Sapphire said playfully jabbing at Timmy's side.

Shyly giggling, Timmy smirked saying.

"My father would probably be smiling ear to ear at that thought, but at the same time I think he'd be interested in seeing what the two companies could do together." Sapphire disappointedly huffed, rolling her eyes and crossing her arms.

"Competition fuels my father. There is no way he would let that happen." She scoffed.

"That's why he doesn't get personal tours." Timmy jokingly sneered before laughing with Sapphire joining suit.

Turning another corner, they were finally met with the shuttle bay entrance. "Here we are." He said inputting a code on the door beside him. In front of them, the metal doors began to slide open revealing an enormous bay that opened to the ocean view just beside the complex. Standing in the center stood proudly an enormous silvery Shining ship that spanned across nearly 100 meters.

"It's a Starship ... a Clipper class ?!" Sapphire exclaimed.

Timmy smiled at her shared astonishment.

"It's classified as one considering its top speed but if we go by the size matrix then it's actually more of a Galleon class." He said trying to add emphasis by extending his hands. "It functions as one too, but with the speed well past that of her ordinary Starship and something more that I'll show you once were out in space." Timmy said grinning ear to ear.

"That's ridiculous..." Sapphire said in awe as both inched closer to the ship.

In the middle of their self-guided tour a man dress business casual with a red and white badge around his neck walked up to the pair first shaking Timmy's hand before speaking.

"Ah Mr. Green, it's a pleasure to see you again." Timmy shook the man's hand and smiled saying.

"Head Researcher Wayden, it's been too long!" The man nodded his head before taking up the tablet in his other hand.

"I couldn't agree more. In fact, I have to say I'm glad that you're back, perhaps if you do some more mapping, the board would be more interested in restarting the project." The Researcher said as he turned his tablet over showing his proposals to Timmy.

Taking the tablet Timmy walked with the man as he began to read it over nodding his head as he sheepishly responded.

"I know, I know, I'm sorry that I haven't been around but the past couple months I've had to focus on... personal matters." The man frowned.

"So, I've seen. From what I've heard you haven't even sent an as much as a single blueprint." He said eyeing Timmy

"Hmm, yeah sounds about right." Timmy regretfully admitted, handing the man back his tablet.

The researcher gave a sigh before shifting his frown to a slight smirk.

"Well luckily for you, you're more of a freelance worker for now. Even though the board would rather cut ties completely from the Greens lineage." The researcher again looked over his tablet shaking his head.

"Which I think would be a very big mistake along with many of my colleagues." Timmy smiled warmly at the sentiment.

"I'm glad we still have so many supporters." he said with the researcher smiling back.

"Of course, if it wasn't for you or your family none of us would be here right now with the opportunities that we have."

Turning to Timmy, the researcher waved his hand at the ship behind him. "We are starting a new frontier of human evolution. Expanding the new renaissance! I truly believed in what your father said." The researcher smiled then holding up his badge saying. "No matter whose name gets plastered on the building." All Timmy could do was smile. Finally diverting his attention from Timmy, the researcher nodded to Sapphire who stood patiently behind him.

"And who is this visiting with us today?" He asked, reaching out to shake her hand. "It's a pleasure Miss..."

She smiled reaching past Timmy to shake the researcher's hand.

"Miss Sapphire Price, it's an honor to be here." The researcher became stunned, cocking an eye questionability peered at Timmy.

"Miss Price? Don't tell me... from-" Timmy interjected holding his hands up pausing the researchers questioning.

"Yes, she is but don't worry she is visiting as a friend." Cautiously eyeing both of them the researcher again gave a sigh.

"I see... you do know this would be troublesome if the board heard about this."

Timmy rolled his eyes.

"I will deal with it then but as far as they're concerned, I am taking my soon to be personal aircraft for a ride and yes I'll do a bit more mapping of ***the Styx***." The word catching Sapphires attention curiously, and yet she held her tongue as the researcher addressed her again.

"Very well I now understand as well why you had me bring this, please miss price if you would kindly sign our waivers." The researcher said, as he handed over the tablet to Sapphire.

"Oh... uh, of course." Sapphire said surprised at first but quickly brushed it aside and gleefully grabbed the device from the researcher's hand.

As she did Timmy stepped aside grabbing two space suits and a few different pill capsules from a nearby storage area. After hurriedly filling out the waiver and handing it back to the researcher, Sapphire looked over to see Timmy, who was making his way back to her. In his hands he held her own suit and a cup of water to which he handed over the cup along with the three pills. She took the suit excitedly with a bright smile across her face. Looking at the pills, however, her joyful demeanor subtly changed with Sapphire tilting her head curiously.

Timmy smiled pointing each of them out individually.

"Radiation poisoning, Space madness, and motion sickness all of them are very important and highly recommended even if I don't imagine us going outside of the ship." Wide eyed Sapphire stared at the three pills with a shocked look until Timmy leaned in whispering. "Not really space madness it's just a type of anxiety med."

Shrugging her shoulders, all she could say was.

"For space!" before throwing back the pills and chugging the water.

"The trip we're taking should be well within safe Alliance territories. So, it should be pretty safe and peaceful." Timmy said.

"Sounds good to me!" she replied as she slowly slid the suit over her clothes. Timmy then slipped on his own suit, as the researcher checked over Sapphires to make sure everything was Secured. Given a green light by the researcher, Sapphire and Timmy gave each other thumbs up before stepping up to the starship's entrance.

Pressing a few buttons on his suit's wrist mounted device, Timmy activated the spacecraft's start up sequence. Its engines whirling as a hydraulic platform lowered slowly to the floor. Stepping on to the aircraft's platform, they began to rise into the bowels of the ship. Leading the way through Sapphires tour of Charon. Timmy pointed out every facet of the ship he could remember.

"The room we're in now is going to be a docking station for a miniature spacecraft, anything from a small Husk class ship to a Brigantine class can be housed in here."

Walking forward to a giant sliding door Timmy pressed more buttons on his wrist monitor causing the door to depressurize. With hydraulics hissing as the door gingerly slid open. Taking a step into a hallway the doors behind the two whistled as the room pressurized and the hydraulics locked up the bay. "Up these stairs and right behind us is the living quarters as well as the ship's gravitational center system" Timmy said leading Sapphire up the stairs as he pointed behind himself. "Pass that is our cooling block." Timmy said.

Smiling to himself proudly he thought back to the model his father had made. "That was actually, something I came up with. A little idea of housing the metric ton of Crystalline Ambrosia that powers the ship." He said shyly. Sapphire shot past him holding him in place with wide eyes as she shouted out.

"Wait you mean there's a metric ton of Crystalline Ambrosia inside this thing! How doesn't it overheat the ship and melt through the hall?"

Giving a nervous chuckle Timmy forgot that most ships barely carried more than 100 kilograms of Crystalline ambrosia at a given time.

"Well unfortunately for now that's why we have half of the ship being a cooling block, all of that is needed right now to keep everything from overheating but because of that we're able to power so much and travel so fast within this type of ship." He said, giving a slight smile to her stunned expression.

"Ah I see..." she muttered.

Taking a step past her he continued his way up the stairs as he led her into another room.

"This right here is the Botanical Garden for the ship it helps provide oxygen as well as farming produce which takes up the rest of the second floor." He said. She lingered a bit tip toing around the garden before fallowing Timmy as he waved his hand onward. Lastly stepping to a glass door Timmy once again pressed more buttons on his wrist monitor as the glass door slid upward revealing the cabin of Charon.

"This is where you fly the ship!" Sapphire's eyes lit up as she roamed about the cabin. Timmy smiled as he watched the twinkle in her eyes and a childlike joy rush over her body as she stared mouth open wide at all the controls and the smooth metallic layout of the ship. "This can't be happening." she said beaming with excitement as she turned to Timmy with joyful tears in her eyes.

Caught in her joyful twirling exploration of the cabin. Timmy couldn't help but peel away the layers of maturity that shackled him. Rediscovered like a lifelong friend he swept the joy with open arms as he toured his new yet cherished acquaintance about the cabin.

"Be careful not to touch anything that looks like it's lighting up and no buttons I gotta do a few more diagnostics on the ship." He said with a smile on his face, managing desperately to part from her simply wanting to continue their intrinsic dance.

She swayed gracefully in her turn to meet his gaze nodding her head before quickly taking a nearby seat.

"Take all the time you need Timmy I've never been more ready for anything in my entire life!" She exclaimed squirming in her chair. Checking the overview and other 'bells and whistles' as Timmy commented. Timmy rescued Sapphire and himself in their seats and finally prepped for takeoff.

Timmy and the control room started to count down their launch over the radios in their helmets. The head researcher giving one last reminder refreshing Timmy that his main objective was to map out more parts of 'the Styx' Timmy nodded his head speaking into the radio confirming That he understood his objectives over the radio. "Mapping out 'the Styx' he mentioned that earlier. What exactly is that?" Sapphire questioned.

"I'll explain a bit more once we get there for now just settle in for the launch." Timmy said priming the navigation and engines. Clearing his throat Timmy spoke loudly as he counted down Charon's launch. "In 5.... 4.. 3... 2... 1." The engines roared as the spacecraft shifted forward before blasting out of the shuttle bay. Jettisoning out of Earth's atmosphere, Sapphire held her breath as the spacecraft shook and trembled as it broke through Earth's atmosphere.

Sliding through space at ludicrous speed. Moons and planets dipping in and out of field of vision. Seconds passed and they had already made it near the edge of our solar system at our asteroid belt. Sapphire was mute, incapable of speech. Wishing that her eyes could convey the range of emotions she felt. Stars passing with each blink it took all she had for her mind to comprehend just how fast they were moving.

Looking over at Timmy she saw his unfazed expression and was taken aback at the fact that he was so calm about everything. The whole time he had been casually responding to the Control Center back on earth stating how they had broken through the atmosphere and made it to the edge of the solar system. Also stating that multiple systems were engaged and functioning properly and that they were beginning to reach 'the Styx'.

Everything was so much faster than Sapphire ever thought was possible regarding space travel. And she felt anxious that her time in space would be up before she could fathom it. "This is final communication until exiting 'the Styx'. Last beacon being dropped 1 astronomical unit away from entrance." Timmy said disengaging a marker to send a signal back to earth.

After turning off the radio Timmy turned to Sapphire asking. "So, you wanted to know what I meant by the Styx?"

"Well duh!" Sapphire replied eagerly.

"From what I remember it was an accident that happened during one of Charon's many test flights. One that was supposed to be a safe, well simulated route so my dad could take me, my mom, and my brother." Timmy said.

Taking a moment to try and scratch his head only to remember his helmet. "I ...Ugh dang thing...But uh when we got to this area we slipped through, popping out into The Styx." Timmy said waving his hand at the cockpit window to the vast emptiness in front of them. Sapphire looked on trying to understand but finding the explanation a bit confusing.

Holding her tongue, Timmy continued his explanation saying. "It's a doorway in space and time allowing someone to travel light-years in seconds." Reactionarily Sapphire shook her head in disbelief.

"Are you serious? That's wild... how haven't we discovered this before?" she said in a frown grasping the side of her helmet as she looked outward.

"Well, there are a few reasons from what I've discovered." Timmy said shyly fidgeting with his hands.

"Before we traveled freely in space, we only discovered what was observable or had an observable effect in the surrounding area in space, when we went to spy on the Mudlurks we traveled in a completely opposite direction. And lastly our solar system had finally made it to a reasonable range to where 'the Styx' was now right outside our solar system." Stunned Sapphire was at a loss for words by Timmy's spontaneous exertion of astronomy.

Solidly surprised Sapphire threw her head back before expressively waving out her hands.

"Woah... uh man that didn't even sound like you." She muttered. Timmy blushed, lowering his head bashfully in response.

"Sorry I just really like space and stuff... I can kinda rant sometimes." He said softly.

"That's nothing to be sorry about... it was actually kinda... uh ... cool." She said with a blush. Catching herself from confessing too much.

Jarringly in the middle of their conversation, instantaneously, and without warning. Charon warped through the Styx entrance as both Sapphire and Timmy traversed the unseen portal into an entirely different plane of existence. One that met Sapphires eyes with a pure void of nothingness. Not a single thing could be seen outside of Charon's cockpit. An absolute absence of light. No matter how hard her eyes strained she couldn't see a thing and all she could do was gasp at the utter emptiness before her.

"It's okay." Timmy cooed his voice soft and comforting.

"We've passed the entrance now." He said and as those words touched her ears her body begin to shift and tense up as now a new sensation trickled across her body. Unbeknownst to her, Charon had been cast into an alternate dimension that treated space less like a vacuum and was instead simulating a flowing ocean.

"What's going on?" her voice was exasperated as she gripped her chair tighter instinctively holding her breath.

Again, Timmy comfortingly whispered to her.

"We've made it. We are now in what my father called the Styx." Timmy said sitting up in his seat. "Which reminds me I don't need the gravitational engine on anymore and I need to put up the sail." Having said this Timmy pressed several buttons on the console in front of him while slowly pulling down a lever as well. Suddenly the feeling of a weight on both their shoulders was lifted. "I still haven't learned to time that right like my father did." Timmy admitted with Sapphire questioning what he meant about the sail and if they would start floating without the gravity device.

"This kind of area doesn't react the same as our world I don't exactly remember everything but from what I do know it's kind of like were the contents within a sandwich." Timmy stated. Holding his hands out in front of himself. "The bottom piece of bread, it's where we just came from which is the same as the top piece of bread which is where we're going." Timmy said as he now layered his hands trying to imitate a sandwich. "In the center, the PB and J if you will, is the Styx... it's the in-between that connects the two." Timmy smiled half-heartedly looking to Sapphire to gauge if she was following.

Slowly she nodded her head yet still held a fixed trance on the sight of the void. “The PB and J isn’t the same as the bread that holds it together, but it melds well with it... I don’t know.” Timmy said with a shrug. “That made more sense to me when I was younger.” Timmy added in sheepishly. Sapphire cocked an eyebrow at the oddly specific explanation of where they were, but before she could utter out a question.

A new more startling discovery captivated her attention.

“Uh okay new question... why ...are your eyes glowing!” she exclaimed. Pointing a finger out to Timmy. Her being able to see a prominent shine in his eyes. Even as it was sheathed by his space helmet.

“Oh shoot, man I’m bad at showing this to new people!” Timmy said, smacking his helmet. “It’s kind of like an ‘evolutionary trait’ from what I’ve been told... something about being in this different environment.” Timmy said, flailing his hands. “My eyes react to it, allowing me to see inside the Styx as opposed to you who doesn’t see anything.” He said as he pointed to her and the void outside.

“When we first passed the entrance accidentally. This is how we were able to get out. It was because me and my brother were the only ones able to see inside of the Styx.” Timmy said with a fidget of his hands. “My parents on the other hand couldn’t.” Locking with his eyes Sapphire held her gaze consciously unbashful.

“They’re heavenly... I’m sorry that sounded really weird but... they look like a soft sparkling gold... I-I can’t look away.” Sapphire whispered in her self-aware trance.

Of which made Timmy all the happier that she couldn’t see the rest of his face which was back to showing a rosy tint of red on his cheeks.

“My mother did call them my special eyes.” Timmy softly confided. “I’m sorry.” Sapphire said as she shook her head trying to peel her mind from its mesmerized state.

"I don't know what came over me...but I gotta say your mother must be right." Sapphire said, so casually said it flustered Timmy causing him to turn his red face away. "This is all so intense, I mean we're in a what? alternate universe, a different dimension. Connected to ours?" she asked.

Thinking aloud as she continued. "And somehow you and your brother were able to see perfectly in here... where I can't see anything. What does it look like?" she asked frantically.

"Well, it's kind of like my eyes, I guess. You said they looked gold, right? I see waves it's... it's like we're in some giant body of water and there's like tree branches, golden tree branches that shine even brighter than my eyes, and there's billions of them!" He said with his outstretched arms. "And they all branch out, leading to different entrances that look like massive sparkling stars!" He exclaimed. "That's what I map out when I come out here. I'm mapping it out so other people can traverse one day through the entrance and across the Styx." His feverish excitement riling up Sapphires own excitement of this new mystical domain.

And in a second, I'll show you how fast it is to cross." Timmy said with a smile. As Charon ferried the two further across the Styx Sapphire began to realize that this new plane of existence was not so empty as it appeared. The noises of possible living creatures sounded in abundance. Surrounding the outside of the ship in a symphony of vibrant sound. Through Timmy's eye's these creatures could be seen. Their iridescent, semi translucent bodies, dashing across the glimmering golden branches. Mimicking strikes of lightning that danced laterally across the mystical body of water.

Intertwined and yet still sporadically divergent, the branches soared even in the Styx's sky. Embracing distant stars and housing flying creatures that coddle themselves within. Calm were the waves in the Styx as they gently splashed up the side of Charon's Hall.

"I hear... wind chimes? glass wind chimes?" Sapphire muttered.

"Oh no that's the residue from the branches hitting the ship." Timmy replied as he steered the ship.

"Is that dangerous?" She asked.

"Hardly on occasion it might get stuck somewhere, but it dissolves on its own." Timmy replied.

"A few more seconds tops and we'll be there." Timmy said pressing buttons on his station, Sapphire could hear the sail collapsing into the ship and the sudden weight of the gravity device being reactivated. And like pushing through a curtain Charon warped itself out of the Styx revealing in a stunning splendor, the Pillars of Creation. Jutting up from her chair Sapphires eyes sparkled with pure wonder as she saw the pillars before her.

A tear fled from her eye and her heart burst with joy. This childhood desire of hers gifted to her off the whim of a kind stranger she met only a day ago.

"Hey uh Saph?" Timmy called for her, slowly peeling her gaze away from the celestial view.

"Oh, hey your eyes there back to normal!" She exclaimed.

"Huh?" Timmy replied forgetting his optical transition. "Oh yeah my eyes don't stay glowing after leaving the Styx." He said.

Pointing ahead of them he ushered her onward as he spoke. "Follow me to the boardwalk it's the best view." As he said this, he unlatched from his seat along with Sapphire. The two of them taking a staircase down to a viewing platform at the front of the cockpit. "Looks like we're in luck usually there is a couple of sightseeing Clipper class ships that normally crowd this spot of the view." Timmy said leaning onto the railing.

"I wouldn't blame them, but it seems like you have good timing...thank you Timmy." She said softly as she looked on at the ancient starry formation. "I mean, seriously... a couple days ago, and I was bored out of my mind. Hating that I would have to just keep pushing day after day of my family's bland company bullshit... and now. I'm in fucking space, with a guy who I just met, but is so nice and brave ... a guy who just saved my life."

Timmy looked at her and in that moment her face Appeared so gentle and warm glowing perfectly under the natural celestial light that peered into Charon. A foreign feeling of butterflies fluttering in his stomach. Mysteriously to him, he could not look away from her beautiful smile. Only for those feelings to be stuffed down as he shamefully denied her praise.

"I... I didn't do anything. All I did was run into you. If anything, I probably made things worse for you." Timmy muttered.

Hanging his head soberly he slouched into his arms that rested on the railing.

"And you could have kept running once you were free of those guys. You could have run and never looked back...but you did, and you got hurt for it... even though you're better now. I still don't take that lightly. You literally took a bullet for me, a stranger you barely know!" She said compassionately as she inched closer to Timmy.

"I just wish I'd quit running. When I was little, I ran from my brother. When my family was murdered, I ran. When I was at the plant I ran because they caught me. That's when I ran into you. And at the hospital, I also ran. Just seems like that's the only good thing I know to do." He looked away from her at this moment, feeling tears build in his eyes.

"I don't believe it." She countered sternly. "I mean, aside from running away when you were a kid. Your family's death, your brother trying to scare you, I mean, those are normal situations for any kid to run. When it comes to the plant that you were at, was anybody in danger?" She asked softly.

"No." Timmy said as he stifled his tears.

"So, then I assume you were outnumbered. I mean, you must have been. Because if you ran from that, but then when you crashed into me suddenly that made you fight off 4 guys Twice your size!" she exclaimed.

"At the hospital, was there anybody in danger?" Sapphire asked. Breaking eye contact,

Timmy nodded his head. "There was the man who died."

Without hesitation Sapphire questioned. "Could you have stopped it?"

Timmy replied plainly. "He was dead before I even got there." Confessing still feeling remorse for the stranger.

"Then what you did was right, you got out of there. You were the only reason why they were there. You getting out of there probably saved more people. If they had seen, you in there they would have started shooting not caring where the bullets went." Timmy thought back to those moments reflecting on what his reactions were in each moment as Sapphire continued. "What about agent Rivers? You could have run from him. But you didn't you stayed, and you fought him Which whether you were trying to protect yourself or were trying to protect me again. Which itself is pretty crazy. You didn't run away. It makes me think that instinctively inside you is a good man who wants to do the right thing. Whether you see it that way or not. For you, you may be running away but deep down. I think you know. What you're doing, when you're doing it. You know when you're being a hero." She said with confidence triumphantly.

Turning to him she grabbed his hand tenderly "So come on, enjoy this moment, be happy...because in my mind, every superhero needs to smile." She said, giving him a soft smile. He stared into her jubilant eyes and smiled back as his heart again fluttered in that foreign feeling which he had no words to describe.

"I like that smile." He admitted through his own smile. "It reminds me of what it means to be happy, to be hopeful..." He said, his words trailing off as another flash of his father hammered his mind and heart until he snapped back to Sapphire. "I'm sorry I just." He paused, finding difficulty in speaking as his sadness returned overwhelming the foreign emotions, wishing they would return.

Sapphire's smile changed to a frown as she moved closer to Timmy.

"Hey, it's okay besides I'm glad I make you feel that way. Trust me the feeling is mutual." She said, putting her hand gently on his shoulder. Causing Timmy to blush as his smile returned. "You know ... I always wanted to have an adventure, I wanted to be like one of the U.M.E soldiers. Out there defending people, protecting the planet, the galaxy! Seeing new places and different species. I... I never thought I'd experience it, at least I know my family would never approve. I guess you don't always choose your adventures though, sometimes they just ... run into you. I guess I'm just kinda happy is all, you know that you're giving me my first adventure." she said, her eyes looking deeply into Timmy's.

"I'm glad to be a part of it..., without you... I think my adventure would have been cut short to tell the truth, if you hadn't helped me." Timmy said giving a short laugh.

"Well, of course, I had to help you I didn't want you to bleed out on me. Do you know how traumatic that would have been?" she said in a sarcastic way, giving a devilish smirk

"Oh no can't have that" Timmy snickered.

"Yeah! And by the way, what about my dry cleaning? Do you even know how much Kartarian silk is? Let alone how much it is to get blood washed out." Sapphire laughed.

"Oh, I'm sure my ghost would've been good for the bill." Timmy said, as the two giggled playfully, before slowly settling into a locked gaze. Celestial light dancing around them with silence filling the room. The silence built itself yet was unnoticed by the pair. For all they cared time could have stopped completely. Innocently entranced, the pairs' hearts were beating in a pure form of harmony. And as they unknowingly inched closer. They had become lost to the stars around them yet found in each other's eyes.

Their displaced and distracted minds soon became tethered back to reality as a blaring alarm sounded from the pilot chairs of the cockpit. Both jerked away startled by the sudden blaring alarm with both of them hurriedly returning to the cockpit.

"What is that?" Sapphire asked wincing at the loudness of the alarm.

"It's the bacon thing that Agent Rivers gave us." Timmy shouted, picking up the bacon from his bag before pressing its flashing blue button.

Once pressed the blue blinking light turned solid and showed a projection of one of agent River's men.

"Mr. Green Pardon the intrusion. This is Staff Sergeant Maci, from Nomadic squad." Timmy shifted into his chair as he set the projection onto Charon's pilot console.

"No worries, Staff Sargent just jumped a bit from the loud alarm and the fact that we can see you so clearly." Maci smiled nodding his head at the pair.

"Top of the line undisclosed satellites used for special missions undertaken by Alliance special forces. And as for the alarm that was my bad didn't mean to send the imminent contact beacon."

Sapphire plopped into the copilot seat as she exclaimed.

"Imminent contact?" Maci waved off her questioning saying.

"It's no concern we can explain the function at a later date." Turning his attention to Timmy, his expression turned serious. "The real purpose of me contacting you is that we've located our targets refuge." Timmys heart stopped, and a cold sweat draped itself over his face. His eyes went wide as he took in what was said, looking on for a confirmation, with Maci clarifying. "It's time for you to make your decision Mr. Green...***we found Escalero.***"

| Page

Chapter 6: Deceit

With little time for deliberation and a fair bit of compassionate encouragement Timmy agreed to return for the fight ahead. Traveling back through the Styx Timmy and Sapphire departed from Charon at Nie Fallen Corp. Getting picked up shortly thereafter by another team working alongside Captain Rivers. Standing in front of a blacked-out terrain vehicle was a tall imposing man whose very presence equally intimidated Timmy just as Captain Rivers had in their first meeting. He wore a similar uniform to Rivers. The only Difference being a different symbol on the man's patch centered on his chest.

Clasping his hands together the man greeted Timmy and Sapphire as they walked up to him.

"Namaskar Mr. Green My name is Jason Rao." He stated. Opening the door Jason stopped briefly, turning to Sapphire, his expression changing from one of humble welcoming, to one that was drastically more uncaring and destitute. "Miss Price, I presume?" He asked,

"Um yes, that would be me." She cautiously replied.

"I see and Why are you still here with us?" He coldly asked.

Timmy shot a look of disbelief at Jason before turning back to look at Sapphire unsurprised to see her equally baffled expression.

"I was under the impression that I was still being protected by Captain Rivers and his group." She Muttered nervously.

"Hm noted." He sternly replied, swiftly facing Timmy brazenly asking him in the same tone. "And you Mr. Green are a child?" Again, Timmy looked at the man incredulously yet still solemnly as to not disrespect such an imposing authority.

"I'm seventeen sir." The man eyed him for a moment as he held a firm grip on the vehicle door. Abruptly saying

"Noted." He then clapped his hands opening the back passenger door before making his round to the driver's side.

Holding still with a reasonable notion of suspicion they both glared at Jason not stepping foot in the vehicle. "Listen kids I know don't trust strangers especially when they are rude." He said, turning back to the pair. "But we don't have time to go on a; I don't like you fit, just like my subordinate Captain Rivers and the rest of Nomadic squad can't come get you as they're busy doing the opposite of their current objective. Of which is dismantle The Final Crusades ability to send out units from project David." Every word heavy and concise. With Jason leaving not a moment to breathe. His sharp wit covered any question the two had.

"So, if you would rather us continue our work instead of going after the Final Crusades most high value general, I'd be very happy to redirect to our primary objective." He facetiously said as he turned from them, starting the vehicle. "I would not be remiss on not capturing him today but if you want Escalero Martí, which I am fairly certain you do, then I would get in the damn car and stop being so afraid." He growled all too apparent in his showing of annoyance as he continued. "The time for fear is over, now is the time for action."

His words seared the both of them and yet they were moved. Hardly controlling her demeanor Sapphire could not help but snap at the man stating.

"I'm hardly scared and I feel I can confirm that for the both of us, but can you really blame us for at least showing an ounce of caution." Jason raised his hands in defeat as he replied.

"Very well, very Well. But I must insist that we do not have much time." Hesitantly the pair looked at each other with Sapphire giving Timmy a reassuring nod before the too begrudgingly entered the vehicle.

Wasting no time the man drove off from Nie Fallen HQ. Tense and silent, the ride was, in Timmy's perspective surprisingly uneventful with Jason practically disregarding them the entire ride. Before pulling up to the run-down shack entrance they had seen before. Again, Some of Captain Rivers men stepped out from behind the shack. Touching the Device on his wrist Jason spoke clearly saying. "Omega One coming in clearance code 'Red River". With Rivers men stepping back allowing the base entrance to rise with everyone traversing down into the bases interior to be met by Captain Rivers and the rest of his squad.

"Well look at that he didn't quit." Shining said at the forefront of the group beside Rivers.

"I had not a doubt in my mind." Apollo said as he placed a hand on Timmy's shoulder. With the rest of Nomad squad welcoming back both Sapphire and Timmy. Finally at the end of the line stood Nimitz who coldly stared arms crossed glaring at Timmy. Speaking first with determination in his voice before Nimitz could even say a word he said.

"I'd say I won't let you down but I'm not doing this for you, I'm not doing this for Captain Rivers, I'm not doing this for Sapphire. I'm doing this for me. because I want Escalero. I'm going to take him down. I want justice for what happened to my parents for what happened to my brother, and I will not rest until I give them that justice."

A Moment passed before Nimitz finally nodded her head in approval a smile cast across Timmy's face but before he could thank her, she added in her own consolation.

"I like your bravado I really do it's brave for a kid like you to feel the way he does shows the sign of you eventually becoming a man." Her eyes narrowed, leaning closely to Timmy till she was but an inch away from his face, eyes like daggers as they pierced into his. "But always keep in mind. If you cost the life of even a single person let alone my squad, I will not hesitate to put you down and label you as a casualty of war understood?"

Tilting his head upward Timmy nodded as he replied swiftly.

"I understand. Thank you, Nimitz." Slipping between the two Rook gently tapped Timmy on the shoulder saying.

"Chief if it's alright with you, I would love to have a word with you Timmy." Rook said with Nimitz stepping aside.

"Go on a head I think I've made my point." Timmy quickly recognized the man as the one who took care of the mechanized creations.

"Is there something you need for me to do?" Timmy had asked.

"Well actually it's more something we need to discuss it's about the test on your blood Captain Rivers had us do." Rook said as he ushered Timmy away.

Wide eyed and taken by surprise Timmy quickly interjected.

"B-Blood tests? When did?" Rook stopped for a moment looking back at Timmy Shocked by his own accidental admission.

"Ah well this is weird but during your confrontation with Captain rivers he was increasingly curious about you and so in the middle of it all he secured a blood sample from you." They both stood there with Timmy looking down at his arms and hands quietly whispering.

"Where?"

"A small little prick on your thumb probably barely even noticeable, barely even felt." Rook said nonchalantly continuing his walk down the hallway. Having created a rather bewildered Timmy.

Entering a new room of the facility. Timmy was introduced to a laboratory filled with beakers, test tubes, and various other scientific pieces of equipment. Timmy stared at them all inquisitively whilst obediently following behind Rook. As they stepped up to a table Rook took a seat, patting the one next to him for Timmy to take a seat as well. "First off let me just say I had no idea who you actually were!" Rook said with a bit of excitement staring ecstatically grinning and throwing his hands upward overcharged with giddy admiration.

"You are Timothy Green, grandson to Eli Green, and second son of Andrew Green. Both renowned in the industry of revolutionizing humanity itself!" He exclaimed. "Truly your grandfather and your father were marvels; if it weren't for them humanity wouldn't be where they are today." Timmy smiled, his face turning flushed and yet still he felt a bit inadequate, as if he had not yet filled the shoes laid before him by his loved ones.

"They we're awesome I agree. My father showed me a number of his inventions and I did help with a few of them...but I don't think I could really compare to him." Timmy said humbly.

Rook shook his head in disagreement.

"Perhaps you just lacked the room to stretch your creativity." Rook said with a smile. "But before I get sidetracked let's continue with your blood sample, I found something remarkable." He said moving rations from infront of his computer before continuing. "Now I had a theory for why this blood is... well. Wait no I shouldn't say that yet. we'll get to that in a second." His whole thought process sporadic and seemingly nonsensical. "Back to that theory I had. See it started off as just a theory about your blood and so I needed some evidence." Rook said.

Opening up a number of different files on his computer. He pointed out one specifically saying. "Now in this file here is Captain Rivers testimony of what happened when you two first interacted." The screen displayed a showing of Rivers perspective of the early morning conflict. "From what river said it was almost a natural snag and grab mission however you started to adapt creating what Rivers states here as: Abilities, hidden abilities, instinctual abilities." Timmy frowned juggling both remembering how the events had played out as well as listening to Rook.

"Your speed and movement capabilities we're almost outside natural possibility. moving much faster than him which might I add he is a seasoned veteran who has had countless combat experience and undergone grueling training that is still blacklisted to this day." These words all hit Timmy with equal amounts of shock, but he could not understand. Only being able to curiously probe Rook on how he might be capable of manifesting such abilities.

Rook put up a finger as he continued clicking on to a video. "Hold up, I'll do my best to explained I shouldn't get off track." He said, his eyes darting chaotically. "This is recorded video of Rivers engagement with you captured by his... personal optical equipment. This is the moment where Rivers was about to subdue you with a Taser but if I press play." Rook pauses for a moment pressing play on the video and before the both of them they could clearly see Timmy standing a few feet away from Rivers before vanishing from his sight.

Timmy was put back staring in confusion.

"I don't remember it like that for me he just started moving slowly I had to get out of the way I didn't know it was a Taser." Timmy said frantically. Still questioning what he had seen himself do.

"Yeah, and that's exactly what I believe you did see from your perspective! See now I slowed it down 3000 frames per second and this is what I found." Rook said as he altered the video before pressing play again rewinding it back to Timmy standing again before Rivers.

The video continuing Timmy watched his eyes glow marble white and yet still a mirror like silver. As they did so, he began to sidestep moving and sliding as he did.

"What? Why are my eyes like that what's going on?" Timmy said. As an immediate sensation of DeJa'Vu struck him.

"Well, it's still going with my theory but let's look at example number two" Rook said exiting out of the file. Clicking on to another opened up police documents statements from nearly 10 years ago.

Reading the timeframe Timmy noted almost immediately what the date was in reference to.

"The night my family was murdered." Timmy whimpered.

"Yes, I had to do as much research as I could in as little a time but starting my research in these two specters, I had already seen what I needed to continue on with my theory and that is the police report the night your family unfortunately passed." Rook said, voice was soft and extremely hesitant, but this was not the first time Timmy's family had been brought up in a conversation. Regardless it's still comforted Timmy that people still attempted to be respectful.

"Eyewitness testimony reports you being in two separate locations. First at the diner on 5th and 7th Street In the center of Ultimo city with the second location being at Verdes Valley." Rooks said pulling up a map of the city.

"That's where I ran to. I panicked, I was scared, I felt like I was being hunted. I couldn't stay there I couldn't, ... I couldn't." Timmy said softly as he hung his head.

"That's okay, that's not the issue. The issue is the inconsistency." Rook said zooming in as he showed off the two locations on the map. "It doesn't make any sense... the distance between both locations Is 20 miles apart the reported time that you were found was only about a minute after your families passing."

Timmy shook his head.

"A minute? I'm confused... I mean it felt like it didn't take long when I ran there but I... I assumed it was just adrenaline."

Rook snapped his fingers. "Ah and remember when you were taking on Captain Rivers. You didn't recall your movement as rivers perceived. It was altogether different from his experience. Your speed alone in that quick burst is reason enough to help my theory." Reaching down and opening a filing cabinet. Rook rummaged through a rather cluttered mess of papers.

Snatching one from the pile and handing it to Timmy. "Which if my math is right, you have a ridiculous ability to move beyond human comprehendible speed!" Rook explained. A still perplexing look holding tightly on Timmy's face. Rook scratched his head for a moment before tapping on the paper he handed Timmy. "Let me break it down the distance between the diner you ran from and the rough location you were found in Verdes Valley, being 20 miles, time traveled being that minute." Rook paused as if to recheck his own math.

Nodding his head accepting his calculation. "You would have had to travel at least 1200 miles per hour!" Rook exclaimed. Timmy's face recoiled, as he leaned back in the chair sliding away slightly from Rook in utter disbelief.

"You're not making any sense I don't understand." Timmy said.

"Yeah, I get the way it sounds but from eyewitness testimony and the video evidence recorded by Rivers neurological implant. It points to that being a possibility." Rook said sounding even excited at the prospect.

"And now the most exciting part going to your blood sample...now I understand why Rivers wanted you tested." Rook said, as he opened another file on the computer pulling up test results. Pointing at the screen, he showed a number of different microorganisms, floating throughout Timmy's blood stream. "This is countless amoebas to be specific; ones that live in Astro-pods." Rook said. Timmy's ears perking up recognizing the name.

"Those things that latch themselves onto starships?" He asked.

"Precisely!" Rook blurted out hardly containing his excitement. "The reason why Astro-pods latch on to starships is because they feed after the energy that is given off by the ambrosia crystals that fuel starships. Right?" Rook said reaching for a confiding conformation. Timmy nodded his head allowing Rook to continue. "Right! Now it's commonly theorized throughout the scientific community that the reason why these Astro-pods even exist is that they are a type of parasitic, symbiotic...whatever you would like to say. Organism that used to feed off life that could travel light speed. Ergo as fast as starships or Gillian class cruisers." Rook said. Waving his hands as if he was showing the separate ships.

"And so, what you're saying is that their blood is in my blood?" Timmy questioned.

"Yes, and more incredibly, your white blood cells are not attacking, and you are perfectly healthy. It seems you have grown symbiotic with the microorganisms, and they are not dying off either instead living off of their host without harming you." Calming himself down Rook sat back in his chair contemplating. "Now that only leaves two questions the first being, how did it get there." Timmy too leaned back in his chair.

Questioning everything and drawing a blank.

"I can't think of anything." He said.

"Perhaps a blood transfusion? Was there any point in your life where you lost blood. Who's your doctor? Did you have any type of exotic food I suppose?" Rook asked rattling off possibilities. Debating each question Timmy thought back, refuting most of the possibilities. That was until he remembered with just the tip of his tongue as he spoke out only two words.

"The shots..." He muttered breathlessly.

"The shots?" Rook questioned.

"The shots my father gave me and my brother..." Timmy breathlessly replied. "They were medicine...he wouldn't." His words sounding more like a question then an assured statement.

"Shots? Your father gave you shots... personally, and he said they were medicine?" Rook continued to question. "Not even real doctors can give their kid shots. a medicine? Your father wasn't even a doctor. An inventor, a genius innovator but... oh my God." Rook said. Struck deeply by the realization of correlating paths.

His mouth hung agape by the stark likelihood.

"Why? I don't understand. Why would he do that? He wouldn't." Timmy said frantically, almost tearing up from the chance of this new possible revelation.

"Now hold on. We don't know what his intentions were. With how smart your father was or at least as smart as he seemed to be. I don't think he would so casually and recklessly use you as a predominant test subject. I'm sure he had countless tests before this" Rook said confidently. Giving a reassuring and comforting gesture.

Fighting back a sullener sunken mood he optimistically made Rook aware of his father's notes.

"There are archives. My father gave me access to all his notes and journals on all his projects in his will. He would have hidden it from me if he didn't care right?" Timmy asked, looking painfully at Rook.

"I can't speak for him all I can do is have hope." Those words hitting Timmy like a hammer. He wondered in the weary years since their passing he had already forgotten what that meaning of hope was.

Yearning to remember, to reignite a spark of hope, he looked back on every fond memory he had of his late father. Until, softly nodding his head, he held tightly to the idea that in the short time he had with his father he knew him well enough to trust him. "Well... now if it's okay with you that still lies the second question. If your ability isn't a random happenstance and you can recreate it..., can it evolve?" Rook asked

leaning in his chair closer to Timmy he babbled on. "If so, you could be the answer to so many things if you're not the only one compatible you could evolve humanity as a species or at the very least you could end the Final Crusade and you could end the war." Rook said holding a gleam of aspiration in his eyes as he said those words to Timmy.

"I could do all that?" Timmy whispered back to Rook.

"Only time will tell and a few tests ...for example." Rook said, trailing off as he left his chair.

Making his way over to what looked like a chest freezer. "I happen to have a little gal I want to introduce you to." Reaching in he grasped some type of creature that writhed around within the tank sputtering about inside it. Cautiously Timmy peered over his shoulder before sliding the chair away from Rook and the ominous commotion. "Don't worry I know it sounds weird but truly they are...Come on Biscuit work with me!" He strained bending his knees and arched back.

Lifting none other than a large Astro-pod out of the tank. Its eyes blinking thoughtlessly as it stared in Timmy's direction.

"What the! Is that a flipping Astro-pod?" Timmy screamed as he jumped on top of the desk.

"Indeed, it is To be specific it is a baby an infant actually." Rook said as he started to step towards Timmy.

"Are you going to try and have the thing eat me or drink my blood?" Timmy shouted.

Balancing himself off the computer behind him. He extended his foot out at the creature as if to kick it.

"Huh? No, no, no. Don't be absurd. They don't even have teeth; they have nothing really to chew or pierce with." Rook said giving another clumsy stomp over to Timmy as he tried to hold onto the moving creature. "All they have is a suction thing it sucks in dead tissue and if anything, it probably sucks out the bacteria leftover from the microorganism that is in your bloodstream. Or at least that's the theory." Rook continued as he inched closer.

"So, it's not like gonna kill me or anything is it?" Timmy asked, as he cautiously stepped down from the desk.

"As I said it's incapable of it, I only wish to test my theory I have about your speed. If what is in your bloodstream and is in their bloodstream. Then you two could form a symbiotic bond. Perhaps Biscuit here is exactly what you need to fully unlock your real potential." Rook said in utter excitement.

Holding out Biscuit, it stared helplessly at Timmy.

"I-I don't know. This is all very new with my dad, with finding out that I have... super speed, it's all a lot to take in." He muttered, cringing slightly at the creature's slick outer coating and its squirming abdomen.

"Oh of course I'd hate to make you feel uncomfortable we can always come back to Biscuit. Would you at least like to touch her? She seems to like you." Rook said still holding out Biscuit as he smiled.

Hesitantly eyeing the creature, it looked like an odd mix between a horseshoe crab, and an isopod. No doubt it's closest living relatives. Timmy inched closer staring back into the simply alien, black beady eyes. Reaching out his hand Timmy touched the very top carapace of Biscuit. Her eyes closing gently as the creature tilted its body to get closer to Timmy's touch.

"I guess it is being nice and looks... oddly cute...in a weird kind of way." Timmy said with a hesitant smile. Abruptly a tapping started to sound from the laboratory doorway. Diverting the attention of the two men.

Sliding into the room was Reaper who cocked an eyebrow as she watched the extrinsic scene before her.

"Oh, Reaper what's going on." Rook said with a noticeably brighter smile.

"Are you really showing off your pet while we're on a mission." She asked using sign language. Giving a half smile and rolling her eyes in the middle of her response.

"It's for research and it's kind of a part of the mission." Rook replied.

Reaper gave a frown which was contradicted by a slightly resisted smirk.

"Yeah, sure whatever. Rivers sent me to grab you and the boy. Wonderland and Maci are back." She signed. Failing in her attempts to show a rougher exterior. Weather directed to himself, or Rook Timmy could not tell.

"Good! Well, here I'll put Biscuit away you go with the Reaper and see Maci and Wonderland." Rook said, already stepping away causing Biscuit to return to its squirming.

During which, Timmy to felt a heaviness on his heart and in his back. Yet he could not discern his unspoken feelings. "I gotta feed her anyways so I'll catch up in a second." Rook said. Unaware of his slight hesitancy, struggling momentarily to depart from Biscuit. Timmy gave her one more pat to the top of Biscuits carapace. Nodding in response to Rook, Timmy then followed Reapers lead back to the meeting room.

Reentering the war room Timmy looked around to see most of Nomadic 5 tucked into a corner of the room quietly speaking with Sapphire, stood Timmy 's Uncle who was visibly nervous as he Hesitantly whispered with her before meeting eyes with Timmy. Immediately he leaped off the wall he had leaned against running to him embracing him tightly in his arms.

"Oh, Timmy thank God! I had hoped what Sapphire was telling me was true these people are here to help us." His Uncle said hugging him tightly.

"BG!" Timmy gasped as body could hardly react to seeing his uncle.

Stunned to see him now here in the base alongside Sapphire, and Jason's team. "You're okay... I-I didn't get a call back from you I was worried." Timmy said, his eyes starting to tear up. BG also starting to get choked up looking back at his young nephew.

"I know, I know. But I couldn't contact you after you left. I tried to call the police tried to have them swarm the hospital and evacuate everybody but luckily this man and his team had swooped in before I could even tell anyone." BG said as he pointed a hand too Jason's direction.

Jason nodding to Timmy in response.

"Mr. Rao told me that a separate group that worked for him was going to get you... Mr. Rao said they had other things to do so they couldn't bring me to this place sooner." Timmy hugged his Uncle back giving a whimper before confiding in him.

"I thought I had lost you too." He muttered.

"Oh, Timmy I could never do that to you I'm not going anywhere." BG said holding Timmy closely as he patted his head. Looking up at his uncle Timmy smiled.

Gently Captain Rivers stepped up to the reuniting family, placing a hand on Timmy's shoulder.

"I don't want to break up this reunion however we have to move forward. Our window for reacting is quickly closing." Timmy turned to Captain Rivers nodding his head and giving another comforted smile to his Uncle as the two separated. "Okay everyone, listen up!" Captain Rivers' voice boomed. "We will no longer be working as a joint operation unit." Rivers said gesturing to Jason's team opposite of the Nomads.

"Omega 1 will be continuing on with our primary objective, figuring out how the Final Crusade got a hold of project David, and hampering any distribution factors that play at hand." Rivers said starting up the War table. "This will be a search and destroy mission for Omega 1. As for Nomadic 5 we will instead be deviating from our original course thanks to the Intel that was gathered." He said Displaying a holographic layout of a city block before continuing.

"During the reconnaissance undergone by Wonderland and Maci, we have discovered this local bar that is a guise for Final Crusader trading." Rivers said his red eyes flickering. With three images appearing next to the view of the city block. "This location is apparently a method at which they launder money, conduct deals, illicit human trafficking, and where they intend to plan the rest of their roots with their contacts for Sending project David across The United nations land bridge between Alaska and Russia." Riverside switching the location to that of the mega continental land bridge.

"Now because the bridge is scrupulous in its travelers as well as being funded by Miss Prices family, we were able to ascertain the identities of who would be collecting project David for the other side." His eyes flickered again and now this time three images of crossed out individuals appeared in front of the land bridge as well as a caravan of vehicles. "Captain Rao's men have already detained and interrogated them." Timmy looked over to Jason surprised to hear such tactics with the man simply nodding to his credited work.

"The individuals disclosed to us that they have not yet met with Escalero nor any of the other members who are at the bar." Jason said in response.

"While that gives us the opportunity to slip into the bar disguised as Trades-hands. Most of us have already had numerous contact with the Final Crusade. None of us here, whether it be from Nomadic or from Omega can go into the bar without the possibility of being identified by someone within their ranks. Luckily for us one of Nomad 's very own refuses to go out without a mask." The same girl who had messed with Shining earlier, Kilo, again played with his mask flirtatiously hearing her lover being mentioned.

"Sergeant Shining will be heading undercover as the lead Trades-hands negotiating to find out any Intel from Escalero during the meeting as well as an ability to distract the general as we surround the building Leaving him unable to escape." Rivers said, his body language suddenly shifting to a more uncomfortable posture as he paused for a moment. The sudden change throwing Timmy off giving him a sinking feeling. "Unfortunately, there is another matter to attend to." Captain Rivers said, turning to Timmy and Sapphire. "The man who Sergeant Shining is to disguise himself as is reportedly coming along with two escorts; one for accounting the units of project David they will be smuggling across the border and the other supposedly a more provocative escort."

Timmy's body shivered hearing this, looking to Sapphire to watch her expression. Seeing how she too was visibly shaken at what Captain Rivers was insinuating. "Both of you have done enough for this cause. I will give you this one last chance. You can work in disguise and help us with our best given chance to detain a highly valued Final Crusader general. To which you will have to be face to face, with minimal protection." Rivers said deliberately staring down Timmy laying emphasis with every word. "Or you can be under our protection as we undergo these missions. You will stay here until all objectives have been neutralized and completed. the choice is yours." Rivers said before taking a step back from Timmy all eyes on him awaiting his choice and although he had felt determined. The shaking sensation of the perilous tasks to come still weighed heavily on his mind.

"You can't be serious he's a child they both practically are!" Timmy's Uncle shouted, waving his hand across the table. The commotion drawing in everyone's attention.

"We understand that Sir, however we need those other escorts to be able to play this off. Without them we'll have no means of properly disguising Sergeant Shining it would be too much of A risk to send him in there alone." Rivers said, upholding a calm unmoving presence despite BGs disgruntled vexation.

"And so, you're telling me sending in a child into a suicide mission is better?" BG shouted back slamming his fists on to the war table.

The loud bang instantly setting off multiple individuals from both Omega 1 as well as Nomadic 5, Nimitz herself charging up to BG, only to be stopped by Rivers himself who extended a handout to halt her.

"BG wait." Timmy pleaded reaching out for his uncle. His uncle swiping his hand aside as he continued to shout.

"No! I refuse to listen to any of this. This is madness you already were shot bleeding out in my restaurant... I nearly lost the last bit of family I have Timothy!" Tears shook from his eyes has he grit his teeth staring down at his nephew.

Timmy was speechless. Eyes wide not having heard his real name in years. It struck with such a heavy weight that appalled the young man. "I am your guardian. I promised I would look after you... I can't just sit here while you and little Saph go out and speak to the man who murdered your parents, murdered your brother, and these people can't even promise to protect you!" BG shouted pointing at the others in the room. The lot of which hung their heads everyone refusing to speak. Thinking quickly and without saying a word Timmy lifted his shirt and pointed to where he was shot.

His uncle paused for a moment flabbergasted at the sudden motion. "What? What are you doing?" He asked before his eyes suddenly shot wide. "Your, your wound!" He exclaimed stumbling over his own words. "I-I saw it with my own eyes I don't even see stitches...what happened?" Timmy 's uncle stopped kneeling down as he examined his body touching where Timmy had been shot. In complete disbelief that a wound so severe that happened Amir day ago had fully healed showing not even a sign of scarring to be left behind. As if the event had never happened. "Did they heal you?" BG muttered.

"It was all himself." Said Rook as he entered the room, a small stack of papers in his hands as he stared down at the two showing off one of them. The paper showing varying evidence and statistics Rook was researching. Timmy and his uncle both turned to him his Uncle speechlessly taken aback. "I had just discussed with Mr. green he possibly has hidden abilities given to him under the guise of medicine by his late father Andrew Green, your brother-in-law." Rook said showing off other research papers.

"These abilities are astounding! Faster human regeneration on an astronomical setting, A ludicrous capability for speed, with a heightened metabolism, Retrofitting his structural integrity almost instantaneously and instinctively as he enters Mach-2! That's breaking a sound barrier mind you!" Rook shouted overtaken with excitement again. The room suddenly fell hush, and all eyes diverted to Timmy.

"That's impossible." His Uncle said. Trailing off as he looked over the papers handed to him.

Anxious with his body feeling cold sweats, Timmy's hands fidgeted has he bit his tongue. Looking into everyone's eyes he knew at that moment he had to prove himself. Show what he could do, that he was capable. That he could fight the Final Crusade, he could put a stop to Escalero, he could finally step into his family's shoes and quite possibly save the universe.

Taking a deep breath, he closed his eyes and stepping back from his uncle his body began to shake. Calming his mind, he listened to the sound of an ocean. hearing its clashing waves feeling the glowing warm branches of life feeling life itself. opening his eyes they glowed as they did when he looked into the Styx. Darting back out of the doorway watching as their eyes were still fixed on the location he had been opposed to where he was now, he felt it was a safe distance for him to show a proper display of his abilities.

Feeling as he had felt that day, running only this time not away, not from fear. Turning his body, he aimed for the other end of the immense underground structure and in a flash, he replicated how fast he ran all those years ago on that fateful night. Crashing into the wall alarms started to wail and the entire complex shook from a sudden burst of pressure. A shockwave fanned over everyone in the war room. ears ranging, adjusting to the spontaneous and chaotic bombardment from the sonic boom Timmy had recreated.

Running out into the main port of the base where Timmy had darted to. Nimitz screamed at the top of her lungs.

"Are you fucking serious!?" Falling slightly off the crater he made in the side of the base wall Timmy winced and cracked his back, rubbing his tense shoulders.

"I had to prove myself that I had the ability to help!" He shouted back as he limped forward before giving a shiver as he shrugged off the pain.

His body quickly loosening from its tense posture. Making his way back to the group, Nimitz continued to chastise Timmy until Captain Rivers stepped in front of them. Nimitz glared at him, spit fire waiting to let loose.

"While I agree with Nimitz that, the display of your abilities was a dangerous and reckless move. I feel this only cemented my interest in your evolution. With proper training and refinement. You could indeed become a powerful asset." Rivers said with Timmy smiling in response.

"Unimaginable!" Rook chimed in. "that was wildly beyond what I imagined it would be! I blinked and he vanished! Your remarkable!" Rook said as Nimitz scoffed folding her arms. Passing them Jason grabbed River's arm, pulling him aside. The two speaking in hushed tones worrying Timmy more than Nimitz had.

Hesitantly making his way to his nephew BG looked past him at the massive crater pushed into the wall as he stared at him stunned.

"Since when could you do that? what was that? Y-you vanished!" He exclaimed, looking back at Sapphire as if to reassure him, he had indeed seen what had transpired.

"Always...I think. I believe I had it back when my parents passed. Even before that, I think. I felt Something similar when I went to the Styx's with you Sapphire...did my eyes glow again?" Timmy asked looking over to Sapphire.

"T-they did... I think... but wait how could you feel it? We aren't in a space or in the Styx for that matter." Sapphire asked, taking a closer look at Timmy's eyes. Blushing slightly from her closeness he shook his head unsure of how to properly convey the sensations.

"I don't know how to explain it... but it felt like I was back in that environment. I could feel the branches, the waves, and I could hear the ocean, even the life inside it. Like I was standing in it." He said looking down at his hands and feet almost envisioning the Styx as if it were surrounding him.

Before Timmy could say much else, both Captains returned to his side with Jason making a clear statement to Rivers saying

"This is on you. Your mission and whatever the outcome, you will be held accountable." Scowling as he said it, being both strict and firm with his tone.

"As if I do not already know that." Rivers responded. Jason nodding his head before clearly stating his leave, rounding up the rest of his squadron to depart on their separate mission.

"Is everything okay?" Timmy asked, with Sapphire commenting.

"Does he always have a stick up his ass?"

Rivers turned to them shaking his head. "He... has a hard time adapting to change." He said with a frown. "But yes, everything is okay. We just have a lot of work ahead of us." Rivers eyes lightly glowed as he stared off. Quickly realizing how spacious he was he cleared his throat looking back at Timmy. "That speed you showed really is impressive. I thought when I saw it before that it might have been a trick of my eyes, but I haven't had a software issue in some time." Timmy smiled proud of his newly understood abilities and curious about what they could do if practiced in the future.

Facing BG once more, frowning at the solemn bit of hesitation that he carried on his face. He could tell his uncle still had reservations and yet now, shown by these two actions of his rapid regeneration and inconceivable speed. It was irrefutable to not think of him possibly being an asset. Instead of either of them saying a word, however, his uncle instead made his way to Captain Rivers. Pointing a finger to his chest as he spoke.

"He's still a boy... maybe not one for much longer which is why I rather not fight him on this, but I do not wanna see him the same way I've been seeing the rest of my family. So, you better take care of him." His uncle growled parental fury unabated by even Rivers intimidating glance.

Surprisingly to Timmy, Rivers nodded in agreement with his uncle.

"With my training nobody would ever be able to touch him." River said confidently. Grievances momentarily settled. The plans could finally be set in motion. Suiting up for the trial ahead, Nomadic took a side Shining, Timmy, and Sapphire to procure tailored suits and dress for their undercover mission. Having already gone through the briefing there was hardly anything else to be told aside from Shining giving demonstrations of minimal signals that he could use in cases of tense and immediate action moments.

With these memorized the three were given an unmarked car and began their drive to the other side of town in what was commonly referred to As ***the Burroughs***. Driving deep into the Boroughs, evidence of the Mudlurks invasion still lingered. Sinkholes stretched into city blocks, burn marks from acidic regurgitation-stained buildings and roads, and glassed over mass graveyards where the Mudlurks had piled their food all stood as healing scars upon the earth.

"I can't believe they still haven't done anything, it's been over 20 years, we're on different fucking planets now. And they still can't come through here and fix these things." Sapphire scoffed.

"And this feeds exactly into what the Final Crusade want. They want to divide, to manipulate, to take all that people have left. Their faith; and weaponize it. All for their own purposes. As man of God myself it makes me ashamed." Shining said with pure disdain in his eyes unblinking.

Timmy looked at him noticing all his scars. They had riddled his face, lacerations across his eyes, a caved in junction on the back of his head leaving a patch of hair missing, a chunk of his ear gone on the left side of his head. Timmy winced and for the first time he considered that others could hurt just like him if not even more.

"It's rare seeing people still have faith in these years. After the invasion people didn't know what to think with aliens being real it seemed hard to believe anymore." Sapphire said. Her voice hurt and remorseful as she underhanded a bit of omission.

"I agree things were hard for a time. My faith was shaken, but a younger me would be surprised that what helped me was fighting in the Alliance. They called us God's children out in the front line said we looked so close to it." Shining said as he looked at his scorn flesh. "They said it was our gentle soft exterior and our passionate driving will" He said softly.

Although Shining had smiled at his quote, it was followed with a sign of guilt. "We are no longer the apex, as if we ever were, and yet still that didn't stop humanity. It gave us a reason to compensate. So, we had to adapt, be stronger, more lethal, more entertaining. And eventually when they started calling us God's children, we had to be more holy." Shining said even more resentfully

"But pride is a sin and with given too much of a good thing I feel like it can go to all of our heads. That's what I feel the Crusade is showin." Gripping the steering wheel tightly with one hand, Shining tapped on a flask that he had placed in the center council. "There's an imbalance in our ability to be humble, we're soaking in our blessings pass our capacity and now we've become drunk with no viable site to sober up." Shining said giving an agitated sigh. "At least not before something dark happens."

Looking back from his front seat with his hand on the back of Sapphires chair. Shining smiled to the both of them, before changing it to a sly grin. "And I'm here to stop things before they get out of hand, to humble those who need it."

"I suddenly feel reassured on our company Timmy." Sapphire said looking back at him with a giggle.

"Mr. Edwick ...Miss Leyden." Shining corrected as he waved his finger and pointed out their given aliases.

"And remember for the time being call me... Nicholson, Mr. Nicholson." Shining playfully smiled. "Okay lady and gentlemen, time to put on your game face. Remember do not say anything unless spoken to, you're only here to punch the numbers... and you're only here to give me a fun time" Shining said snapping his fingers to Timmy and winking at Sapphire. "Go along with everything. Roll with the punches, take nothing personal. Treat this as a game of hide and seek, but with your feelings, and never... forget each other's names." He said patting Timmy's shoulder.

Leaning past him Shining reached into the center council, grabbing a small box and his flask, stuffing them into his suit pocket. "Well, out we go let's try not to die." He says reaching for his earpiece stating. "I landed at the hotel and we're about to get checked in." Before pulling off the earpiece and tossing it into the car. "Can't have that distract me, now let's go chuckle nuts." Shutting the door, he stepped around to Sapphires side opening the door for her. "Shall we?" He steamily whispered, attempting to make his voice more rustic.

Extending out his arm Sapphire peaked over her seat looking at Timmy blushing a bit as she stepped out of the car. Timmy following shortly after. Taking a look at each other, they were both pleasantly surprised at both their appearances, as they had made it too hastily into the vehicle beforehand. Having not gotten a proper chance to see their new attire.

"The suit... suits you Mr. Edwick." Sapphire said with a smile.

"And your dress has me breathless Miss Leyden." Timmy replied hardly missing a beat in his delivery yet still oblivious of his own suave and rather bold comment. Sapphire's eyes widening from the surprisingly sudden brashness. And her cheeks a bit redder, even over her already applied blush.

"Hey, whoa Casanova remember your part. Don't overdo it." Shining jokingly sneered.

The same tone given thereafter to Sapphire as he patted her hand.

"And I'm sorry love, I'm already spoken for so don't get to attached." He chuckled with the both of them. The three finally walking up to the sleazy shut in bar. Timmy looked around and not once had he seen Rivers or any of his other squad members. As far as he knew they were completely alone.

It was at this point his nerves began to tense and the realization that this was now the time for him to act. There was no more planning. No more intel to be gained. No secondary target to be focused on. After 11 long years of everything he obsessed over everything he fought and cried over blinked on the other side of a brightly lit neon entrance in a tucked away barely held together borough town.

Masqueraded as a rundown backend hole-in-the-wall. This place hid its shadowy vile intentions in plain sight and backed into its borrow was a venomous hyper-lethal snake whose rattle could be felt in Timmy's chest. He truly wondered how prepared he was for this moment, as if any amount of preparation would have been enough. as if in mere moments his vengeful wrath would be Hushed.

Flashing images of all he worked for all the pain he endured. It's magnum opus just steps away. Concrete filled his shoes as they dragged along the pavement and in this chilled night sky, he felt a warmth that radiated. Biting into his tongue he worried his teeth would almost puncture the flesh. and as they reached under the humming neon sign a bouncer stepped forward placing his hand on to Shining.

Timmy choked on his held breath staring into the man's eyes.

"The line." the man said pointing to the left of him.

"Very funny... you must not see what's in my hand...Not this hand, although she is fuckin gorgeous, I'll admit." Shining said, his whole demeanor changing as he more lustfully eyed Sapphire. The look slightly causing Timmy's stomach to squirm. "Eyes over here big boy, the gold ticket... I'm here to see your boss's fuckin boss." Shining snapped as he tossed the gold ticket like a pamphlet at the bouncer.

"Well fuckin excuse me, booth on your right far back of the bar." The man said rolling his eyes as he rips the ticket in half stuffing it into his suit jacket and stepping aside. The three of them making their way into the bar entrance. Timmy half expecting the man to grab at his throat or to swing at him. Timmy's eyes never leaving sight of the bouncer. Only departing as he began to hear the heavy base inside pound against his chest.

From the moment he entered the building he felt as if he shifted into a solely new domain. He could feel it, through the music, and the talking. He could feel it in his very soul. Pure unbridled terror ached in every pore of his body as he took another step inside. Each step gave him a new urge to scream and run, far away from that discomforting place. A discomfort that matched what he had felt when he stepped to that burning car that his parents resided in, A discomfort that hurt to even be close to.

Unbearable in its presence. It was then that he saw him. It was unmistakable, he was sitting between two men tucked into a corner booth by themselves. Timmy watched him steadily as his nostrils flared, and then despite the varied crowds that passed by, he locked eyes with Escalero. He had stringy wet gray hair that mopped over his head. His eyes were once blue, it had shown residuals of such a thing. But now they were overtaken by a sickly yellow that mirrored the light that infested the room like a poisonous fog.

It was at that moment that Escalero slowly peeled his mouth open revealing metallic dagger like teeth that he used to give Timmy a horrid smile. One of his decrepit slimy hands with fingertips that matched his teeth inched toward Timmy, as he ushered for him to meet his side. Timmy's gut retched from a putrid sensation of dread. A sensation that he felt all those years ago amidst the carnage that scorched his family. A feeling that crept around the entire room. A feeling of being prey just before the eyes of its predator, of being toyed with, of being hunted.

"Blessed be, and what an honor this truly is to be before one of our most Holy Generals." Shining said tearing through the tension as he led the others to the booth.

"Praise be to the new Messiah." Escalero happily breathed. Extending out his hand ushering his guests to the booth opposite to him. "Please have a seat. I assume you're our master Trades-Hand." The two shaking hands. Timmy watching intensively as he slid first into the booth followed by Sapphire.

A feeling of unease dug into his back. Fighting desperately to hide his fear and anxiety being an arm's length away from Escalero.

"That would be correct, most Holy General Martí. On our far end is Mr. Edwick he is my most trusted accountant he shall make sure the transfer is fully recorded and that we have enough people on our side to easily bring across The Units." Shining said waving his hand to Timmy. Escalero and his two men looking over to Timmy smiling a causing a shiver to strike across his back.

Mustering the best acting he could, Timmy met them with a smile of his own. Shining thankfully, in Timmy's eyes, drew back their attention. "And in-between the both of us is, well a lovely woman by the name of Miss Leyden. Whose only here to make the trip back more fun." Shining said with a wink to Sapphire as he took his seat placing a hand on her lap. Sapphire giving a giggle as she placed her hand on Shining's shoulder. Confusing Timmy again with his newfound conflicting emotions.

"I have a feeling that fun would be an understatement, she looks... delicious." Escalero crudely said. Chipping slightly at Sapphires enactment her hand retreating to Timmy's under the table. He held it softly whilst still contracting his own character to play. In his mind continuously repeating his fake name. *"Mr.Edwick...Mr.Edwick... Mr.Edwick."* he reminded himself in his head.

"Ha, my thoughts exactly. Seems like a full crowd tonight and the special occasion?" Shining expressed looking behind himself at the bar full of Final Crusaders. Surprising Timmy that nearly every patron was an enemy. Further pushing an imposing nature to everything. Timmy wishing, he could recede deeper into the booth.

"What other reason does there need to be other than treating my holy followers." Escalero whispered with a sinister smile.

"And humble are we to accept such blessings." Shining replied gratitude forcing its way out of every pore of Shining's overly eccentric personality.

Shifting in his seat, Shining looked over to Timmy snapping his fingers. Signaling for Timmy to retrieve a book given to him on records from the Crusades envoy.

"All of this being said maybe we should move on with our transfer we do after all have a long journey back..." Shining started, before being immediately interrupted by a loud screeching from Escalero's metallic claw like fingers across the glass tabletop.

"Ah, ah, ah, why the rush?" Escalero's witheringly scowled voice called.

Having even put off Shining's extravagantly acted persona.

"As ordered by our Holy leader, Of course." Shining finally replied, regaining his calm and collected inflection.

"I, am...your holy leader." Escalero growled. The men beside him grimacing as they shifted in the booth, spiking Timmy's heart rate.

"There is no doubt, but I refer to our Lord the new Messiah." Shining said in attempt to recover level heading. Tapping the glass table Escalero's eyes diverted from the three. A smirk slightly slicing open, a glint of his metal teeth reflecting the disgusting yellow lighting which only brought attention back to his diseased eyes.

Breaking the silence by clacking his alloyed fingers together he ushered over a waiter.

"As I said before though, I treat all my followers. Would you do such a harm to my reputation as to deny a gift from me?" He said holding his chest, turning to the approaching waiter. Snottily he cooed for him to bring some drinks "Negroni Sbagliato for each of us." Hearing this the men beside Escalero relaxed leaning back in their booth which helped alleviate the tension. Slowly Timmy turned his attention to Shining. Who was now giving the most genuine smile of the night, practically jumping out of his seat applauding Escalero.

"Now that's more my language! ... However, I should ask to exempt the boy I need him properly oriented." Shining smirked.

Viciously Escalero glared at him, with his painful yellow eyes. Clanking his fingers he clashed them gently yet loudly against each other as they scraped against themselves.

"Five it is then." Escalero hissed his breath pressing sharply between his dagger teeth. Licking one of his teeth. He smiled despicably as the group was suddenly served their drinks. The first of which to give a toast being that of Shining holding up his glass.

"To our, Holy General. May our new lord, our Messiah bless his General with a righteous soul and may he command this Final Crusade to The Lords true vision." Shining chanted. Surprising Timmy with how natural the Final Crusades rhetoric was to him.

Raising a glass in response Escalero finished the chant saying.

"To a flood stronger than any other. One more of encompassing cleansing blood, then the lords holy water." Timmy anxiously squirmed in his seat as the others cheered and drank to their toast. Setting his drink down Escalero's eyes traversed across his guests. Seemingly, they lit up once fixated on Timmy. He froze biting his tongue until he could taste his own blood as to keep himself still. But what he couldn't help but shiver towards was the possible notion of what he had seen. For if he didn't know any better, he could have sworn that he had seen Escalero's nostrils flare again as if he had smelled the freshly pierced tongue that was now exuding the smallest stream of blood.

"We should play a game, That way each of my splendid guests are entertained." Escalero said, as he slicked back his hair. "A simple game one where we go around and tell each other a story about ourselves." He exerted waving his hand lastly to Timmy. Raising his glass and gulping down another drink, Shining however volunteered himself. Afraid of the possibility that Escalero was beginning the question Timmy's character.

"Wonderful! I have a number of stories I could tell!" Shining exclaimed.

Waving his hand Escalero denied Shining's request instead placing his metallic claws to his own chest as he spoke.

"Please, please I am your host, and what kind of host would I be if I were to expect my guest to tell a story about themselves before, I tell one of myself." Shining taking a quiet sigh of relief as he sat back in the booth.

"So graceful and humble is our host. Please we would love to listen to what stories you may tell us." Raising a finger in thought. The word seeded the perfect segue for Escalero to start his story.

"Such a fine choice of words!" Escalero declared, acting as if he had rediscovered a lost epiphany. "A humble story. That is a wonderful idea, and no humbler of a story is there, then how one began. After all, I was not always such a holy general of this fine Crusade. Indeed many, many years ago I was but a humble boy." Escalero omitted. Looking off to either side of him with his sycophant men nodding their heads in a non-conflicting approval of his story choice.

"In my younger years I lived on a farm. It was quite outdated even for the Pre-invasion Era. It was me, my father, and my mother. Before the invasion of earth, we were seen as plentiful. Providing quite a bit for my small village. But during the invasion and sub-sequentially after, Our farm became tainted and nearly inoperative." Escalero frowned, swirling the ice in his glass As he reminisced on the days of the invasion. Surprising Timmy with how old Escalero truly was.

Returning his gaze to his guests, Escalero continued. "Thusly after the Invasion my father had begun to do what all working men would do, he would go and scavenge between the Mudlurks machinery. Gathering their technology for the governments that managed to survive." He said a sign of resentment slashing across his face as he scoffed. "What little land we could produce from became rationed. So that not even our food, from our land, could be given to us."

He took a long sip from his glass, his metal teeth clanging against it that made Timmy wince instinctively from the noise. "We were starved and working till our fingers bled. And no matter how hard we worked, no matter how connected and unified our government said we were. We still starved, we still ached, we still became restless." Escalero growled.

Looking down at his nearly empty drink, Escalero gave it a disgusted look. Causing Timmy to wonder, was he disapproving of the things of the past, his woefully aging appearance, or the drink. "Eventually one day my father became so restless with the endlessness of working to no end, for no result. That he selfishly abandoned us, losing himself to drinking, a factor of which my mother despised." Remorsefully Escalero achingly mourned his father pushing a weird type of sympathy over Timmy.

To which he quickly reminded himself of just what Escalero had done to his family. "Fading his aching bones and distancing his mind from reality. My father drowned himself to death all from what my mother said was that putrid bottle." He spat, seemingly mocking his mother's words. "With my father gone, we became that much more deprived. Lacking our main source of rations and commerce. It became apparent to my mother that we would begin to fight over crumbs." He hissed rubbing his claws together as if to wipe the metaphorical crumbs off.

Contemptuously rolling back his eyes, Escalero scathingly recalled his mother's plan. "And so sowed a thought so ingenious, I'm surprised her famished mine could even conceive such a thought. Tossing me below the house, my mother left me alone in the void of that cellar." His voice becoming more vicious, more croaked.

"Withering and rotting as she saved a larger portion of the rations for herself. Burying my father, yet never marking that he had passed." He said shaking his head. "Months or even years would pass yet my withering consciousness could only grasp aimlessly at the passage of time, I had begun to lose any sense of reality I had in that dark, damp, rotting cellar." He said his teeth clenching scraping against each other as he snarled.

"And so patiently waiting. Holding out for an inkling of liberation. I began biting my time until my mother made a mistake." Escalero said stretching out one of his hands. The sudden motion making Timmy jerk away only to realize he was only accentuating his memories. "Testing my luck, I felt around the cellar and sure enough an exit showed itself resourcefully to me. Having not known the full layout of the cellar. My mother failed to block a window, that's hinges were rusted and falling off." He said proudly acting as if he had crushed the rusted hinges in his hand.

"Needing minimal effort, I managed to kick the window out and pull myself from my solitary prison. Making way into our house a revelation occurred to me." His eyes widened as hatred filled his lungs. "The 'Alliance' had made its self-present in the Earth's shortcomings, thus allowing for what people would later call the 'Inner Galactic Renaissance.'" Every word sounded sarcastic. His lack of credit to the Alliance made plainly visible.

"My mother was no longer starving; she did not lock me away in the cellar to survive. No, she only hid me away, so the last remnants of my father we're out of sight." Escalero grumbled as his claw-like fingers dug their metallic points into his drinking glass. "When I entered the house, I found food was littered on the counters like trash. Sprawled out as if she was preparing for a feast!" He began to shout.

"All those years she had sprinkled down crumbs into that cellar for me to barely survive...while she was fattening herself like a pig!" ***Ksh!*** Shattered glass and ice spewed from his hand. Blood dripping from his hand as he swore to himself. The sudden burst causing everyone to jump. Escalero's left guard reached out to clean the mess with his right guard sitting up and snapping his fingers for a nearby waitress.

"Hey! Bring us a towel!" He shouted sitting up from the booth.

Escalero nodded his head, as he held his hand tightly, thanking both of his men. Following the guard on his right, he got up from the booth to meet the waitress who, visibly shaken, stepped to Escalero. Nervously out stretching her arm as to hand him the towel She was stunned to instead be met with him reaching past her outstretched arm and instead grasping onto her blouse rubbing his bleeding alcohol-soaked hand across her plain white dress shirt. The young girl froze struggling to not squirm from his touch nor to make a single noise, as if playing dead, all while his men laughed in response.

The misfortune woman waiting for Escalero to turn away from her, before leaving. Soft subtle whimpers came from her as she hurried off to the opposite side of the bar. Disgustedly Timmy recoiled from the scene. Goosebumps covering sapphires arm. The hair off the back of her neck standing up as Timmy watched her balling up a fist in rage. Yet all Timmy could do was hope that they still hid their true reactions well enough from Escalero.

Smirking proudly Escalero clapped his hands together as he readdressed his guests and compatriots.

"How rude of me. I apologize for the unexpected outburst but reliving and retelling fond memories often excites me, I suppose we should all be grateful however that I haven't gathered an appetite yet..." Escalero said licking his lips revolting both Timmy and Sapphire. "Speaking of...let me continue my story." His guard that left the booth with him holding out his hand allowing Escalero to slip back in. Only for Escalero to shake his head, wanting to stand as he continued his vivid recollection. "I was shaking at even the sight of fruit! I grasped the first thing I could... an orange, and bit straight into it. Right through even the rind!"

Pulling his hand closely to his mouth he curled his fingers into a ball as if to grasp tightly onto the orange as if he was willing to die rather than lose this metaphysical piece of fruit. Baring his teeth, he chomped down on to the imaginary fruit and when he parted his lips from his hand he muttered out in ecstasy. "And it was so juicy, so succulent...It tasted as if it were the best thing I had ever eaten, at that point in my life." His arms jutting out expressively, sending a shock throughout Timmy's body.

Fear dug deeply, every cell of his being petrified at the thought of Escalero leaping across the table and gouging into Timmy's trembling body. "Looking beside me, I took another fruit, and another after that, and another after that. I had eaten so fast that I thought I would choke... that I would die right there having not eaten a proper meal, and yet my body could not stop." Escalero rustically whispered a sign of relief escaping Timmy's lips is he thanked God that Escalero was merely an eccentric storyteller. "Five pieces of fruit. Five pieces were all that I managed to scarf down my weathered throat. It was all my frail body had managed to digest...that is... before my mother entered back into our house."

Escalero's vision spaced as a menacing growl slip through his jagged teeth. "Words I had never heard before, screaming as if the bombs laid bare from the invasion once again. She kicked, and she screamed, and my body recoiled like a kite in the wind!" Escalero exclaimed, swiping his hands across the table seemingly mimicking his mother's assault from all those years ago. "She tossed me effortlessly across counters, and into tables, and into chairs. Grabbing the nearest thing she could and bashing my teeth out." He said his metal fingers clanging against the metal edging of the glass table as he slammed his fist down onto it.

"And with all the hypocrisy in her lungs, she screamed; 'You pig! You pig! How will you eat now with your broken teeth!'" He screamed. Tearing to meet his guard who still stood idly beside him. Escalero 's hand drove into his face, claws in bedding within the flesh. Restraining even a simple gasp of pain his guard shook and tensed his body, eyes now locked with his leader. As Escalero inched closer perfectly replicating his mother as he hatefully whispered to his guard. "Her spit flying across my beaten and swollen face."

"And as I barely winced, peering at her through my swollen eyes. She snatched me again yanking me over a chopping board, and grabbing a butcher's knife she said so coldly, so alien to me. Her own flesh and blood!" Tears and blood streaked down his guard's face and yet he seemed compelled not to even twitch from Escalero's brazen torment. Timmy and sapphire squirmed in their seats with even Shining gripping the holster hidden just out of sight as he steadily watched. "For every piece of fruit, you ate I will be paid back in flesh and blood! So effortlessly, so swiftly, so blindly she chopped off four fingers and the thumb!" Escalero shouted, retracting his hand from his guard's face. The man slumping against the wall as Escalero returned to meet his guests showing off is brutish mothers' handiwork.

Fuming with passion he breathed a deep meditating sigh before continuing again with his speech. "White hot, searing, itching, pain wracked my face and my hand. Breath could not be uttered from my mouth, as I lay there in a pool of my blood, gasping desperately for things to stop as she continued to berate me. Hysterical in her proclamation! 'Selfish, spoiled sow'" He disgustingly spat looking down at the table clearly envisioning himself talking down to his mother.

Suddenly a decrepit smile creased along his twisted conniving face "But as if an act of mercy from God. She slipped on the seeds she sowed. Falling on to the pool of blood of her own kin, that she had created." He cheerfully said, his hand raising to the ceiling as he looked upwards. "Collapsed before me... the beast she had so callously named me in her belligerent rant...emerged..." He hungrily breathlessly growled his accent singing every word, loosely delivering them to each of his listeners.

"I was far more vicious than any of her lashings. I leapt on to her like a scavenging predator would to any wounded defenseless prey... And I butchered her!" his voice lowering, joyful and ravenous as his smile attempted to stretch past even its normal capacity the edges of his mouth slightly tearing his face morphing into an unrecognizable purely animalistic contortion.

Tightening his hand into a bold grip, hissing as he pridefully cherished his retribution, unrelenting in his self-awarding deviation of moral humanity, he continued. "Using the very cleaver, she used on me, I chipped away at her body until it became unrecognizable." He madly exclaimed a psychotic look in his eyes that even his men could hardly endure. "And in the aftermath, once I had stopped my bleeding, and the pain had disappeared. I became ... hungry... so very hungry." He was a rapid animal practically frothing at the mouth.

Truly his mother had starved any sane part of his somehow functioning mind. "And it was at that moment that I noticed a very flavorsome taste, all together new in its texture. An experience so unique to my young mind, that I had become feral." He said, bringing his metallic fingertips that still carried the fresh stain of his own guard's blood to his mouth. Unable to look away, Timmy watched as he licked his fingers clean. Timmy nearly gagging on his empty stomach as he attempted to hide his hand covering his face. “Eating until my famished body for the first time in years was full! My humanity, peeled from its fleshy cocoon birthing a beast that hungered in the shadows.” Escalero said his aggression dripping from his face as he slowly slid back into his side of the booth.

His guard hesitantly slipped back into the booth after him as he held his still bleeding face. “From that came the birth of Bestia Hispaniae, as I traveled along the countryside, feasting upon my fellow locals.” Escalero continued. His tone having drastically shifted to the way it was when he first greeted them. “As all good things however, my end of being Bestia Hispaniae came all too soon.” He said, giving a disappointing frown that nearly mimicked a pouting child.

Picking at the grooves in his metal teeth. Escalero was mesmerized, completely enthralled whilst remembering his first gruesome cannibalistic meal. During which, within a mere fraction of a second, Timmy perceived one of Escalero’s edge tipped fingers protracting and curving under a farther tooth to pick at before returning it to a normal finger length without anyone else noticing. Timmy held his breath paralyzed as Escalero returned to his story. “I was caught...eating off my most recent catch. A nun who I managed to catch out of a newly constructed church.” He snickered.

Producing an off-putting laugh as he traced his fingers slowly from his lips to his chin. “I must have looked quite literally like a dog caught with shit in his mouth ha-ha! Her muscle and blood dripping from my chin.” Suddenly a loud gag was heard to the left of Timmy. Sapphire heaved, tearing away from the table. Fully repulsed by Escalero’s egregious description of his heinous actions. Stumbling and nearly tripping over Shining as she scrambled to get away, she retreated to a undiscernible region of the bar.

The booth went silent as everyone's attention lingered on Sapphires' retreat. Timmy bolted upward, beginning to exit the booth only to be halted immediately in his attempt to chase after her. Cold, slightly moist, metal gripped tightly on to Timmy's arm as Escalero coiled his fingers around his arm. "Playthings are a dime a dozen. No need to make a fuss over them." Escalero emotionlessly proclaimed. A swirling mixture of hate and terror cascaded his goosebump covered arms. And now so intensely Timmy and Escalero stared each other down.

Even in that loud bar with all the sounds of the kitchen and the music in the celebratory chanting of distant Final Crusaders. To the most prominent noise was still The uproarious deafening beat of Timmy's heart, and the shifting metal that coiled tightly like a constricting snake around Timmy's arm. ***Click, click, click***. A new sound had appeared. the origins of which coming from Shining. Who flicked a lighter as he pulled out his small rectangular box from earlier. Retrieving a neatly wrapped cigar from it.

Placing the cigar slowly in his mouth he brought his lighter in close igniting the tip. Dragging the attention of the booth to himself as he inhaled deeply savoring the flavor of his cigar before sending out a cloud of smoke that rolled from his mouth.

"I hope you don't mind I've just been itching to have a puff... Ahh that's smooth ...I agree. dime a dozen, but she's only doing her job; entertaining me." Shining said twirling the cigar in his fingers. "Obviously she didn't expect there to be such a vivid tale, and my assistant..." Shining stopped taking another puff of his cigar. "Well, he's just doing his job of, you know, being accountable for things."

Though Timmy was undoubtedly sweating Shining remarkably continued his resolute statuette demeanor. It was no wonder that Captain Rivers chose Shining to partake in this particular mission. Shining undoubtedly was a respected equal to Captain Rivers. "And me? Well, I'm doing my job of being a most gracious Trades-Hand while enjoying a humbling tale told by my most Holy host." Shining said waving both his hands in a surrendering motion. "To which I must implore you to continue. After all I was just starting to get fuckin entertained." Shining smiled leaning back fully relaxed in the booth as he placed his cigar back in his mouth.

Loosening his metallic tendrils from Timmy's arm, Escalero sat back in his booth as he slid his fingers through his greasy hair.

"You know what, you're right. As a matter of fact, I was just getting to the best part of my tale." He said softly his men having calmed themselves as well whilst Timmy sat back down in the booth. "Caught like a dog with my tail tucked between my legs. I expected to be executed. for me to end starving, cold, and alone just as I had begun this journey." Escalero said somberly

Bowing his head Escalero held his hand together in a type of prayer. "Instead, I was ushered into the welcoming warm divinity that is our true lord, our most holy Messiah." He said, raising his hands to the sky. "And what he relinquished from me that day I shall forever worship. A burden of fear." He maliciously smiled, his eyes darting quickly to Timmy as he lingered on the Final word.

"No longer would I feel her chilling touch. For on the side of Abhorrence you find true acceptance with the reality of inevitability and are at peace with all creation." Escalero chanted. Timmy switching within a second from looking at Escalero to Shining, noticing that his face was discernibly conflicted with what he had said. Yet Timmy could not tell why. Instead returning his attention to Escalero. "In his embrace I was reborn similarly as my holy cohort who sadly is not here with us this present moment." Escalero said one of his metal fingers creeping across the others as he picked at more of his metal grooves.

Were the men beside him or his Messiah not considered his 'cohort', Timmy wondered. "Promised to me in my rebirth and repentance was that I would never go hungry again." Escalero proclaimed slapping his stomach as he continued. "And most certainly I am fed to bursting!" He loudly laughed. His men chuckling alongside them as they raised their glasses even despite the one guard's lacerations. They still cheered in unison. "For the glory of our God, and all his Creation! Blessed be the New Messiah!"

Startlingly, even some of the other patrons cheered in hearing their oath. "How magnificent this Crusade is indeed." Escalero smiled, nodding his head. "As now I feast on much more than the richness of man. Now indulging myself in those creatures. Out in the stars." He said expressively waving his hands about. A thought quickly developing in his mind. Eyes excitedly shifting between his remaining guests. "Tell me are either of you familiar with the species called Brachyurans?" Escalero asked.

Shining's ears peaked. Shifting up from his laid-back position, suddenly he became more interested in the topic change.

"Yeah actually, funny enough I had a type of blood transfusion with one of them saved my life back in the day." Shining said. "And uh well I suppose I'm a testament to their abilities. Part of the reason why my blind ass can see you lovely fellas." He smiled pointing his cigar to the three men before him.

Loudly snapping his metal fingers Escalero's smile resurfaced.

"Precisely, and so you know well enough of their decedent physiology, but my poor boy, hapless are you to have experienced it in such a bland way." He dismissively waved at Shining. Shaking his head in disappointment. "Only by devouring such a unique specimen can you truly encapsulate the enjoyment of both their flavor and power." Escalero passionately said grinning whilst licking his lips.

His metallic fingers extending towards Shining. Continuing his own experience of the Brachyurans' special abilities. "While their blood blessed you with sight, I can see now on so many spectrums, smell a bounty of new aromas, taste like it is the first I've eaten in my entire life." Escalero proudly said. Briefly bringing back his crazed exhilaration. "And one does not simply forget such a lingering sensation such as fear, isn't that right... Timothy?" Escalero coldly shifted that tearing uncanny smile that recollected more to that of a demon than that of a man. His eyes dilating, no longer a moderate look of curiosity. But that of an Insatiable hunger.

Dread. It was the only word needed to adequately convey the vacuum of emotion that dug free from the pit of his stomach. Only to be replace by raw terror that planted itself in his heart. Stricken down by a manic laugher that jolted the room. In the corner pulling one more drag of his cigar Shining cackled before lining his view with Escalero.

"Cazzo..." he muttered playing with his cigar between his fingers. "that's not his name... his name is fucking Edwick." Flicking his fingers, he shot his cigar at Escalero dashing it across his face.

Jumping up from his seat Shining withdrew his Desert Eagle aiming directly at the 'Holy General'. Before he could get a shot off however, Escalero's Guard to the right of him smacked Shining's gun upward causing, the rounds intended for Escalero to shoot through the roof. Grumbling at his failed attempt Shining gripped the table shoving it against the opposition. Firing off another two rounds through the glass table shattering it, blood splattering on the back wall.

Escalero's right guard narrowly pushing Escalero aside sacrificing himself. Bolting over top the table Escalero surprised Shining with his agility as he ran past him. "Shit!" Shining exclaimed turning to aim at Escalero. Loosening his grip on the table however allowed the left guard to launch it into Shining's side knocking him to the ground. "Dickhead!" Shining grunted, turning back and holding his side. The left guard scrambling to un-holster his own gun.

Throughout the whole ordeal Timmy had watched frozen by the initial shock of violence and aggression. Now seeing himself as the only thing standing between Shining's life and him glancing at deaths door. He burst from his seat leaping across the table kicking the guards, now withdrawn gun aside. Clambering overtop the guard pushing them both into the booth as Timmy jabbed him in the face quickly knocking him unconscious from his quick swings.

Hopping off the guard and reaching for Shining's hand the bar suddenly erupted in even more screams as several blasts blew out the entrances from various angles. Covering his ears Timmy crouched down as he held himself still as the building shook. "Over here!" Shining shouted waving his hand out. Hiding behind a booth Shining checked his magazine pointing forward. "Escalero ran that way I think he left out a side entrance." Pushing Timmy forward Shining sat up firing at more of Escalero's nearby men.

Running off in pursuit of Escalero Timmy twisted and swerved past the terrified crowd in front of him. perking his ears Timmy heard a blade as it screamed through the air just to his right. His eyes shifted in a fraction of a second as he dashed away fully facing his would-be attacker. A fully armored man cladded in silver and white. With red bold crosses on his decorative sashes that laid on his shoulders, chest and waist. The attacker stood firm, the point of their sword but a meter away from Timmy. The man held a proud stature with a look of distain.

"The wicked flee when no man pursueth; but the righteous are as bold as a lion." The man growled before lunging forward.

Cascading waves roared in Timmy's ear, and his eyes shined in that evangelically gilded emboldened sight. Dashing to the side he became a whisper in the wind. The man was still for a moment, perturbed by the abrupt disappearance of Timmy. Glancing to his side the man scowled as he ferociously barked at Timmy. "An act of heresy! Before that of a Noble you must be begging for The new Messiahs penance!" The Noble snatched his helmet from his belt clip concealing himself as he stepped forward his helmet bright white pristine in its marble like appearance.

His visor shaped itself in the pattern of a cross. Its color was tinted black momentarily before flashing to a fiery red. "I may not be worthy to deliver the Lord's sentence, but I will be enough." A ringing crackle snapped from behind the Noble as he stunted forward.

"Go Timmy, Escalero is the main target! I'll handle this Noble!" Shining shouted. The Noble grunted detaching the banners on the side of his biceps.

Draping down they unraveled over his forearms and hands to which he snapped them more securely around him. Glistening in the same silver as his pauldron. Pulling off a shield attached to his back he whipped backwards as he lunged at Shining. Timmy took a step back contemplating still helping Shining. Realizing the growing distance that circumstantially was transpiring, making Timmy rush out of the bar in a resurgent pursuit of Escalero.

Taking cover behind a vehicle, three members of Nomadic 5 held their position with Kilo patching up a visibly wounded Maci. Wonderland providing covering fire upon emerging Last Crusader reinforcements.

"Is everyone okay? Can I help?" Dropping slightly as he attempted to kneel beside them. Maci waved him off through strained wincing.

"I'm fine kid, Escalero just caught me off guard." He winced again as Kilo tightened his bandage. "Captain Rivers is already on his way. Go help him the ladies can take care of me."

Turning back Wonderland shouted over the mob of Crusaders that bared down on them.

"Escalero ran up the fire escape of that building over there." Timmy spun to where she pointed, looking back at the group giving a reassuring nod, he then took off onto the aforementioned trail. Pulling himself over the escape way, vaulting with ease as he surfaced to the rooftops. Vacancy met him, noticing the absence of Escalero, as Timmy's eyes skimmed the rooftop. Panicked at the thought of losing Escalero, Timmy began to dizzily comb the area. Jerking his head side to side checking for any sign of where he might have pathed himself.

Jumping over a roof barrier Timmy instantaneously sprung back, hearing the creeping malevolently coiling metallic tendrils of Escalero's so called fingers.

"How odd, the prey chasing its hunter." Escalero tormentingly belittled, whispering in Timmy's ear. Without any leeway for Timmy to use his latten abilities Escalero skewered him tearing through his arm and digging into his shoulder with his remaining worming metal fingers.

Deafening wailing through gasped short breaths of agonizing pain crippled Timmy as he first dropped to his knees before being pulled up higher by Escalero. "Hmm ah." Escalero wretchedly inhaled breathing in Timmy's aura. "Dismay, Dismay what delicious taste I am blessed to have lingering on my tongue." He unsympathetically said. Timmy's body falling limp as his mind disassociated from the pain.

"Ah ah ah no my dear boy stay awake a while longer." Escalero Hummed as he slapped the side of Timmy's face with his free hand. "I refuse to let another dish go to waste. Truth be told I despised the order I was given to murder your family." He said, inching closer to Timmy's face a bit of twisted sorrow emulating from him. "I mean don't get me wrong I'm certainly one to have praise for a warm meal. Nor am I a man to be picky of the gifts the Lord hath given me. But I will always hate burning my food." Indignation toiled building in a crescendo thrashing aside the weakening feeling of fear and pain.

Grinding teeth and snarling quivering lips displayed a furious gravitas. "Oh, now that is something new. In all my years of hunting never before have I been met with this type of change." Escalero happily growled contrasting Timmy's overflowing rage. Escalero snapping to look behind himself hearing heavy footsteps approaching.

"Escalero Martí! Release him now!" Captain Rivers shouted. His rifle drawn steadily at Escalero. Rivers' red eyes menacingly searing through the nearly pitch-black night.

Surprising Escalero, he faced Rivers pulling Timmy more in-between them. Calling out to the hyper lethal Captain.

"A Heretic in the flesh? 'The Red Eyed Devil' here on Earth. And what possibly could bring you here of all places?" Escalero tauntingly questioned. Rivers, ignoring him as he again shouted to Escalero.

"I did not give you a request Escalero! That was a demand! And I am authorized shoot to kill." Rivers said remaining completely still as he waited for a better line of fire.

Escalero hummed looking over at Timmy who could do nothing more than grit his teeth through the pain.

"Being a soldier of the Lord, I have been down many paths that would show me deaths door. And I can see it yet again" Escalero smiled Whipping his hand across Timmy bring a few drops of blood to his mouth. Giving a gratified sigh as he ingested his blood. "The only question that remains then dear Heretic do you care for my leftovers more than I do?" Escalero diabolically exclaimed before hurling Timmy over the roof, retracting his fingers from Timmy's arm and shoulder.

"No!" Rivers shouted slinging back his gun as he dove to the ground reaching Timmy's struggling hand that held him up along with his tearing suit. "Hold on, hold on Timmy!" Rivers shouted, grasping him desperately pulling him over. Timmy collapsed onto his back, as he exerted pants breathing sharply through the pulsing pain from his various wounds.

"Why !... Why ! this whole time you... You were all telling me to be prepared to do what was needed..." Timmy painfully cried. "Why did you grab me! ... You should have-" Timmy stopped after noticing a lack of debate from Rivers.

Turning to look at him, he found that Rivers body had frozen still, his eyes shining that deep red they had before. His body shook ever so slightly, unnoticeable to those not trying to openly perceive his body language. "We don't have time for this!" Timmy coldly shouted. Looking off to see Escalero had already run off. Sitting up with an excruciating level of suffering in his arm. Luckily his newfound disgust toward Escalero dragged his body along pushing through the cumbersome aching throughout his shoulder and arm. staggering to another escapeway on the opposite side of the building.

"Timmy!" Rivers suddenly called out. Only to be blatantly ignored Timmy, disappointed in Escalero's escape.

Struggling down, opposed to his swift clambering earlier. Reaching the bottom, however, showed no improved restitution. Frustrated, he pulled out his X-board that he had stashed on his back underneath his suit with tape. Unfolding it as he started to pull out the boards arm controller from his deep pockets strapping it to himself. "Timmy!" Rivers shouted. Timmy whipping back to him a gust of wind pushing back against Rivers, who braced himself from the shock wave.

Tears in his eyes Timmy yelled back at him.

"What Rivers!? I did everything I could! I bit my tongue, I stood inches away from that freak, I didn't run or hide like some kid!" Wincing as he held his injured arm. Timmy's anger and confusion demanding explanation. Slowly walking closer to Timmy, Rivers held out his hand pointing to Timmy's wound. "No! why!? Why did you save me! I said I didn't matter... that all I wanted was him gone! You should have taken the shot!" He said continuing to shout at Rivers. Still allowing him however to inch close enough for Rivers to tear off Timmy's suits sleeve.

"Enough!" Rivers yelled back as he addressed Timmy's slightly oozing wounds. "Escalero is not where this ends. You know as well as I do that The Final Crusade is an ongoing conflict." He said, as he pulled out a medical kit to patch Timmy up. "Do not allow yourself to be controlled by your emotions." Jerking away slightly Timmy shook his head.

"That's rich coming from you...seeing how you just went still up there for a second." Timmy scoffed. Rivers pulling Timmy's arm back in place. Taking a saline solution to his arm washing away what he could from Timmy's heavily lacerated arm.

Stopping for a moment the red in Rivers eyes twitched as he reflected.

"A lapse in fortitude, something new that I struggle with along with a great many things." He confessed, giving a sigh. A surprised look flashed over River's face as he began to pack Timmy's wounds. "Regardless. You must affectively analyze the words I said.

Remember them properly this time Timmy." Rivers said sternly. "I first gauged your comprehensiveness, and the probability that you might falter. I then reassured you over Nimitz rash behavior. I will only remind you of this once more. So, pay attention this time Timmy." Rivers said softly, his rustic voice managing to somehow calm Timmy's adrenaline filled aggression.

Gently Rivers wrapped Timmys arm in gauze before continuing. "War is long and brutal, unfair and uncaring. Survival is the definition of victory in war. If bodies traded eye for an eye every time, then there would be no victory, because there would be no one alive to see it." Rivers said testing the feeling in Timmys arm. "Can you feel my hand?" He asked to which Timmy nodded in reply. "We still need you, Timmy. Do not throw away your life in pursuit of revenge." Rivers said with his eyes returning to normal.

The two held a mutual silence with Timmy thanking Rivers for the aid. Abruptly Rivers' eyes shifted red as he held his earpiece. "I copy Nimitz do you need reinforcements? are they pushing us back?" Rivers worriedly asked, shifting to hold a better grip on his rifle.

"Was there to many back at the bar?" Timmy asked Rivers. Going quiet Rivers frowned, turning away from Timmy as he swore under his breath.

"No, they managed to handle the Crusaders and the lone Noble...But we have a code black however...Sapphire is missing"

| Page

Chapter 7: Frenzy

Speeding down the darkened pothole infested glassed over ghettos Timmy once again snarled at Rivers.

"I could have been there by now." Looking at Rivers however he held a coldly focused face. "If you had just handed me the tracker instead of making me head off to find a vehicle with you." Timmy started, raising his voice at Rivers. Slowly riling himself up in the passenger seat.

"Arguing about the method of tracking her down will not bring her back." Rivers barked. Timmy scoffed turning in his seat.

"I...I guess you're right." Timmy said, defusing himself. Somberly presuming the worst. Tears filled his eyes as he hollowly looked at the similarly broken-down buildings they passed by.

"Do not do that either." Rivers chimed.

Timmy spun back to look at him with a face of muted pain before hissing out only a single word. "What?"

To which Rivers more calmly replied. "Do not mourn her."

Surprised, Timmy asked for clarification. "You act as if she is already lost. She is not. I see her vitals and through the tracker I implemented with the two of you." Rivers said softly as he for the first time comfortingly looked at Timmy reassuringly. "She is scared. But alive. We are going to make sure she stays alive." Timmy's burdensome tempered state gradually evaporated. Releasing a relieved sigh his shoulders slacked only slightly.

"Where is she headed?" Timmy asked softly.

"The tracker is still triangulating a location. I'll tell you when I know more." Rivers said. The truth however was that he knew where she was. And had known for some time. But in that same note he also knew that if Timmy were aware of where she was. All of his strength could not contain Timmy's absolute Rampage. She in fact was running out of time by the second. Beta, however, knew they could not afford to go at the situation emotionally. To which he refrained from telling the truth, in a possible way to calm Timmy's nerves.

"Reach in the back, there is a black bag with a leather case inside. Carefully... grab it for me." Rivers said. Timmy looked at Rivers curiously before obliging to his request. Doing as he said he retrieved the black leather-bound case from his heavy similarly colored military rucksack. Looking over the case it had no inscription, no name or tag to state who it belonged to.

Asking in an almost hushed whisper Timmy said. "What is this? what's it for?" Rivers did not depart his gaze from the road simply replying with.

"It is medicine for me, can you take out one of the bottles of pills and hand it to me." Once again Timmy did as what was asked of him, unclipping the latches and opening the briefcase.

Timmy looked on at a few photos, one of a man and a woman nearly identical in appearance to Rivers. Also, inside was a number of dog tags with scratched out names, a single assault rifle magazine with oddly colored tips similar to that of the Mudlurks Hak-ya-guh metal, a broken gold necklace with an emerald gem, and the aforementioned pill bottle.

In the bottle were black pills that contained a semi crystallized, semi liquid black substance. Stuck on the pill bottle was a white label which read: **Thirty 20mg dosage. Prescribed twice a day for Beta Rivera.** In smaller print it prescribed the side effects. **Increased hallucinations, increased heart rate, increased swelling in the veins. Sensitive senses, vomiting, internal bleeding, cracked skin, loss of vision, black veins, muscle growth, and possible death.**

In such a brief amount of time Timmy had become perplexed by an overdosing of information. He had stammered and stuttered over lost words and an investigative disoriented mind.

Finally fumbling his words, he curiously mumbled. “Is this crystal ambrosia?”

“It is.” Rivers calmly affirmed.

“And the name on the label?” Timmy asked.

“Beta Rivera, a privilege I allow you to know. But I request you did not disclose publicly or frequently.” He said gravely.

Timmy again checked the pill bottle, rereading his companion’s newly discovered name again and again.

“Beta Rivera... Beta.” Timmy said aloud intrigued by the uniqueness of his name.

“You don’t follow orders too well do you Timmy?” Beta said giving a slightly annoyed look.

“Oh sorry... Rivers.” Timmy replied apologetically.

“I suppose it is fine for now we are not technically in public.” He said and for a moment Timmy thought he glimpsed a smile.

Before he could question this possible trick of the eyes Beta called out for his medication. “Timmy would you kindly hand me one of the black pills?”

Timmy paused for a second before wearily asking. “It’s Crystalline Ambrosia you want this?” Beta nodded his head extending a hand to Timmy. Carefully pulling one of the black pills from its container. Timmy reached over gently dropping the pill in his hand.

“It has been, about a year now...” Beta started to say as he gulped dryly swallowing the pill. “I was captured, and nearly drowned in this drug when I had become compromised by the War Council or Mudlurks as most call them.” “Since then, I’ve had to use these ambrosia pills to postpone the side effects of the drug and diminish my ... addiction” Beta said hesitantly seeming prying the confession off his chest.

Refocusing his attention on the road Rivers snapped his fingers motioning for him to put back the case. "We are closing in on the supposed location Remember it is just the two of us and most likely we will not be capable of calling for backup if things go South. Furthermore, I must add that what we might see when we enter this location... it might not be promising." Beta said.

"You might see some things that could express an undesirable outcome. Try as best you can to not let your emotions control you, it could determine whether we are capable of rescuing Sapphire." Beta said with Timmy nodding his head. "Just down the street." Beta said parking a few blocks away from Sapphires possible location.

His eyes glowing red as he went quiet. Seconds later stepping from the car waving for Timmy to follow.

"What's going on?" Timmy whisperingly asked.

"I had a satellite pull up live footage of the perimeter." Beta said quietly his red eyes blinking on as he reviewed the information. "It appears that recently they had entered an adjacent building with about three vehicles." Beta said motioning to the left side of the building.

"They then Took a terrace entrance on the right side of the building and entered the building that is in front of us." Timmy rushed forward ready to charge the building by himself. Only to be stopped firmly in his tracks by Beta, who quickly grasped his arm. "Emotions in control." Beta reiterated. "We make the wrong move. React the wrong way and suddenly things go to shit very quickly." Beta said Assertively giving Timmy a serious look.

Reaching into his bag Beta pulled out 2 suppressors screwing one on to his rifle and the other onto his side arm. "So, we are going through this efficiently and preferably stealthily." Beta Continued as he opened a holographic layout onto his wrist mounted tablet. "You will go through the top terrace that they entered, and I will breach from an entrance on the ground level we should be able to meet somewhere in between." Beta said Tapping Timmy's intergalactic responder which was fastened to his belt.

"If we come into trouble we will divert, I repeat we will divert from anything we are doing and regroup immediately am I clear." Beta Said Timmy anxiously awaiting the go ahead.

"I understand you Beta." Timmy Replied.

"Good. Use that speed to your advantage, be that blinding blur that I had seen...who knows you might even get it done faster than me." His voice was still stern and rasping appearing 'so serious and yet a joke?' Timmy smiling nonetheless at Betas attempt.

Overshadowed now by a building fury. That he planned to direct at anyone who could be in his path. Splitting up from Beta Timmy slowly snuck over to the terrace. Mindfully placing extra care into each silent step, he made. Vaulting over a small, locked gate Timmy had reached the entrance to which the men had taken Sapphire.

Holding back his anger he adopted for a different approach as opposed to kicking in the door. Which had been his first thought. Slipping beside the door to a nearby window, he peered inside glancing around the room. Trying to look for any possible Crusader men, or at the worst Sapphire. Sucking in his breath sharply he gasped noticing a feminine shaped outline huddled in a corner with a blanket over top of them.

Quickly taking his knife from his holster he pried open the window sliding it upward before entering the room. Dashing quietly to the figures side he hesitantly grasped the cover slowly pulling it off them. Shamefully, he was relieved he did not see Sapphire. Instead, it was a very bruised breathless woman of similar age but altogether different in appearance.

Remorsefully he covered the young woman and after doing so he frowned gritting his teeth. Once again hearing the crashing waves of an ocean. His body began to shake and tremble, his heart aching whilst he yearned for justice. He thought of how fast he could be with his resurfaced abilities and yet still he questioned; 'would he be too late to save another?'

These thoughts corrupted his mind and in a blitz of motion. He leapt to his feet and at the wrong time, and at the wrong place. A Crusader had entered the room, becoming the first proprietor of Timmy 's unbridled rage. grasping the closest thing beside him he took up a hammer and charge the man before his mind could even perceive what laid before him. His bodies mutilation began first with Timmy smashing down on the man's knees dropping him to the floor.

Timmy swinging again swiftly to the head with the back of his hand, before the man could even exert a sign of pain. Stepping out to the hallway there was a multitude of doors all closed and at the very end of the hallway hanging slightly out of a window was a man smoking a cigarette as well as a man beside him Who leisurely held his Rifle in hand. Hearing their compatriot collapsed to the floor they swung back only to be met with a distorted blurry censorship of Timmy's mortal body, visually paranormal and acting with celerity. The men before him only able to perceive his actions, as the doors burst open, one by one in a zigzag pattern. Each door being flung nearly off their hinges. One door in particular being slammed outward smashing a hallway light, dimming the corridor. And another slamming down on a radio that had been playing.

Its tune now eerily distorted as it played down the hall. Rapidly a multitude of holes started to concave into the walls coming from the far end of the hallway before quickly approaching the men. Paint and drywall crumbled over the immersing crater until without warning a hammer flung to the smoking man clocking him in the head. The man dropped to the ground motionless and his friend beside him shakily aimed his gun down the seemingly haunted corridor.

In just a single blink of his eyes, however, the gun he aimed had started to rattle and disintegrate before him. Terrified the man tried to pull away from his dissolving gun, but before he could take a step away the butt of the gun was lunged forward bashing the man's nose. With the straps that were attached to the gun being yanked forth slamming him face down on the ground knocking him unconscious.

Standing over the man's body Timmy felt his own body tremble, as he felt the Styx's ocean sway him side to side. A cosmic feeling of unimaginable reach coursed through his veins. This oceanic leviathan sized storm was raging through every pore of his body and every essence of his soul which nearly drove his mind beyond the scope of sanity. And were it not for his passionate will to find, to rescue, to protect Sapphire. He would be swept away within the frothing crescendo of waves.

Looking on word there were two rooms left. As he burst forth the hallway started to evolve, becoming drenched with visions of the Styx, and as he ran across those golden definitively epic branches that casted out in all directions. He tore through the door to the left of him demolishing it into splinters and in an uproarious fashion after spotting a woman lying still on a bed before him surrounded by men.

He barreled into a whipping bolt of lightning, jutting forth at each man, knocking them into the ground. They screamed in terror, blinded by the whirlwind that swept them off their feet, threw them into walls, and crash them through windows. One attempted to get up and yet he was knocked back down to the ground where he laid still. Another tried to run for the door, and Timmy leaped upon him with animalistic ferocity, planting his feet upon the man's back pulling back his arms as he stomped onto his back.

The man collapsed to the ground writhing with pain as he begged for mercy, yet Timmy showed him none, stomping onto his back as a cracked and squashed under the pressure of his repetitive Trampling. Slick with sweat Timmy slipped off the man repealing his punishment. As Timmy stumbled back panting loudly, his sounds carried a disorienting ominous tone. Turning to the woman who had now shifted to her knees, he watched her as she looked on at him with an odd mixture of fear and gratitude.

Focusing intently Timmy attempted to hold himself as still as he could to see the woman but still uncontrollably vibrated to a nearly invisible form, all she could see clearly, we're his golden glowing majestic eyes. He wished to stay to help this woman who had very clearly not been Sapphire and yet his feet already began to move again. Dashing across the hallway and through the door adjacent to the room he was in.

Holding a firm stance before him was a single man who shouted out aggressively in Timmy's direction.

"I told you fuckers that I would be first! I brought her here so I get-" The man stopped as he had turned around to look who had interrupted him. Stark with fright he looked on slack jawed, entranced by a primal takeover of emotions that shot up the hairs on his back and froze him so completely still.

Uttering not even a scream Timmy flashed moving down the hallway and back again having retrieved the hammer from the man he threw it at mere moments ago. Like something akin to booming thunder and lightning, he struck down the self-entitled sinner with a spiteful unrelenting wrath. Dropping lifelessly the hammer still protruding from his skull Timmy stopped.

Hyperventilating as his body slowly reappeared fading back to his normal human form. In front of him laid a single mattress dingy and smelly. The stench of everything in that building finally brought solely to his attention, the distorted radio singing slightly louder, the crumbling of a nearby door frame. Everything rocked his trembling fragile body and yet not even one, either from this plane of existence or the existence of that oceanic other world could push him more towards discomfort and pain than to look down at a hollow dried teared topless Sapphire.

Stifling his cries he took hold of his brother's hoodie, looking away from her exposed body as he shambled painfully slow to the edge of the bed. Miraculously Sapphire began to part from her shellshocked status. Meeting a similar expression as the girl in the room behind Timmy had felt, fear and gratitude. Now truly awakened to the fantastical and now horrific powers that had only recently begun to be used by her savior.

Sitting up she looked to his watery bloodshot eyes, which still held a glittery gold sparkle in them. Holding out his brother's hoodie he slipped it over Sapphire. Trying desperately to not look or touch her pure, soft, white, goosebumps' riddled skin. Merely looking to spot the possibility of bruising or cuts. Prayers answered Timmy nearly cried at the fact that he had not spotted either. Having fully draped her in the hoodie his body finally gave in to his heart's despair.

Falling limply to his knees he could hold back no longer. Grief endured to a breaking and with one final look at the cost of his actions in saving Sapphire, in the fact that he could not shield her from such torment, he wept. Babbling incoherently, he mumbled apologies and begged for forgiveness through sorrowed screams and draining nostrils. He balled inward compressing himself as much as he could, in an attempt to hide himself from the terrible world.

Cold breezes from the domain of the Styx washed over him and he shivered through a growing cold sweat. His throat growing horse as he swayed back and forth on the ground and shook his head.

"Why, Why, why!" He wailed, hitting the side of his head trying to smack away the thoughts of seeing the man bloodied and destroyed. Of the women exposed and molested. Of his inability to protect the innocent.

Stretching his head to the heavens his eyes trying to tear the roof asunder as if to ask God himself why he could not be better. Why he could not protect them or her. And the with a violent gasp his eyes shot in front of him. Through the manic episode of sheer lament, Sapphire crawled to meet his side. Despite her own harrowing treatment, she ached to see Timmy in such a way.

And so ever so gently, she embraced him. Holding him closely to herself, as she fought back tears of her own. As she ran a hand through his silky jet-black hair their eyes met. And peacefully they rested their heads against each other's. Silently restoring a semblance of stability and comfort. After a short minute, the pair slowly regained enough composure to leave.

Practically tied together, the wedged pair were on top of each other's heels as they made their way down the corridor.

"There are... other women here. Aren't there?" Sapphire asked as she looked in the passing rooms.

"Yes." Timmy heavily whispered. "I'll tell Beta, hopefully he and his group can do something for them... right now it's just us three." Timmy said as Sapphire gripped his shirt.

"Beta? Who is that? and only three of us ... so you and only one other person did all of this?" Sapphire quietly exclaimed.

"Oh, shoot I ... I gotta remember to not say that too often... Beta is Captain Rivers real name." Timmy whispered.

"Wait his name is ... Beta? what an odd name... I wonder how his family came up with that." Sapphire whispered back.

"Yeah, wish I knew myself... and uh as for the mess... that was only me ... Rivers is downstairs." Timmy said.

"What?!" Sapphire nearly shouted out. "You did all of this?" she said looking around at all the busted doors, lights, and walls as well as the unconscious men.

"Holy shit... Timmy it's like a hurricane went through here." Before Timmy could speak more a loud bang shook the building.

"Oh no! Captain Rivers!" Timmy shouted out. The both of them rushing down the rest of the corridor, meeting a flight of stairs. Stealthily cautious they side stepped down the stairs both catching a strong scent of gun powder and blood. Slipping around the bend of the stairway Timmy and Sapphire peered slowly into the new hallway.

A single light illuminated the hall with a twitching flicker, as a man bloodied and battered slowly pulled himself from the room in front of them before laying in place his eyes glassing over as he reached out for a distant gun. Past him laid more scattered, gun downed men. A river of blood flowing down the hall finally bringing to attention another man who was crawling to the main entrance. Pulling himself just under the blinking hallway light, an unmistakable shadow peeled from the unlit walls as red eyes slowly beamed to life.

Slow heavy steps of his boots echoed repetitively until he stood overtop the crawling man. Reloading his magazine Beta shot two rounds into the man who now slumped forward abruptly. Both Sapphire and Timmy looking completely appalled of the total carnage painted by its ruthless artist. Beta glanced back to the pair as the flickering light suddenly held his shine over him casting a perfect shadow. Hardly showing his face and more visually showing off Betas red mechanical eyes.

"Well Timmy, it would seem you got done faster than me... or perhaps I just wanted to be more...efficient."

| Page

Chapter 8: Beneath

Disturbed and harshly silent, the entire ride back to the base seemed abnormally longer this time around. Sapphire throughout the ride was hardly an inch away from Timmy's side. Clutching his arm to a discomforting degree. Timmy, the entire time, not disclosing a single notion that it was. Instead, was simply pained by the jarring juxtaposition of her character.

Gratifyingly the shack in the desert appeared before them in the headlights. With familiar security Sapphire sighed in relief, loosening Timmy's now tender arm. "I have been given an update on the women who were rescued from The Last Crusades human trafficking." Beta said as they receded into the base. "About seven out of ten of the survivors are in stable conditions. The others are in critical condition but with favorable outcomes in sight." Beta said, as a bit of talk slipped from the earpiece in his ear.

"Thank god..." Sapphire breathlessly whispered. Timmy's heart excitedly jumped, stunned with her first words spoken since they left that forsaken nasty hellhole filled of depravity.

"I thought you would want to know." Beta softly replied as they pulled into the base's vehicle bay. A morbid curiosity suddenly played its hand in Timmy's mind, as he wondered about the soldiers he had fought, as well as all the dispatched dead men. Specifically, the man he had killed.

Distorted as he might have looked to the man, Timmy could clearly see him. From defining features of his face, to his slowly differing reaction of anger, that transitioned into fear. It was mortifying. No one had ever looked at him with such horrid contempt. It writhed in his stomach as a terrifically conflicting battle.

He understood he needed to save and protect Sapphire. However, the split second of the man falling limp, the almost instinctual adrenaline-imposed action of swinging the hammer, met with the morbidity of self-indulgence of taking out his retribution.

It was so cathartic, but even reliving it briefly gagged him. He couldn't help but compare himself to Escalero. Remembering just how happy that disgusting monster was at his own brutality, and that he might carry something in common, disturbed him. Appeasing his haunted mind was his uncle who happily greeted him and Sapphire as they stepped from the vehicle.

"Thank god you're both okay!" He said hugging them both. It comforted Timmy, Sapphire however dropped her head looking away from B.G., giving a weak whisper as she took a step back from him saying.

"I need some rest." She paused for a moment seemingly reflecting on her words and the night's events.

Looking beside her, she gave Timmy a weakly warming smile.

"Thank you ... again... hero." She said before looking off at a nearby Reaper who took her arm and led her off to the base's barracks.

"Did... is everything okay?" B.G. said frowning with concern. Timmy held back his urge to cry out. Swallowing his dread, he too dropped his head with a lack of will to confide in his blissfully ignorant uncle.

"We will discuss everything in due time." Beta said walking up to the two. Timmy sent a silent thank you to Beta in his mind.

Placing a hand on Timmy's shoulder as he continued. "We need to talk, follow me please." Beta said.

"I'll be okay BG; I should probably help Captain Rivera with whatever he needs..." Timmy tried to reassure his Uncle. BG's frown grew but begrudgingly nodded, allowing Timmy to follow Rivers down a differing wing of the base.

"So, from what I understand you have taken your first life." Beta spoke bluntly, absolutely relentless in his frigid stature.

Briefly looking to his bold compeer, Timmy was stunned at his very nature, he was so human and flexible and yet at the same time so robotic and stiff. Definitively callous yet so questionably compassionate. A fighting, walking, talking contradiction of incomplete personality. He marched with a purpose but still had an expression of being lost.

"I ... I did..." Timmy said frowning, a shiver clawing on his arms thinking of the refutable action he had made.

"I am surprised it had not happened sooner." Beta replied with a shrug.

"What do you mean?" Timmy asked, surprised by Rivers bold statements.

"Example's being the Church, the Plant, the Construction yard, Last Salvation Plaza, the Hospital, and even our confrontation." Beta listed.

"Wait... you've been following me all that time?" Timmy exclaimed stopping in his tracks.

"I have had tabs on you for months now." He replied turning back to face Timmy. "Only recently have I taken the reconnaissance into my own hands as a matter of formally introducing myself to you." Beta said.

"The only time I noticed you was after the hospital." Timmy said back rethinking the moments Beta had listed off.

Indeed, not recalling spotting him any sooner.

"Really? Although I suppose that explains your more sporadic behavior when we first met face to face." Beta replied. "I wonder then. How did you think the Construction yard went down?" Beta asked with a frown.

"The automated crane happening to malfunction, and crash into the vehicle...the one guard who was shot?" Timmy questioned the sudden realization striking him. "That was all you?" He whispered in disbelief.

"The crane yes, the man being dispatched however I will give full credit to Carolina and her marksmanship." Beta replied carrying a bit of pride for his own squad member.

Timmy paused cocking an eyebrow at the unfamiliar name.

"Carolina?" He asked.

"Right, you know her as Reaper. A place like this we are safe so we can discuss names in the open." Beta said, "But remember only speak casually in safe zones." He sternly re-affirmed. Timmy nodding his head understanding the seriousness.

"I guess I owe you a lot then. You saved me back there." Timmy smiled scratching his head. Feeling a bit humbled at the prospect that he was in fact not alone and having quite a bit of help throughout his recent ordeals.

"I saw a potential informant but was surprised to acquire something more consequential." Beta replied.

"Hmm...but I couldn't get Escalero." Timmy said disappointed that even with help they still had few results.

"For doing what you have managed, as a kid, alone and untrained. It is admirable." Beta said reassuringly patting Timmy's shoulder. Giving a stiff but still notably genuine smile.

"I don't know..." Timmy started to say. With Beta quickly interjecting.

"Learn when to take acknowledgement. It will help you balance criticism." Rivers advised.

Turning away from Timmy Beta ushered him onward before continuing. "Both will be granted accordingly during our training sessions." He said.

"Wait training? You're going to train me?" Timmy asked, walking in a faster pace in order to catch back up with Beta.

"I intend to teach you as much as I can. But the scope of your abilities and the way you access the peak of them might be beyond what I can do." Beta said entering a new room with large monitors covering a wall.

Reaching under a desk and into a refrigerated attachment Beta retrieved a mysterious jar. Placing it on top of the desk Beta continued to speak on his plans for Timmy. "First step is realizing that both war and fighting in a war is dirty." Beta said, his eyes turning red as he began to look for other things in the room. "Although tactics and simulations can help, things can still differ when head-to-head with an opponent." He said grabbing a type of baton from a wall mounted weapon case that carried several more.

"Realize and acknowledge they will not go easy. They will not pull punches; they will not hesitate on a trigger." He said handing the baton to Timmy as he glanced at the monitors seemingly turning them on with his red eyes. Taking the baton Timmy looked it over curiously while watching Beta. Interested in how seemingly natural it was for him to use his red eyes with the surrounding technology. Wondering how his father might have reacted if he had the chance to meet him.

Snapping his fingers Beta recalled Timmy's attention as he continued. "Focus. When you are on the battlefield you will not have time to daydream." He berated as he imposingly stood over him. "They will fight grizzly and brutish. Kicking, punching, biting, scratching, gouging with any opportunity they can take." Beta said. With Timmy wincing at the thought of violence again. ***Bang!*** Beta hit the table shocking Timmy refocusing him again.

"Come to terms with the fact that they will not show you mercy! As they do not expect it from you!" Beta snapped at Timmy.

Rolling his eyes Beta stepped away. Gathering more inconspicuous equipment as he continued to lecture Timmy. "Furthermore, when an enemy is not killed, rendered unconscious, or incapacitated. They will continue to be a threat. Do not yield until they are one of those three." Beta said, Timmy trying to memorize all the drilled in information. Giving no time to digest the information Beta moved on to his next plan for Timmy. "For your second step: I will be teaching you a more effective manner of running." His eyes shifted side to side as if he were looking at something.

Reactively, Timmy looked down trying to see what Beta might be looking at but seeing nothing. "If what Rooks reported is correct, then you're miraculously capable of speeds that are double some of the fastest land vehicles." Beta said, blinking in an awkwardly deliberate fashion that looked almost mechanical before looking back at Timmy. Jerking his own eyes away trying to hide his discomfort from watching Betas movements.

"That status and capability of yours was roughly when you were six is that correct, traveling at 1200 miles per hour?" Beta asked. Timmy frowned shrugging his shoulders still in a bit of disbelief at what Rook had theorized. Now however, after the events at that human trafficking ring, it was hard for him to completely rebuke that he has a remarkable ability of speed. but 1200 miles an hour? It was hard for him to even comprehend it.

"That's how old I was when my parents passed, and I ran from the diner yes." Timmy replied softly.

Beta was continually amazed by Timmy's remarkable abilities. His own military feats were considered unimaginable. But if Timmy had the same upbringing as him, he wondered what he might be capable of.

"If you were capable of such speeds at such an early age without any prior training of proper running technique..." Beta said thinking aloud. "The sheer possibility of your potential is astronomical and for all intents and purposes inhuman." He said, pausing for a moment to think of the increasingly perplexing situation.

"It adds to a mystery that bends reality as we know it. but I am not one to tip in the science that fun can be set aside for Rook and doc." Beta said casting aside his thoughts. "Lastly I want to put you through proper military training I have reasons to believe that you will outperform even myself." Beta said as Timmy gave a chuckle of disbelief. Which immediately was struck down as Timmy looked back at Beta who stared him down deadpanned. "We have a war on the horizon. A paradox that no one will ever see if we do things properly, and you will be one of our strongest assets." Beta said projecting a number of threads onto the monitor behind him.

Again, it showed lists of groups within the Final Crusades hierarchy: The Lords of the new Messiah, The Holy Generals, The Knights, and The Nobles. But now adding events and intel including White Rose asylum and A Raffiniert named Gurt. He read every name curiously. Comparing what he did know with what Beta had uncovered separately. It was entirely off-putting that he indeed only scraped the surface of what the Final Crusade truly consisted of. "I want you to be a part of a crew, Timmy. Handpicked solely by me, to do what our military and Alliance cannot." Beta said as Timmy continued to read the names.

Within the overarching web of connections was one category labeled High Value Assets. Shocked to see his own planted within the webbing attachments to the Final Crusade. He read off each assets file as Beta switched through them. Subject 1: TIMOTHY GREEN, Age: 17, Location: Último City; New California, Status: Under Review. Next were two identical files of men who shared the same last name. Subject 2: THOMAS DEMENTO, Age: 27,

Location: Bridgeport; Michigan, Status: Monitored. Subject 3: ISSAC DEMENTO, Age: 27, Location: Mega City 3(Old Chicago); Illinois, Status: Monitored. Under review... monitored? Timmy thought to himself.

So many questions lingered after reading just a sample of Betas intel. Why was he the to be under review, and who exactly were with these two men? More importantly, who was the fourth individual within the High Value Assets category. Looking at their file was like seeing a type of black ink coated classified document. Unlike the others who clearly had photos of themselves. Timmy noticed his photo was from a company get together that happened a year before his family's passing. The two men having what appeared to be driver's license photos being shown. But the 4th had no photo whatsoever.

Next to the normal moniker of subject #4 was a type of side note which read as: Name/Alias; Az/PROTECTOR. What kind of name was 'Az' and Protector? Was that some type of title? The man was also the oldest of the group being 30. Which only further confused Timmy at the prospect of Beta wanting someone as young as him. Lastly Timmy read that this mysterious 4th man's location was also a mystery being labeled as Europe instead of any specific country and or city state within the region. Despite the differences this one mysterious man carried, he was still under the status of being monitored.

Quietly thinking to himself, Timmy's sporadic train of thought was quickly derailed as Beta continued to mention his training. "A normal U.M.E initiate will undergo a normal routine of two months boot camp." Beta said exiting out of the files for the other members of his yet to be assembled crew. "Followed by two months basic training and then be given the choice to further their career becoming U.M.E special forces, Alliance cooperatives, or naval

Starfighters." The monitor now switching to images of said different fields. These were the brave men and women his father had mentioned years ago. The soldiers on the front lines who fought against their fears for the sake of other, for a better tomorrow.

Timmy thought to himself looking at these images, could he really stand up with these brave men and women? Could he do what Beta wanted, could he do whatever it took, even when those brave men and women could not? "Each of these fields are a grueling undertaking and require training that is designed at a level of impossibility with an expected failure rating of 96%." Beta said. His words served only to imbed the feeling of doubt further into Timmy's mind. "In total the whole progress can take upwards of a year, however I was capable of completing my own venture within half the time." Beta said. In another "blink and you miss it" moment, Timmy could barely notice a showing of pride as beta stated his own abilities.

Looking back to Timmy a compassionate smile that warmly reminded him of his father flashed over Beta's face. "I will expect you to do the same if not better." Timmy's heart swelled by an uplifting vigor that was contagious. Truly the Captain of Nomadic 5 was a natural in both combat and the innate ability to inspire. For the first time in years Timmy felt an urge to make someone proud. "I will make nothing easy. I will strain you until your body aches and your bones become brittle. You will feel in the coming months as if you are already at war but with yourself you will either succumb or I will prefect you." Beta said the smile vanishing as he held his head high raising it for Timmy to meet his expectations.

Sitting up straight Timmy too raised his head nodding in compliance as he braced himself for the coming storm. "For now, we will do what we can in the short time we are given to hone in a minuscule fraction of your capabilities." Beta said his red eyes flickering as he discreetly sent a signal for Reaper to join them.

Entering the room Beta signaled her to the monitor. Before continuing. "I do not intend this battle to be long. But I want you prepared for whatever might happen when we go on the offensive again." Beta said with Timmy only partly listening more surprised at how sudden and nonchalant Reaper had appeared. "Thus commences a very controversial training, something that was created by me and so far, used only by the members within Nomadic 5." He said now ushering to the tools placed beside Timmy.

"It has been deemed the black book training..." Beta said taking out the same briefcase that carried his pills from the nearby desk. Placing the briefcase on the table opening it, he retrieved the aforementioned Black book. Waving it in front of Timmy. "In short it is designed to give a heightened sense of instinctual performance and result. You will learn to fight to survive with this training because if you do not, you will die." Beta said the last words stunning Timmy as he jerked backwards in response.

"You're kidding right you don't actually intend to kill me Beta..." Timmy asked with a nervously quiet chuckle.

Looking over at Reaper, Timmy tried desperately to pry a more human response expecting her to smile or show some sign the Beta had over exaggerated. Instead, she showed a practical mirror image to her Captain which only further strengthened Timmy's anxiety.

"I intend to push you to your limits and even further beyond." Beta replied stepping closer to Timmy. "Round one of your black book training starts now, Nomadic 5 will hunt you." Beta said gearing up with his own equipment "You have a 5 second lead." He said as the room fell silent and the lights turned off. A red hue flashing over the room. Low and raspy Beta cocked back his gun as he menacingly called out for his subordinate. "Carolina...start the simulation."

Approximately six month later

Timmy ran through the nearly pitch-black underground base, trying his hardest to control his breathing. The environment barely navigable aside from a flashing red that slightly illuminated his tired jaded sprint. Panicked, his eyes shot from side to side. An unknown shadowed silhouette trailing just beyond his peripheral vision. Collapsing behind a vehicle in exhaustion. He quietly strained to control his timid breathing. The warehouse so silent, no footsteps, or breathing could be heard.

Timmy held his chest disgruntled at the fact that his own heartbeat might betray him. With how loudly it pounded in his chest. Then, before even Timmy could react, his eyes glowed that shining gold, as he dashed away from his cover. Barreling to face what had impeded on to him. Bracing the metallic beam that he held in his hand Timmy lunged at the figure, being blocked on several fronts, before swiftly knocking them off their feet.

Placing the metal beam to the silhouette's throat he shouted out at it. "Yield!"

And the familiar voice barked back in disappointment.

"I will not yield until you make me!" Without another word, the silhouette un-holstered his gun and fired shooting Timmy in the head. Stiffly Timmy's body froze, collapsing backwards with a loud thud. Stepping to his feet the silhouette slipped out from the darkness chastising Timmy 's performance. "This is the second time you've failed to eliminate an obvious threat. I know what you're capable of and it's upsetting to see you not match those results." The silhouetted figure replied with a shake of his head.

"It feels pointless to continuously reiterate and drill into your head the concept that others will not yield and will not show you mercy like you do." Kneeling Beta pulled off a paralyzing rubberized bullet from Timmy's forehead. Timmy's body drooping limply from his frigid state. His arms and legs falling to his side as he quickly sat up rubbing his forehead.

Tears slightly forming in his eyes as he yelped out in pain. "Ouch! God that flippin stings!"

Smacking his arm Beta continued to chastise Timmy

"Please, you were shot 10 times as much by Reaper the first time." Timmy winced checking his forehead for blood, feeling only that there was a slightly tender bruise.

"Yeah, but she shot me in my butt." He winced in retort.

"Get up." Beta barked ignoring Timmy's cries. "As it would show, you have failed your first attempt at black book training, but we will give you your third round anyways reposition and get ready for your final round." He said sternly as he walked off.

"Head over to Carolina for another dose of the distortion berries. Remember not to chew for too long, spit it out immediately after you've bit down on it!" Beta yelled out before entering the observation room. Making his way to Carolina she quietly signed for him to take the smaller as it would be the safer dose for his body weight. Timmy looked at Rook who had been prepping for the final round beside her.

"Oh, she is saying take the smaller ones, it's best for you." He translated.

Timmy nodding his head taking one and doing as Beta had said before saying thank you to them both. Carolina reading his lips and gave a soft smile and a friendly nod back. Taking the small dark orange berry with black dots he quickly popped it in his mouth and in the same beat spit it out in a trashcan beside him. Before even turning his breath felt slowed and his eyes grew heavy. Already he began to slowly adjust however to the steep effects of the distortion berries. His body adapting significantly more than the other participants as he even in the other rounds showed a faster response, less fatigue, and a more alert mind.

Again, as in previous times a voice came over the bases intercom system announcing the hunters as Rook, Maci, Wonderland, Queenie, and X-ray. Followed by a recap of set rules: 'Only hunters are allowed firearms. Boundaries are set to only within the main training room, the mess hall, and vehicle storage bay. Finally for the round to be over all five hunters or the hunted must be eliminated by forfeit, paralysis bullets or melee, or rendered incapable of continued combat.'

With the rules displayed and the base transitioning to lock down. Timmy slipped from the training room and into the nearby mess hall. Despite the previous round having a favorable outcome where he had held his ground in the training room. He recognized that this was only because of an element of surprise as they did not anticipate him waiting in place for them to appear. Instead, they had expected him to rely more prominently on his ever-evolving abilities.

This time Timmy devised an altogether new strategy, more planned out and thorough. This time he would use his first rounds knowledge of running around scouting and familiarizing his environment. Able to now map it out even in the dark to a near one to one. As well as using the two former rounds notice that each team member had accustomed almost natural pathing. He determined they had grown with confidence with the overall layout of their base. Using both understandings and his speed he would shift everything slightly as to being a hindrance without being too obvious.

And at the same time dismantling doorways or lighted areas in which he felt would give him a better chance to hide. He even went as far as placing the given training weapons in multiple locations as to allow more options in case he lost his current one. Attuned ears drawn in by the first sound of steps of his slowly approaching opposition sprung Timmy into a course of action. Hastily he dismantled the doorways, repositioning tables chairs and trash cans in a jagged pattern

Hiding low behind where a light was originally illuminated. Stepping slowly into the mess hall the group checked corners flashing their lights in a strobe in hopes to at first disorient Timmy. He was fortunately hiding just beyond their affective range. The other half of the team then pushed open the second door with its sabotage becoming apparent as one of its hinges came lose. Queenie the one having cracked the door open fell forward along with the door. Timmy shifted to this, taking advantage of the opening he had been striving for.

Taking the opportune moment, he burst forth to their now open blind side as they had been checking on Queenie. Jabbing the paralyzing weapon twice at Maci's neck his body violently freezing before dropping hard to the ground. Timmy retreating to his haven past their sightline, Xray being the first to react to Maci being eliminated. Strobing his light in a widespread and firing off a few paralyses rounds before pulling Maci back out into the hall yelling for the others to fallback as well.

What proceeded was a methodical and slow game of cat and mouse which pushed Timmy into various creative methods of isolation control and spontaneous Guerilla warfare that rewarded him in three more eliminations. Wonderland found herself being shut in a room alone after Timmy locked the door behind her teammates. At one point, Timmy crawled under a vehicle to lash at an unsuspecting Queenie's legs. Later, a fierce two against one hand to hand combat in which Xray and Rook cornered Timmy back in the training room.

The open area was working to their advantage as they set off glow sticks to illuminate the room giving Timmy little cover resulting in him using a more personal face to face approach at combat. Using his imperceivable form to disregard their advantage blurring in a side-stepped motion as he swung at Xray.

"Dayshon cover your eyes!" Rook shouted to Xray as he pulled out a blinding device that shocked Timmy as if he had stared at the sun, causing him to narrowly miss Xray.

Reacting slowly from the distortion berry it felt like hours that Timmy was staring into the burning light before he could finally stumble back and scurry out of the training room. Turning off the light, Rook breathed a sigh of relief. "Damn that was close he was right as your throat Dayshon..." He trailed off having noticed that although Timmy had missed his initial hit point on Xray. In the period that the distortion berry took its affect he jabbed Xray several more times in his side paralyzing him. Rook now alone ventured back out the final impediment of Timmys last round of Black book training.

Separately, Beta looked on at a monitor along with the rest of Nomadic 5. Notably Nimitz, BG, and Sapphire shared the most intrigue besides Beta. Having attentively watched every detailed choice and reaction made by the amateur fighter.

"Astounding, that bullet to the head must have really resonated with him." Nimitz coyly snarled. "At this rate maybe, we shouldn't have given him the crutch of only handling a half of Nomadic at a time." She mockingly scoffed.

"Careful Nimitz that almost sounded like a compliment." Shining commented from behind. The playful smirk clear as day despite his covered face.

"Can it Jack. I'm simply suggesting that if we wanted to test the boy, we should have done it to the proper standers of this so-called black book training." She scathingly hissed. Beta waved his hand dismissing both of their behaviors.

“Be fair with the kid, Nimitz he is unrefined and undisciplined, but his mind is creative and weather he knows it or not he is becoming more intrepid by the second.” He said intensively watching and recording every move of both participants with his red eyes.

“He chooses to take on two soldiers head on instead of running away and currently is looking for a new weapon after having dropped his in the scuffle with the two.” Beta continued, a pleased intrigue sliding past the cracks of his stiff appraisal. “He is not shaken. He is determined. If anything, the two being the last ones is the best possible outcome in this training session. It’s a good test for both.” He said moving the main monitors view to look over Rook.

“John has struggled a few times in black book training.” He disappointedly affirmed. “It's hard for him to push back the fight or flight, along with the compatriot aspect of black book training.” He said with a sigh looking over to Nimitz.

“This will make it increasingly difficult considering his overall interest in Timmy as well as his abilities.” She noted stepping closer to Beta.

Switching the monitor back to Timmy’s location as Beta continued his observation.

“As for Timmy, this is the first round where he has been capable of doing what he needed to eliminate all the five aggressors.” Beta added.

“His Ingenuity is refreshing and that perseverance...” Shining replied, stating. “It’s no easy feat staring blankly into a Supernova Unit without eye protection and being able to just walk it off.” Both sapphire and BG quietly watching in the corner understanding very little of the professionals’ comments.

Nevertheless, they were still thoroughly impressed by what they could see from Timmy's black book training.

"Beta, look Rook is closing in on him." Another member of Nomadic called out. The group redirecting their eyes to his position. Slowly the Staff Sargent followed Timmy into the base's vehicle Bay.

Nimitz quickly grit her teeth as she growled. "What the hell is he doing!" Timmy rubbed his strained eyes as he hid behind a half-disassembled starship.

"Mr. Green?" Rook called out. Stepping slowly into the vehicle bay gun drawn as he flashed his light around. "Mr.Green?" He said again only louder this time.

Still remaining silent Rook realized Timmy was in fact taking things a bit more serious than himself. "Oh, right I suppose it's smart not to reply." He whispered retrieving small devices from his rucksack. "Smart choice, I mean I know you must be in here though." Rook admitted as he began to place the devices around himself. "The frantic running caused you to hit a wall on the way in cracking it. Along with your melee that you had now sitting a few steps down the hall." He said with Timmy gently smacking his head having not even thought of the possibility.

"I'm sorry I used the supernova, but I couldn't see any other way..." Rook said returning Timmy's train of thought. "which brings be to what I wanted to say." He said taking a look at his surroundings before giving a sigh as he continued. "If there was anyone else to stand against you like Carolina or Jack...I mean Reaper or Shining... sorry you must still be getting use to our names." He paused his derailing thoughts showing a glimpse again. "Captain Rivers...I feel like they would at least stand a chance on this one-on-one." He half-heartedly confessed.

The concept taking Timmy off guard. He too had felt the same way, that he was inadequate compared to all of Nomadic 5. And in a unique way Rooks statement comforted him. Deciding to continue to listen in his hidden location. "But me I'm new to all this. I was taught to fight Mudlurks, to travel in space, fight in the stars." Rook started up again. "As wild as it sounds that's what I aimed for even as a kid. To join the U.M.E and the Alliance." His softly spoken mindset finally bringing a more casual and less ruthlessly tactical side 2 Nomadic fives Overall conveyed image. Reminding Timmy more of Apollo.

"I never realized I'd have to fight and kill my own." Rook said aching regret clearly audible in his voice. "To be honest I'm surprised I survived even a week with Captain Rivers." He said almost giving a chuckle.

"And he says these challenges ain't even the worst of the storm to come." Rook said, hardly believing his own words as he leaned against a disassembled Starship. "That I'll see and do things that I'm not even ready for..." His voice trailing off leaving Timmy to think for a moment remembering one of the first things Beta had mentioned.

The idea of how much more was at play. Of the fact that there was more than just Escalero. That truly the Final Crusade as a whole and the overarching galactic war we're still foreboding and hanging over the heads of every individual within the universe. Gripping his shotgun tightly Rooks tone shifted. As he more loudly proclaimed. "And yet my Captain picked me to be in Nomadic squad!" A wave of determination sent crashing against Timmy. Rooks' confidence attempting to even erode Timmy's hesitant and ever doubtful nature. "My Captain believes in me to get any job he wants done, done!" Rook shouted, as his adrenaline rushed him.

Setting up from his slouched posture he checked over his location retrieving even more devices and laying them about in front of himself. “So, I might not be super powered like you, might not be super human like him, might not even be the best in my class like the others in Nomad.” Rook breathed Heavily is nervous hands gripping painfully on to his shotgun. “But my Captain believes in me! My Captain sees potential... just like he sees potential in you!” Rook shouted, hoping that his own attempts to hype himself up we're working for his friendly adversary. “I don't intend to hold anyin back! I'm braving the coming storm. I'm not running from this even if that means I had to come at you head on.” Unaware that his words struck a familiar chord the final phrase reminding Timmy of his father.

Steadily the two prime themselves ready for action as they both simultaneously an unknowingly ready themselves for another surge of combat. “So why don't we give them a show... make them see something more than what they see in us already!” Rook screamed out in a war cry as he racked another paralysis shell into his shotguns chamber. “On your go Mr. Green!” Determination set forth by his friendly adversary. Timmy rushed his opponent ripping around the corner as he swung out his melee. Rook held his ground against a horizontally backing spaceship.

Aiming his shotgun outward he expelled around from left to right the paralysis buckshot spreading in a wide diameter covering every angle in front of him. Timmy ‘s eyes widen as the fray of bullets tore through the air to get to him. with golden eyes he flashed contorting around bending and leaping out of each individual spread of the paralysis buck shot. While simultaneously advancing on John's position. Suddenly amidst his advance Timmy began to hear Fast-paced mechanical clicking that surrounded him at his feet.

Looking down to his feet he noticed a multitude of rigged paralysis traps encircled Rooks perimeter. Dashing back just in time he narrowly escaped the radius of each consecutive blast of paralysis ammunition. And in a weary sense of repetition John again racked more shells throwing out more traps as he fiercely held his position. Jolting back to a farther location Timmy surveyed this situation, devising a plan while deciphering an opening.

An idea struck him decisively and without hesitation he began implementation. Tossing his melee to the canopy of the spacecraft. Making Rooks attention immediately divert, causing him to look upwards as Timmy's melee clanged loudly from above him. Instinctively Rook shot upwards sparks flying off the spacecraft as the paralysis bullets sparked outwards. "Fucking Zero!" Rook swore. An immediate response of shock and regret rocking his face as his adrenaline surged.

Tearing through the air, Rook swiped his gun down. But was all too late, as Timmy had covered the distance short and in one swift swing cracked upwards across Rook's jawline with a second melee that Timmy had concealed. Convulsed Johns body attempted to resist its paralyzing effect but could only hold it off for a moment before freezing completely and dropping to the ground.

Standing triumphantly in the dark Timmy jerked as the lights soon beamed around him and the darkness disappeared. Crouching down Timmy took Rook throwing his arm over his shoulder. Pulling him to the rest of Nomadic squad who met Timmy with a round of applause and various cheering in celebration of his first win of black book training. Doc and kilo speeding past the others taking Rook in their arms as Doc began to administer the opiate antagonists for the distortion berries.

Letting go of Rook Timmy shyly smiled at the rest of Nomadic 5 as Beta proudly stepped forward giving Timmy a nod.

"You did well for your final round of black book training." Beta said, Yet not fully celebrating the occasion as he reminded Timmy. "but do not hold this too highly above yourself. In the three rounds you only succeeded in this final round." Beta said with a frown as Timmy knowingly hung his head in disappointment.

"That being said, I'm pleased with this outcome. it continues to show the potential and the promise of a more renowned fighter with you." Still feeling a bit conceited to his constructive criticism Timmy felt a bit disheartened about failing his first attempt. Shining detecting this from his own abilities, chimed in.

"Hey now, don't stress too much a few of us haven't passed our first go around the black book training still." He said motioning to the rest of Nomadic squad.

"Heck even our second-best fighter Master Sergeant Nimitz, didn't pass her first attempt at black book training." Tempered eyes scorched into the back of Shining's head as Nimitz barked out at her subordinate.

"The only reason I failed the first time was because I don't take this 'black book training' or whatever the hell you want to call it seriously!" She barked out as Beta step between the two as he gave a deliberate signal to end the discussion.

Turning back to Timmy after giving a harsh look Beta corrected Nimitz saying. "What the Master Sergeant is trying to say is that it is still an unconventional method of training." Now turning his sternly cold gaze towards her. "However, even she can attest to its effectiveness am I correct Nimitz?" He asked already knowing the answer. Giving a sigh and rolling her eyes.

Begrudgingly Nimitz confirmed her Captains statement saying. "I suppose I can agree that black book training has proven to be Effective in everyone's development And productiveness in the field."

Giving another disapproving sigh before both Nimitz and Beta we're abruptly shooed aside by Doc pushing past them.

"Those things aside I need to run a diagnostic on Mr. Green here and we all know I take priority in this." He said, ushering Timmy to a nearby chair as he knelt beside him.

"Understood Doc." The others said giving him space as they returned to the observation room.

"Hmm fancy that... just as the previous rounds you show remarkable resilience." Doc said astounded by Timmy's cognitive attributes as he tested his eyes and reaction time. "At this rate you're becoming a bit immune to the distortion berries." Doc continued.

Taking a look at a chart he then began to question Timmy, saying. "But just to be safe what is today's date?" Timmy took a second to think before giving an unconfident reply.

"Um May 27th, 2057?" Timmy said. Smiling Doc nodded his head.

"Good, you still kept track that it has been only twelve hours and not the year distortion due to the berries." He said before being interrupted by Rook. Who was in far worse shape due to the distortion berries.

"Uh yeah about that. Can I get some Eugeroics, cause I feel like I've been sitting in this chair for five hours." Rook sheepishly asked.

Shaking his head Doc waved his hand looking about for Kilo.

"Kilo would you please?" He said focusing more on Timmy.

"Already on it." She grumbled neither of the men realizing that she was already administering the Eugeroics. Rook being far too disoriented to realize.

"Whoa shit longest year of my life! And here I thought black book training with Carolina was bad!" Rook exclaimed rubbing his sore jaw line while also giving a thumbs up to Kilo.

"You weren't an easy target to take on yourself Rook." Timmy replied with a smile.

Quietly Doc interrupted the too whispering to Timmy that he was clear before making his leave. Both Rook and Timmy waving off Doc and Kilo. Returning to their conversation Rook waved for Timmy to follow. "Where was I? ... oh yeah, If I hadn't moved quick enough or didn't think fast enough you would have got me for sure." Timmy said conceding to how close the match truly was.

"Hmm says the one who isn't even out of breath." Rooks scoffed. Causing Timmy to briefly pause realizing he indeed hadn't even broken into a sweat.

"Ha-ha thanks." Timmy shyly smirked Remembering Betas words of accepting criticism but also embracing praise.

Rook nudged at Timmy shoulder

"Just don't hold that distraction to close to home." He said with a smirk. "That may have worked this time, but I doubt it'd work so easily again."

He laughed with Timmy smiling already eager for another go at black book training. "Unrelated to the training though have you given any thoughts on Biscuit." Rook hopefully asked a tone of pleading excitement carrying his voice.

"Oh ... well... I don't know." Timmy hesitantly shivered remembering the creature's cold black eyes and its completely alien appearance despite its supposedly earthly heritage.

Conceding only slightly, Rook held up his hands.

"I completely understand it's a lot to take in... how about you at least touch her this time?" He said apprehensively giving a hopeful smile. Hesitantly empathetic Timmy wavered to the minor peer pressure.

"Well... I guess that wouldn't hurt... she doesn't bite, does she?" He asked nervously.

“No, no of course not!” Rook smiled, happy with the new compromise. “She doesn’t even have teeth, instead she has a sucker that normally holds on to ship halls.” He described.

Still, it itched Timmy’s nerves.

“Hmm okay...” Timmy replied as he began to pay more attention to his surroundings. Realizing Rook had taken them down a different path. Cutting through a middle section between them and the lab with Biscuit was a type of botanical garden. “Wow... what is this room?” Timmy said amazed by all the alien and colorful plant species that surrounded the room. Entering Rook waved his hand about the room.

“Ah yes our Preservation food supply we use this green house to grow different foods and medicinal herbs.” Rook said proudly showing off the room.

Multiple large beds lined the middle and walls of the room filled with plant life. Each plant, luminescent with varying colors of red and purple. Aromatic in fresh scents that enriched Timmy with rejuvenation in each breath he took. “Most are from the Insectoid home world of Apiary 1, as their planet has the richest environment for plant life.” Rook said pointing out a few of the specific plants. “But a few like Spore-stim or the distortion berries are from some of the other species’ planets them being the Goliathan home world of Gathabyss and the Astrocynos home world of The Den respectively.” Rook said.

Tilting his head Timmy recoiled in hearing the ladder mentioned name of The Den.

“Kind of a weird name for that last one... seems kinda bland?” Timmy said jokingly.

"Home world name aside, Astrocynos are actually some of the most renowned in the Alliance second only to the Goliathans." Rook replied before adding. "In fact, they're very presence alone can intimidate even some of the Mudlurks." Timmy took a step back, a look of shock quickly striking his face as he reactively looked over to Rook.

"I never heard of anything that could scare a Mudlurk." Timmy exclaimed.

He wondered to himself. If there were things that could scare Mudlurks, perhaps he could be enough to at least defeat them. To not only take on the Final Crusade but help in the Galactic war itself. Timmy smiled at the prospect as he looked around the room. Completely enthralled by the beauty of the vividly vibrant life before him. Wondering if the other species in the Alliance had such captivating plant life. How beautiful were their planets themselves. Could he ever see them?

"Oh whoa! Sorry ... still having the berries wear off I feel like I spaced out for a while." Rook said shaking his face a bit as he slapped his cheek trying to reorient his mind. The sudden reaction snapping Timmy from his own trance. The two of them leaving the Garden Room and reentering the lab.

"Anyways Go ahead get comfortable I'll bring her to you." Rook said stepping over to the holding unit. Still nervous even being in the same room as the alien creature. Timmy refused to sit instead his body tensed. all the while Rook unlocked the unit and slowly pulled out Biscuit. Again, her blank drifting beady black eyes looked on expressionless, seemingly thoughtless as Rook turned to fully face Timmy.

"Ta-da!" Rook exclaimed. Almost exactly as last time Biscuit perked up tilting its body curiously before wiggling excitedly as it tried to shimmy closer to Timmy. Reluctantly Timmy fought back his urge to push back as Rook stepped forward. Jerking only slightly in his timid approach at opening up to the creature. "Go on Timmy touch her!" Looking up Rook reassuringly nodded with his own bit of excitement nearly matching the creatures.

And so, with a big sigh Timmy closed his eyes and patted his hand gently on the creatures head. Holding his hand for a moment in place Timmy opened his eyes noting the creature had stopped moving and instead began to peacefully hum and click as it closed its eyes blissfully.

"Y-you know what... I I guess she isn't so bad. she is kinda cute...good girl Biscuit." Timmy said softly as his nerves finally relaxed with him becoming more accustomed to the creature.

"She really is." Rook smiled proudly. "Honestly I've never seen her so happy and energetic." He said as he held Biscuit higher "Feeling a bit braver for a test?" Rook asked once again giving a hopeful smile. Giving us slow nod Timmy relented now seeing Biscuit in a gentler light.

"Um s-sure..." Timmy replied. Excited with his response Rook rushed behind Timmy.

"Okay I'll be putting her on your back." Rook said excitedly.

"On me?" Timmy exclaimed. Reactively slouching his posture. fighting to be a bit braver and more open towards Biscuit.

"Yes, she'll suction on to your back and the thought is she will tap a bit more into your energy." Rook said reassuringly.

Putting on a brave face to me straightened his back as he very slightly turned his head to Rook.

"I ... will she let go? Will it hurt?" Timmy asked.

"No, no... she shouldn't..." Rook replied to the bit of hesitance in his voice not helping Timmy's wavering feelings. "I wonder if her suction can hold through ... it does! It holds through clothes!" Rook exclaimed firmly placing Biscuit on to Timmy's back.

"Eh and I can feel it, it's kinda slimy but... wait! I feel weird all of a sudden." Timmy said squirming slightly before beginning to feel a weight lifted from his shoulders.

Rook snapped his fingers and bolted from behind Timmy as he ran to grab pencil and paper.

"Hold on let me write this down. What kinda weird." Rook asked as he intently watched the new pairing.

"Well, when I use my abilities, I start to feel a pressure in my legs, eyes, and lower back but once you put Biscuit on me ... it's...it's all gone !?" Timmy exclaimed expressively moving himself in a freer manner.

"Really that's wild! Wait so then the theory might be true she feeds of residual waste from the cosmic blood cells in your system." Rook shouted pacing back and forth as they began to ponder the possibilities.

Wide eyed Rook snap back to Timmy excitedly proclaiming. "And now she's freeing things up for you." Timmy took a step back stunned at the new revelation. Twisting back Timmy turned his head to face Biscuit.

"Is that true little one?" Timmy timidly asked before giving the simple-minded creature a smile. "If so, I don't mind you sticking on me just don't get hurt... or damage my brothers hoodie please." Timmy said as he reached back patting Biscuit on the head.

"Oh, na you don't gotta worry about Biscuit." Rook smiled As he shook his head. "Hell, when they latch onto the sides of starships, they're more liable to survive a star-fight than the ship itself." Rook said.

Timmy stared at Rook in disbelief, 'What a powerful creature even despite its size', Timmy thought.

"Really so she kinda doubles as a shield on my back?" Timmy said excitedly is he once again turned himself to look back at Biscuit.

"Yeah, yeah you could say that." Rook said. Surprising himself that he had never thought of the comparison. "Truly symbiotic, she feeds off your abilities waste, and you get a tension release and a sick little shield buddy." Rook laughed.

Smiling in response Timmy wondered how he looked with his new friendly addition.

"Nice, so what now?" He asked looking back over to Rook.

Taking a second Rook pointed at the pair saying. "Well now you hold onto her...or she holds onto you ... and you update me regularly about any effects she has on you."

Timmy laughed saying. "Gotcha." As he patted Biscuit her giving a joyful hum in response.

"For now, treat her like an empty backpack even though she's on their pretty snug. Which reminds me." Rook said spinning around and grabbing something from inside Biscuits holding unit. "This is a smaller fuel canister for carrying starship fuel. If you ever want her off or if she starts latching on to tight." Rook said making his way back to the pair.

Timmy looked at it curiously before allowing Rook to demonstrate. "She should be drawn to the higher food source for..." He said before pausing for a moment as he tried to pull Biscuit from Timmy's back. "Hmm that's odd normally she's... oh there we go." He said as Biscuit released her suction from Timmy's back. Grabbing hold of her she again seemed to be indecisive, unsure of whether or not Timmy or the canister was exuding more power. Leaving Rook lost for words before an abrupt knock at the lab door drew both Rook and Timmy's attention.

Standing in the doorway Beta waved At the two with Rook scrambling in attempt to salute his Captain. Struggling to lift the heavy fuel canister along with holding Biscuits squirming body.

"At ease John, are you done with Timmy? I would like to show him something." Beta said as he made his way into the lab.

"Yes Sir, just wrapping up here." Rook said as he placed Biscuit on Timmy's back again.

"What's the report?" Beta asked, giving a curious look to the creature latched to Timmy's back.

"I'll have to give you a more thorough e-mail later, but it seems my theory is correct." Rook replied excitedly.

"Is that right?" Beta asked, looking over to Timmy for confirmation.

"Yeah, the pressure I was feeling on my back, and in other areas it's gone now. I don't even feel it anymore." Timmy replied with a smile before adding in. "Actually, I feel better than ever! A bit more hyper even!" Rook's eyes widened as he grabbed his papers and rushed to the lab door.

"That that right there I need to go talk to doc excuse me Sir I need to tell him these developments!" Rook exclaimed rushing down the hall.

Beta gave a deep slightly annoyed sigh as he refocused on Timmy. "I suppose this means you are free now. Come with me I would like to show you something." Following Beta they left the lab, making their way to a vault like door. "While I cannot personally cooperate in your ideology, I still can give you the means to successfully defend yourself and others." Beta said. His red eyes appearing once again with them flickering. And then a reminiscent sound to Timmy's family Starship the vault door began to whistle. It's hydraulic mechanisms unveiling a tightly sealed room. An Armory of insurmountable proportions with various weaponry and equipment never seen before by Timmy's eyes.

"Holy cow!" Timmy yelled out. They had enough firepower to be the equivalent of a small army, Timmy thought to himself.

"This is the totality of Nomadic 5s Armory and equipment." Beta said as he made his way to the end of the Armory. "From here on with express supervision you have a limited access to anything within here." Timmy jumped at the thought. His eyes intensely staring at the litany of guns and explosives and shuttered. As if on cue Beta added. "Not that you would be too interested in using any of this equipment anyways that is a sign from one piece." Beta said softly.

Reaching above a glass cabinet. he grasped onto a specially handcrafted glass container filled to the brim in the special liquid that held and uniquely shaped tool in suspension. "In this case here is a gift given to me for saving the life of a fellow comrade, a Goliathan." Beta said as he returned to Timmy side placing the case before him. "He was a very good comrade, loyal to his end. like a force of nature when he fought." Beta said sadly. The first time Timmy had noticed a tone of depression coming from the stone hearted and robotic Captain. "This weapon in a Goliathan's hands what only amplifying such capabilities. This tool is known as a Kusari-Huitl." Every word Beta spoke attached the air with a resounding sound of pride and respect.

The tool itself undoubtedly deserving of being used by a Goliathan. It most closely resembled either a hammer or a Mace with a long slab of metal as Its main body. Three extended pillars protruding from either side with one pillar erected from the top of the slab. On each of the side pillars was a uniquely carved wooden amulet that hung from each perspective pillar from that of a chain. the hilt was made seemingly of a type of Hickory style wood and was curved. coming from the pommel of the handle was what looked to be a type of chain but in a uniquely alien pattern unlike the chains crafted on earth instead having a more vine like appearance.

Timmy stared wide eyed taken by its design. Such a remarkable piece of craftsmanship with hardly a single flaw seen on either the metal working or the woodworking. "Pick it up." Beta said undoing the cases lid. Hesitantly Timmy looked to Beta, receiving a reassuring nod before finally reaching into the liquid and taking hold of the tool.

"It's surprisingly lightweight." Timmy whispered, feeling an almost instant electric-like connection to the tool.

"Versatile, that is how most handmade Goliathan weaponry is aside from their firearms." Beta replied.

Timmy smiled, as all the talk of the Goliathan's reminded him I've earlier times with his father.

"I believe it, before my father passed, he actually had a few discussions with several alien species engineers including Goliathan." He said with a sparkle in his eye like how he looked at his father's Starship. "From what little I did here they were I'm very strong very family oriented very in tuned with nature species." Timmy said, feeling over the coarseness of the metal and the soft texture of the handle. "My father always said that we could learn more than just a thing or two from them." In his mind and in his heart, he would hold all that his father did and said as closely as he could Timmy thought to himself.

Again, Beta smiled and as he reached over to the case, he closed the lid looking over to the tool in Timmy's hand before speaking.

"I am glad you think So highly of them, as I intend to bestow this gift given to me, on to you." Timmy gasped in shock, taking an instinctive step back as he attempted to hand back the tool.

"What!? B-but it was a gift for you! it's yours!" Timmy stutteringly exclaimed.

"In Goliathan culture it is commonplace to give new members of a tribe or of their family a tool or weapon to symbolize a merging and a trust between the new members." Beta began to say as he pushed the tool closer to Timmy.

Betas eyes flashed red although his face showed no sign of anger instead of soft reminiscence. "It was not a lightly thought of thing giving me this weapon. It was given to me as a symbolization of my bravery and empathy toward one not even of my own kind." Beta said as a smile crept from his lips. "With it in my possession I regretfully admit it has had very little use." He frowned, pausing for a moment before continuing. "This is where your training comes in, however. From what I have seen you are learning to take the necessary steps to ensure your survival." His red eyes faded, and so too did his reminiscence is he more sternly coldly stared down Timmy.

"That is not enough. In my group I will have nothing less than perfection. You are not there yet." The words hurt and yet Timmy knew it to be true he frowned looking down at the tool. But before he could say another word Beta continued. "I will make you get to that level. This tool will help you accomplish this." Beta said is Timmy looked up to him with hope in his eyes. "It seems fitting... out of all their arsenal this one is mostly used as a means of defense. Used more like a guard protecting their post." Beta said, trying to touch more into Timmy's passive nature.

Timmy looked curiously at the tool contemplating how he would use it. Struggling to not think of the man he killed when looking at it. "How does it feel for you?" Beta asked.

"It's odd and I'd have to get used to it." Timmy admitted.

"That is fair." Beta said in a near whisper. Thinking for a moment, Beta recalled a way that might help Timmy act collaborative with the tool. "Another way of getting more comfortable with their weapon is the act of naming it. Giving it a type of meaningful attachment." Beta said ushering for Timmy to try and name the tool.

"Hmm I guess I could try...calling it something other than K-Kusari-Huitl would be a bit easier..." Timmy laughed holding the tool closely. Him and his father were never the best with names. Rather his mother and brother were more creative. Timmy focused intensely. Wondering what his mother use to call him. What his mother would name this tool, and then it struck him. "How about ... Astrapí?" Timmy cheerfully cooed as he held his new tool to his heart.

"Greek?" Beta asked, cocking an eyebrow.

"Yes, more so on my mother's side." Timmy nodded.

"She always used to call me that. 'Mikrí mou astrapí' or my little lightning, said I always ran circles around her." Timmy said with a warmth in his heart. "My dad wasn't sure how they ever kept up." Timmy laughed wondering what they would think now of his newfound abilities.

"Sounds good... I am sure the name is suitable." Beta said patting Timmy on the back. "Let's go, bring it with you, we are making a final discussion on the whereabouts of Escalero and the units of Project David." Beta said.

Making their way back to the War-room with the holographic table, Timmy and Beta Entering silently. A few members saluting Beta as he walked in. The newer faces being members of Jason's Omega 1 squad. Their leader being on the opposite end of the holographic table.

"Showing up a little late I see, don't say it was the boy. I've seen how fast he moves." Jason snidely snapped at Beta.

"Irrelevant." Beta said ignoring his comment. "Let's get started with this meeting." Beta aggressively asserted.

"Very well." Jason said waving his hands defensively as he stepped forward putting in a memory card into the table. Doing so displayed red dotted lines that trailed along the city outskirts. As well as a few diversions through the city center.

Turning to face the room Jason cleared his throat as he began the debrief. "These here are the routes taken by both suppliers and recipients within Escalero's regiment." Jason said as he waved his hand to the lines. "Things have been going pretty standard... that is until events at a certain plant caused things to spiral outward a bit." He said looking over to Timmy. Whose face quickly flashed red as he shyly ducked his eye level. "Luckily for us at that same given time possibly due to Escalero's abrupt appearance things mellowed back out." Jason said as he continued, refusing to hide his tone of annoyance.

"Or due to the informant." Shining said coyly, leaning back in his chair as he playfully kicked his feet.

"Doubtful." Snapped Jason, who growled at Shining. "We've had no leaks of either my squad or Nomadic 5 having even departed from the rest of Division 180." He said assertively Jabbing his finger down on the war table. "Our presence here is completely covert, or at least it was until the hit on Escalero himself." Jason hissed before angrily glaring at Beta.

The tense interaction surprising Timmy, Sapphire, and BG. Each of which looked to Beta, anticipating his response. Calm minded as ever he hardly blinked in response to Jason's harshness. Causing the other Captain to forfeit their staring match as he continued the debriefing. "Since then, things spiraled again into a panic." Pressing a button on his gauntlet device a new routing pattern showed itself. "This one indeed being much more sporadic and incoherent." Jason said.

And indeed, unlike the previous map This one presented much shorter routes. With quick turns unvarying tunnel systems throughout the city. "Thus lies our current predicament. As the final route traced led through this highway tunnel to which then vanished off our traces." Jason said as he pointed out the tunnel system Timmy had just eyed.

"Vanished?" Nimitz asked. The rest of the room equally carrying puzzled faces.

"Possibly a signal jammer used because they were on to us." Jason replied.

"Did they ditch the vehicle? Swap out for a new one?" Wonderland asked leaning over the map as she attempted to find a possible location where they would enact a transfer.

"With their cargo? It'd be Impossible to smuggle it out that fast." Jason countered. With one of Jason's men adding in. "The second half of Omega 1 lost them in a highway tunnel, with no similar vehicle leaving the tunnel system." Making Nimitz scoff.

"They slipped you up while driving in a semi?" She scowled.

"Perhaps if I had had more resources in covering the entire city like I asked! Then we wouldn't have lost their whereabouts!" Jason defensively shouted. With Omega 1 apprehensively sitting on edge as they watched both Captains body language. While Nomadic 5s group mostly watched Nimitz. Who angrily balled her fists, taking a step to the Captain.

"Enough!" Beta barked, His eyes flashing red as the lights in the room and the war table glitched and flickered. Turning fully dark before coming back on. Everyone in the room now solely looking at Beta.

The room was tormenting in its silence. Everyone incredibly unnerved By both the Captains appearance and abilities everyone that is save the other Captain who disgustedly stared down his fellow compatriot. The factor at which only Timmy had noticed as it had happened within the blink of an eye as the lights came back on. The notion of which was far more unnerving than what Beta had done.

Giving a sigh of distaste Jason cleared his throat as he ushered everyone back to the war table.

"Regardless of why we came to our outcome we need to move past it. I didn't ask for this meeting so that we could bicker on why the search has gone cold." He said looking over to Beta with expectation of a possible plan.

"Was that all Jason?" Beta asked coldly.

"You have the floor now Captain." Jason replied equally frigid, sitting back in his chair.

Having a seat of his own Beta gestured for both his Master Sargent and Sargent First Class as he spoke.

"Shining...Reaper, go ahead and display your information." The two of them sitting up with Reaper stepping over to the war table. Placing a memory card of their own into the table. Shining, with gusto, waved off Reaper saying.

"Don't worry I got this!" with a smiled that grinned through his skull patterned mask. "So, my time to speak now fabulous!" He exclaimed, clapping his hands together. His expressiveness alone was enough to change the entire room.

Shining could even give an Angelon a run for its money on how well he affects others. Timmy thought. "From what I've seen along with Reaper here is that throughout the city this particular symbol is pretty darn abundant." He said. Tapping the table with the symbol of a set of wings, attached to a diamond, with a red sword in the middle. Appearing in the middle of the war table. "Now, for any of us here, we should easily spot, and understand the meaning of the symbol." Shining said as he looked to everyone else in the room.

"Anytime we saw this out in the field, we came across different insurgents, various supplies, and heavy Final Crusade presence." Shining said, tapping the table allowing images of each thing said to appear next to the symbol on the war table. "Which brings us to the concerning detail. This symbol is damn near on every square foot of this city." This wasn't surprising in the slightest to Timmy. who saw plenty of evidence in regard to how intricately intertwined the Final Crusade truly was at both the plant and the church.

What Timmy could not understand was why the symbol itself was unnerving. true he had seen it before but now it was lost to thought where he had noticed a symbol such as this. "From me and Reaper alone we've spotted them at least several dozen times on small businesses commercial businesses residential buildings and even on some vehicles." Shining said tapping at the table again which appeared exactly what he said. and it was indeed everywhere. 'Perhaps this is why he could not pinpoint exactly where he noticed it because he noticed it in so many locations?' Timmy thought to himself.

"Now when putting this into a search engine, it appears that they've been able to rewrite it to accompanying the symbol with a peaceful organization that does humanitarian benefits." Shining said practically scoffing at the idea of the Final Crusade hiding under such a banner. "Reaper and I have investigated nearly all of the residential and small business locations that carried this symbol and so far, we've come up with next to nothing." Shining said dejectedly as he scratched the back of his head.

Taking a deep breath Shining sighed, before adding is plan going forward. "I understand that going through with what I'm about to say is gonna be pressed for time, but it's our best possible route given we have no idea where they went." Shining said tapping the table again I'm allowing for multiple high-end businesses to appear on the war table. "Now as for the commercial buildings it's a bit harder for us to get in there." His voice was hesitant and far less confident than when he began.

Timmy could tell enough that the plan was going to be a stretch before Shining even had a chance to describe it. He balled his fist in anger wishing he had been enough to catch Escalero that night at the bar. Wishing he had something to give and that's when he noticed throughout the column of buildings. Throughout all the enterprises within the city that carried that symbol. The one that made him recall the symbol the most. "neither do I believe we have the time or the resources to covertly infiltrate these buildings and facilities-" Shining began to say before he was abruptly interrupted by Timmy screaming across the room.

"Wait I recognize the symbol now!" Timmy blurted out a cold sweated shock derailing his mind. Jason harshly eyed Timmy From across the room.

"I'm sure you do kid." He retorted in an irritated tone.

"Hold on for a moment Jason." Beta called out, diffusing the other Captain. "Go on where do you recall them?" He said waving for Timmy to continue.

"Well... there was the plant, but also the church where I found out more about Escalero and that he was going to show up in town." Timmy shakenly answered as he tried to avoid eye contact with Jason.

His heart racing, he pointed to one of the several buildings that line the war table before saying. "The place that I'm a bit more worried about is my family's business." The room shifted with even Shining snapping to Reaper his abilities taking in her equal shock to the matter.

"Your family's business?" Rook asked with a stun expression on his face.

"Wait Nie Fallen Corporation?" His uncle BG questioned, leaning over Sapphire. Timmy nodded his head to the questions

Of all people, the head scientists in charge of his family's research was the one he could recall the most. Who plain as day carried the double meaning symbol on his lab coat.

"Yeah... that humanitarian stuff, the business with this symbol, that's the company that bought a part of my parent's company from the shareholders." Timmy said as he pointed to the symbol on the war table.

"Can you gain access to anything within your family's company." Shining asked.

"Not immediately but I might have a way of freezing things. My company is big in trading so they must be using our channels to help them" Timmy replied.

Giving a moment of thought, Timmy recalled his father's laptop still at his home. "I still have my father's computer, and they never booted him out of the system Because they were just going to give me access once I turned 18." He mentioned. "But they don't know I kind of always had access. my father shared the password with me years before he passed." Timmy said excitedly as he leaped up from his seat.

"Where would this laptop be?" One of Jason's men questioned.

"Back at my house." Timmy stated his nerves slightly fading. he was being trusted not just by Nomadic 5 but now Omega 1 was looking to him for a possible new route in their dead ends.

"When was the last time you were there?" The same member asked.

"Four or five days... I've been on the move ever since I snuck into the plant." Timmy admitted with Sapphire shyly adding in.

"That's right and when he wasn't on the move he was staying at my place." The eyes in the room shifting to her as she quietly and nervously shifted her seat closer to Timmy.

"That's probably a good thing since you're back on Escalero's sights." Beta said as he folded his arms. "I wouldn't doubt that he may have a trap waiting for you either in or around you home." He added in.

"With my Captains green light, Omega 1 could search the building, recover the laptop, and possibly detour any Final Crusader involvement with your residence." Jason's team member stated.

Jason looked over to him briefly before giving a sigh.

"I suppose that collecting another means of halting their more of their Trades-Hand would be at our best interest." He said giving a long stretch and cracking his neck loudly. "That leaves however many units of Project David still in circulation without the knowledge of their whereabouts." Jason said, reminding everyone in the room. Suddenly jolting from behind Timmy. Sapphire sprung from her chair.

"I...um might have an idea?" She said, her excited demeanor quickly fading as she remembered all the imposing figures that surrounded the war table.

Sure, enough Jason scolding stared her down before speaking.

"Get on with it." He growled

"There is an area where I too noticed this symbol but..." She said, as Timmy could tell there was a clear hesitance and trembling in her voice. And yet it didn't seem to stem from Jason. in fact, she didn't seem afraid outside of being only the slightest bit intimidated. instead, her voice sounded more protective.

"If you're going to say something, say it." Jason barked raising his voice.

"Jason... Go on Sapphire." Beta said raising his own voice before calmly turning to sapphire and pleading for her to continue.

She eyed them both but giving Beta a reassuring nod and receiving a hopeful smile from Timmy she spoke up.

"It... its where an old refugee city is located. A type of retrofitted bunker like this one but larger and more for families." She said softly as she scooted closer to the war table. "It's called Sanctuary...but before I say where. You have to understand, the people who live there have lived there since the Invasion." She began to say speaking more erratically and desperate.

Her eyes became painfully sympathetic as she looked to everyone in the room. "There are families down there. Women and children...and if I helped some kinda crazy shoot out down there and some kid got..." Her lip quivered and her hands begin to shake as she lowered her head. Timmy's heart ached he was stunned to think that Sanctuary. a place of such familial and communal peace would be the epicenter of such a diabolical organization.

Slowly Beta took a step closer to her.

"Sapphire, we do not intend to put anyone in harm's way." He said softly his rustic soothing voice again peeling away at his robotically stiff personality. "If the Final Crusade is there however, we must act trillions of lives could be at stake. Not just this city or even the earth but the wide array of countless Alliance home worlds." Beta stated resting a hand on her shoulder.

"I just find it hard to believe that all this rests in sanctuary! There are good people there!" Sapphire yelled in frustration. An aching resentment hugging her tightly.

Timmy could see that she had already resigned herself to believing Sanctuary as the place that Nomadic and Omega one needed. But could equally tell of how deeply she cared for Sanctuary and its people. stepping forward Shining called out to Sapphire.

"Mrs. Price, the car ride, you remember what I said huh? The Final Crusade abuses that good nature. Twists it to gain power to misguide the faithful." Shining said, him clearly empathizing and understanding her compassion for the good people trapped between this growing conflict. Even behind the mask his sincerity uplifting Sapphire.

"I believe you and your concern for the people at this Sanctuary place. But we can't let these people smuggle these weapons all that's gonna come from that is a lot of death." Shining insisted. Cautious still, Sapphire gave another second before finally giving a plan for Nomadic.

"There's a couple of places to have entrance into Sanctuary...A few of those routes have been blocked off for some time now... God I think that makes sense." She said her eyes widening as the words left her breathless lips. "You mentioned something about those trucks disappearing in tunnels?" She asked looking over to Jason.

He cocked an eyebrow as himself and a few of his members confirmed. "Well, a few years ago the city requested that Sanctuary make itself a bit more open to the public." She said pointing to the map on the war table. Specifically, that of the tunnel entrances before she continued. "That wasn't an issue, and a lot of people agreed with it, but suddenly the main influencers in Sanctuary just gave up on it out of nowhere and the city never asked again and no one understood why!" She exclaimed, stunned to discover the possibility herself.

"So, what you're saying is that the Final Crusade might have stopped the city?" X-ray asked from the back of the room. The squads whispering amongst themselves before another question was asked

"Were they bribed perhaps? To not opening passageways to keep their organization a little more discreet?" Asked Wonderland, both squads looking to Sapphire.

"I'm not going to jump to conclusions, but we never found out why the city stopped caring." Sapphire whispered folding her arms as she began to bite her nail anxiously.

Beta stepped away from Sapphire, now looking over to Jason the two immediately making eye contact. and with a single nod between Captains Omega 1 left the war room.

"I would say that is reason enough for Nomadic to investigate." Beta said before turning back to Sapphire. "If you can draw us up a quick survey of the area. Do you have any pictures anything that might give away some information?" He asked. Snapping her fingers sapphire took out her phone.

"I took pictures one time when I was coming down it shows a picture of the entire city." She said leaning over as she revealed the layout of Sanctuary.

Briefly Betas eyes flashed red as he scanned the photo.

"That will do." He said to Sapphire with a nod returning his attention to the rest of Nomadic. "Kilo get the Scorpion-Wasp up and ready. Everyone else get geared up." Beta clearly asserted. A new layout of Sanctuary appearing over the war table. And with gravitating declaration, he spoke both to Timmy and Nomadic 5. "We will be sieging on Sanctuary at 0400."

Chapter 9: Overwhelmed

Soaring from the desert, the relatively quiet Scorpion-Wasp whispered across torn through air as it entered the city limits. "Kilo what's our ETA?" Beta asked over the radio.

"10 minutes out...we're a little bit away Still this parking lot Sapphire told us about is in the city center." Kilo responded.

"Everybody remember the layout of Sanctuary, correct?" Beta said addressing everyone in the loading bay.

"Yes, Sir!" The whole of Nomadic squad replied.

"This underground city looks like it goes on for about a hundred miles!" Maci exclaimed.

The others joining him in looking at the photos given by Sapphire on their forearm monitors.

"This entrance is towards the beginning of Sanctuary; the other parameters are somewhere towards the outskirts of the city." Beta said. His eyes flashing as he sent out a 3D scan of Sanctuary to everyone.

"You said hostile presence is unknown? we're going in blind?" Wonderland asked.

"Essentially, Sapphire has reported that she had never seen a single Crusade militant." Nimitz Replied.

"Meaning they could be hiding in plain sight?" Wonderland reiterated cringing at the thought.

"As civilians yes so that means treat everyone as a possible hostile checking corners and being aware of red zones." Nimitz affirmed, as she glanced to all her subordinates. "These people have been down here for years...who knows the amount of planning they went on reinforcing and trapping the location." She said worriedly. With Shining shaking his head

"Great so we're going into a burning rat hole just fuckin fabulous!" He shouted, checking over his gun.

"That is why we are going in the morning. Hope will be that 90% of the population is still asleep." Beta said before adding in. "We will do this covertly, quickly, and efficiently. We will arouse little to no suspicion when ascertaining the high value targets." Apollo who sat across from Timmy watched him. A blank and quiet expression on his face since Timmy had left sapphire and his uncle behind.

"Kill order on Escalero?" Apollo hesitantly asked.

As easy as the snapping twig. Timmy's trance was shattered crumbling beneath the weight of Apollos question. Lifting his head Timmy met with Apollo's sympathetic eyes who gave him a reassuring smile and a pat on the knee.

"Dead or alive Either would work perfectly." Nimitz declared, the entire loading Bay giving the slightest sideways glance to Timmy. With a heavy heart he knew what he would need to do if Escalero gave him no other choice.

Looking to the side of his hip Timmy quietly reached to his side taking hold of Astrapí.

"Splitting into the normal teams of two?" X-ray asked.

"Yes, we will have Timmy apart of team one, supplementing Kilo returning to base." Beta confirmed, as Reaper gave Timmy a playful punch to the shoulder. Making him shift to a lighter expression as he gave her a smile.

"And As for Omega 1? shouldn't take them this whole time just recovering a laptop." Shining mocked. With Beta shooting an irritated look to the Master Sargent.

"That is if they come across little to no resistance at Mr. greens residence." Beta retorted.

Giving a sigh before leaning back in his chair. "The plan is that they will regroup with us and help containing any fleeting Final Crusade members." Beta announced. Looking not just to Shining but the whole of Nomadic.

"One minute till landing." Kilo called out over everyone's radio. The loading bay echoing with the sound of checking rifle chambers and sightlines. Timmy's heart leapt as he gripped Astrapí tighter. A flash of the previous confrontation with Escalero striking at his mind.

The only anchor for him being Beta, who loudly addressed his squad.

"Nomadic 5 we know the parameters. Let's get this mission done!" Violent propulsions of wind gusts emanated on either side of the scorpions heavily fitted propeller. As the beast of the machine descended. All of Nomadic, along with Timmy, stood up in unison as a green light flashed in the loading Bay. "Move!" Beta ordered with the entire team filing out of the scorpion. Guns were drawn on different positions as they held their formation.

Timmy designated specifically by Beta, to strictly only stay behind him until given direct orders. The Bay door of the scorpion slowly lifted up behind Timmy. Sending a gust of wind up his back. Making him shiver as he turned reactively. Watching as the Scorpion lifted back up off the parking lot. Spinning out in a 180 degrees before disappearing quickly into the early morning night. Timmy 's body shivered as the cold air hugged him tightly.

And as he breathed, he could see his breath flowing over the view of a singular parking lot light. Looking around to the members of Nomadic beside him, he felt surprised in their differing appearance, correspondent to how they appeared within the confines of the M.O.B. Now outfitted with tactical blacked out gear, strapped head to toe with U.M.E weaponry, and equipment. And despite their varying personalities, They, at first glance, seemed more unified now out in the field, aside from their personal animal themed shoulder plates.

The differing appearance was not solely for the members of Nomadic however, As once Timmy glanced at himself in a nearby puddle, he was able to fully grasp how different he appeared to be as well. Looking through the reflective surface in the dimly lit parking lot he appeared to look tired. He hadn't eaten in days and had gone without sleep even longer. Over his brother's beloved hoodie was now a tightly fitted Bulletproof vest. Attached to his back was now an alien creature, To his hip a practical weapon of war. In retrofitted to his other side with mechanical brackets his father's X-board.

He felt out of place, as if he was a coating of paint that could be washed away just as easily as it could be applied. He did not feel like his younger self anymore but neither did he feel like one of the members of Nomadic. Instead, he felt like an unconfident, muted, misplaced fragment. Lacking a roll to fit into properly. He wondered, what would his parents think? How would they feel about the situation he's put himself in. Could he justify it? The life he took. The lives he's willing to take.

Anchoring once more Timmy snapped his attention to Beta. "Move up." The Captain whispered, as Timmy and Nomadic formed up, converging on the parking lots elevator. Stepping inside both teams huddled firmly in place. Betas eyes glowed as he searched for the panel that Sapphire and Timmy had mentioned. The circuitry catching his eye, prompting him to smack at it with the butt of his gun. The false panel sliding from its secretive placement.

Pressing the downward button the elevator came to life as it slowly descended into Sanctuary. A darkness filled the elevator almost as abruptly as the silence. Not even breathing could be heard from a single soldier. Startled, Timmy perked his ears, shocked at the indifference towards the silence by any of his companions. Unease finally reached Nomadic with light creeping at their feet, inciting some of the soldiers to raised their weapons.

"It must be the simulated sun or the moon." Timmy said softly, gesturing with his hands for everyone to lower their weapons.

Not a second later the shine from Sanctuary's procedurally generated moon, cast over the group through the glass elevator.

"No shit... I thought the picture looked pretty bright for an underground city." X-ray muttered.

"Sapphire had mentioned that. If some of you paid a bit more attention you wouldn't have been as startled." Nimitz hissed, snapping at the others.

"Holding the elevator." Beta said, bending down and pressing a lever on the control panel causing the elevator to stop in its descent.

"Shining, wanna give me a hand?" Apollo said. The two of them maneuvering to the front, using a tool to pull open the elevator doors before stepping back.

"Team two. This is our stop." Nimitz said, pulling out a grapple and harnessing herself to one end. Aiming the grappling device, she launched it onto some scaffolding on the ceiling of the underground city. Giving a quick test pull, she nodded to both Apollo and Beta before swinging out hanging slightly from the scaffolding. Sequentially the rest of team two consisting of Apollo, Messi, Wonderland, X-ray, and Queenie all grappled across to their team lead. Taking differing approaches as they took off towards the city center. Seeing them off Beta closed off the elevator doors. Starting it up as Team one once again lowered to the floor level of Sanctuary.

Lowering to the foundation of Sanctuary Timmy looked on at the impactful glow of its artificial yet inviting moonlight. That hurdled delicately across the high-rise peaks of the cityscape. Transfixed he admired the city's beauty. Illuminated only by the soft bluish hue, and equally warm yellow dimly shining glow that dotted around the city bends, which came from handcrafted streetlights. In the beginning, Sanctuary was built together hastily. The only thought in mind being survival and fortification.

The community that now called this refuge home, lovingly rejuvenated the overall architecture and atmosphere. Perfecting it to the point of rivaling the city above. Timmy felt immensely disheartened, conflicted with the beautiful tranquility that rested with the people of Sanctuary. They did not ask for this conflict. They did not intend to harbor individuals of malice. No loving parent would ever call a place a home if they could help it. A small part of him had hoped they would not find Escalero. That they would not find the Final Crusade lying in wait. That they would not uncover various units of Project David.

His gut churned as it disapprovingly knew better. What made every hair on his body stand and caused his heart to sink however, was the sudden static of everyone's radio, as Nimitz came over declaring that team one had an unknown individual converging on their location.

"Are they armed." Beta radioed back. Looking at the streets of Sanctuary.

"They don't appear to be." Nimitz replied.

"Is your current location compromised." Betas gravelly voice asked. A moment of radio silence filled the elevator. With Timmy jerking as Nimitz came back over the radio stating.

"Negative, but yours is."

Beta's eyes went red as he tried to identify the person, but Timmy had noticed sooner. It was a rather familiar face, that of Raph the man who had first welcomed both himself and Sapphire into Sanctuary. Touching down to the streets of Sanctuary the glass elevator door slowly opened with Timmy squeezing through the narrow half open gap in order to confront Raph first.

Beta tried to reach for him but was to slow, as Timmy rushed to Raph.

"Uh do I know you bud?" He cautiously asked before looking over Timmy's shoulder at the others.

"Raph, its Timmy we met a few days ago. Sapphire brought me down here." Timmy hurriedly muttered.

"Oh, I think I remember...but uh your friends here." Raph began to say before stepping past Timmy to the others. "Hey you guys' cops? Nothing happened down here... been quiet for a while." Raph said eyeing each member of team one. Rook and Reaper moving to his sides as Beta and Shining inched closer to him. "I didn't even hear that any of you guys were coming down... what district are you guys from?" He asked, Timmy clearly able to see the hairs on the back of his neck standing up.

Team one, stayed quiet, instead only stepping closer, weapons held tightly. "Packing quite a bit of firepower..." Raph began to mutter before he leaned back to Timmy and whispered in his ear.

"Listen kid if you got into some shit this was not the place to bring it... but if you're in trouble say the word." Timmy's eyes widened as he took a step between Raph and Nomadic.

"What? No these aren't bad people. They're-" Timmy began to explain in a panic only to be cut off by Beta.

"He's with them Timmy."

A chill rushed up Timmy's back as his head twisted back to face Beta. Too stunned to even question his statement.

"With who?" Raph stammered shuffling back a step.

"Huh? How do you know?" Timmy asked defensively.

"The symbol on the side of his neck, a branding." Rook said in a more aggressive tone than Timmy had heard prior, which startled him. Before anything else could be said, Reaper and Shining both aimed their weapons at Raph.

"Hey whoa whoa whoa whoa whoa!" Timmy repeated in a quick panic holding his hands out between Raph in the rest of team one. Raph equal in Timmy's surprise raised his hands.

Clicking his holster open. Beta lowered his rifle to his side as he looked to Timmy.

"You've been here only once Timmy. You know only a fraction of the people and this location." Beta began to say, coldly staring past Timmy as he withdrew his sidearm. "We on the other hand know next to nothing. This is for our safety and protection do not get in the way." Beta said as Shining closed in quickly, stepping past Timmy and restraining Raph with a cable tie.

"Ouch! Shit, okay-okay. Just tell me what you guys want!" Raph yelled out, with Shining easily overpowering him. Reluctantly Timmy held his tongue as Raph was restrained. With a look of shame on his face towards both Beta and Raph. "What do you think I'm apart of?" Raph asked as he was raised to his feet.

"The symbol on your neck. It is for the Crusade is it not?" Beta asked as he holstered his weapon.

Raph winced as he attempted to move in his restraints.

"The what? Buddy this symbol it was a dare it's for the organization I work with you-you gotta know them Spoken Valor?" Raph said looking to each member of team one. "You know soup kitchens community funding restoration they're big in the city." Feeling the sincerity through his aura, Shining lowered his weapon.

"The alias for the Crusade?" Shining whispered to Beta.

"Listen we're here for a single individual by the name of Escalero Martí and a number of different semi-trucks carrying heavy cargo." Beta stated stepping closer to Raph.

Raph shot a frown as he questioned Beta. "Semis down here? Buddy, you came down next to the only entrance that we have." He replied dumbfounded. "We can't have vehicles down here! I mean... that's what we're trying to work on, making it more accessible to the city but." He continued to say before Shining interrupted.

"He doesn't seem to know anything." Shining said to Beta. Suddenly Reaper to lowered her weapon.

"Could be a cover." She signed, as she glared at Raph.

"I can read sign language! A cover? A cover for what?" Raph exclaimed, with most of Team One ignoring him, aside from Timmy.

Again, Shining inched over to Beta.

"It would make sense Captain. Think about it, back at White Rose asylum? Those scientists." Shining said, as a world of questions ran through Timmy's mind.

"They had nothing to do with the organization. They also talked about this Spoken Valor." Shining reiterated, with Betas eyes turning red startling Raph for a moment as he recalled said events.

"I guess that's the pseudonym for the cover up company." Beta muttered as he held his own chin in thought.

Still utterly lost, Raph shook his head.

"You guys aren't making any sense." He said looking the Timmy for explanation. Only to be met with an equally unsure expression.

"Let's take a new approach to this." Beta said standing but a foot away from Raph.

"Where are the leaders of this Spoken Valor organization." He said his red eyes fading. The uncanny nature clearly having a effect on Raph who nervously spoke.

"Leaders? Uhh ...The main people in charge should be on the other end of the city...By the bigger buildings." He muttered gesturing with his head to the other end of the city. Pushing aside a shiver Raph looked pleadingly to Timmy, speaking out right "I don't know who you think you guys are looking for, but this group is for refugees, fundraising, aid for the needy." He exclaimed gesturing to the homes on either side of Team One. "People that are down here just live down here man...families." He emphasized.

A rush of guilt hammering at Timmy, even some of Team One appearing more hesitant. "Kids in darn near every house. It's a safe place even if it is underground and tucked away!" Raph continued taking a step to Beta. The steely eyed Captain eyeing Raph. With Timmy unable to tell how Beta felt. Him now seeing the more robotically cold side of the Captain resurface.

"We have reason to suspect otherwise. Get him moving we will take him with." Beta demanded as Team One finally started their trek into the heart of Sanctuary.

Walking in towards the center of Sanctuary Timmy noticed something different as opposed to his first time visiting with Sapphire. Unlike the city above, that even in its nighttime carried noise from construction, loud vehicles, and insects. The city below held no noise. Echoing in the streets were only Team Ones subtle footsteps, and the air systems that circulated fresh air through the underground city. Adding to the dissimilarities to the city above which held a crisp, cold morning air. Sanctuary oppositely cooked Timmy in his brother's hoodie. Undoubtedly due to the warmth of the massive procedurally generated moons screen that now hung above them.

The whole of Sanctuary gave a much more suffocating atmosphere as opposed to his first visit. "You mentioned other entrances what do you know of them?" Beta asked Raph looking back at him as he still continued his way to the outskirts of Sanctuary.

"From what I know they've been under construction but that's been years since that started." Raph confirmed an apparent irritation in his voice. the possible incompetence of Sanctuaries higher ups affecting him and the other locals.

“The two that work are the elevator and the big tunnel that leads to Salvation plaza.” Raph nodding at the latter mentioned location. Indeed, as Timmy looked back the way they had come he could more clearly see a wide cavern like entrance just passed the residential district they left. “It’s kinda packed with random stuff right now though. Things for Sanctuary celebrations and the big parade.” Raph said

“One that we’re passing now had collapsed a few years after the invasion... that did a number on sanctuary from what I heard back in the day.” He said nodding to the right of everyone. This one also had an outline of a massive cavern. But was caved in by a mountain of dirt and the surrounding earth beside it. Timmy winced wondering if anybody had been in the tunnel entrance during the collapse. “And then the last two are at the end but like I said are being worked on.” Raph said motioning forward. The outskirts of Sanctuary still being too far away for any exit to be seen yet.

“One leads up to the main highway in the city, and the other is too I believe some construction yard.” Raph said sounding unsure of his own words. “I thought it was to make another highway, but I don’t know the city just gave up on it from what I heard.” He said disappointedly. The tone and statement similar to Sapphires when she discovered the Final Crusades possible involvement in Sanctuary.

“Nimitz, you copy this?” Beta said over his radio.

“Already relaying the information to Omega 1.” She quickly replied over everyone’s radio.

The chatter audible enough for Raph to hear Nimitz’s voice.

“How many of you are there?” He exclaimed looking to either Beta or Timmy.

“Hold!” Nimitz ordered, Team One immediately stopping in their tracks. The act of which sending Timmy’s adrenaline reeling as he grabbed hold of Astrapí.

"Keep him quiet." Beta preemptively ordered as he pointed to Raph.

"What wait-" being all that Raph could mutter before being bound by Shining.

"What's the situation Nimitz." Beta asked over the radio as Team One slipped to the corners of nearby buildings.

Timmy looked above trying to gauge Team Twos location, before looking back. As a creeping feeling of angst crawled up his spine and breathed down his neck.

"Spotting at least 10 plus mobiles armed closing in, straight ahead of your position." Nimitz declared. Timmy's eyes struck with fear as he looked forward yet seeing nothing. The only calming notion being that of the rest of Team One. That held themselves still.

"Copy, Team One holding position. Waiting for contact." Beta stated over the radio as Timmy finally noticed Beta and the rest of Team One held their weapons drawn down the city street.

Holding the handle of Astrapí until his knuckles turned white. Timmy held his breath.

"They knew we were coming." Shining growled. With Beta quick to reply.

"Possible they were just prepared but-." Devastation; uproariously erupted, trembling the totality of Sanctuary. As several explosions burst across the main entrance of the city. Shockwaves rocketing across the residential, and center districts. Warming the already tense dry air, as smoke clouds barreled down over top Team One.

Exasperated coughs filled the smoke choked air as Team One called out after the disorienting chaos.

"Team Two! What's your status!?" Beta radioed, with Nimitz staggered coughing echoing through everyone's radio

"We're okay! ... Secured... but shaken." She said through coughs and heavy breathing. "That blast nearly hit us!" She exclaimed.

"What are you seeing?" Beta asked, activating his red eyes as he retrained his sights down the now cloudy city streets.

"Multiple buildings exploded along the residential district; fires are spreading along the main entrance!" She yelled out. Timmy turned quickly and even through the thick cloud of dust he could see a raging mass of fire growing in the distance.

His heart sunk as he stepped forward unsure of what to do. "Civilians are waking up, some sound trapped! Odds are heavy casualties!" Nimitz said, Timmy now clenching his fist as he held himself back.

"Dear God, what just happened?" Raph shouted, turning back in horror to see the fire that was now consuming the residential area.

"The fuckin Crusade that's what!" Shining snarled through gritted teeth.

"Escalero knew?" Doc asked, helping up Rook who had fallen during the explosions.

"Seems likely." Reaper signed in reply to him.

"What's the move Captain we keep steady or divert to the civilians?" Rook asked, rearming himself.

"Why is that even a debate! There are children out there!" Raph yelled at Team One in disbelief. ***Snap!***

"Contact! Contact! I'm hearing Whistling!" Shining yelled out holding Raph closer to the ground. Screaming bullets fired in burst over Team One.

"Hold positions!" Beta commanded as he fell back to Shining's side. The two exchanging a subtle nod as Beta took Raph and guided him to Timmy.

"Your friend here is right. You need to save those lives. Have him show you where the tunnel leading to Salvation Plaza is." Beta said ushering Raph to Timmy's side. "Once you've secured him in the location use your abilities and transport as many people as you can." Beta said as more shots rang out, with the rest of Team One now firing back.

Betas red eyes flickered as he began to think for a second. "Your top speed recorded is well above what you would need." He muttered. "In order to avoid killing those you are going to evacuate you must remember the substantial G force of which someone can sustain. Do you know what that is?" Beta asked, staring at him more directly.

"I-I believe I heard about it... About 4- 6 G's of force?" Timmy replied hesitantly.

"If not endured for too long." Beta added. "Keep into account your velocity and acceleration, can you figure out how fast you could go from that and still have people survive?" Beta asked seemingly already knowing the answer. Showing signs of him nearly saying it.

"Uh ... let's see with an acceleration of 5 g that would equal a rate of chance in velocity of about 110 miles per hour?" Timmy said his eyes darting back and forth as he checked the math in his head.

"109 miles per hour but yes. You did that fast." Beta corrected with a look of surprise and amusement.

"Well, my dad taught me to fly spaceships at an early age." Timmy shyly smiled.

"We will continue this discussion later." Beta said placing a hand on Timmy's shoulder. "Right now, you need to save those people. Be their hero Timmy." Timmy smiled giving Beta a nod.

Pushed to a higher more amped rush of adrenaline Timmy lifted Raph over his back and positioned himself in a running stance. Focusing his mind, he cut a path down Sanctuaries winding alleyways, and photographically mapped out his route. I'll be back! and with that final shout he committed to running headfirst into a raging collapsing inferno that encapsulated the residence of Sanctuary.

Raph gasped harshly as Timmy curved and tore down corners and around bends. The sounds of his feet clashing against the ground as he kicked up clouds of dust and smoke before skidding to a slowing stop at the tunnel. Catching his breath Raph was set down by Timmy.

"What the heck?! How did you just ... how did you just do that? What did you just do?" Raph stammered, his mind struggling to comprehend Timmy's actions.

"No time I gotta go back and help those people!" Timmy said in a panic already stepping back to the city.

"Okay-okay but untie me first." Raph said, inching his back to Timmy as he held out his cable-tied hands.

Timmy stopped for a mere moment as he grabbed his knife from his pocket.

"I...uh...Well I would but...Rivers." Timmy hesitantly whispered.

"Dude, the kids, I just wanna make sure they're safe." Raph pleaded with Timmy.

"Don't...don't make me regret this... I'm only doing this because sapphire would trust you." Timmy admitted before slicing the cable-ties.

"Fair." Raph replied rubbing his freed wrists. "I'll try to get everyone who's nearby in here and have them head to the surface. You grab everyone on the far end." Raph said waving to the other side of town, before holding out his fist to Timmy.

With a smile, Timmy shouted.

"On it!" As he bumped fists with Raph. A second later, in a disorienting surge of wind, he blasted away back into the wall of smoke and fire. Unseen through his first trek across the bombarded cityscape Timmy now watched in horror a city smoldering and suffocating. Desperately clinging to life. Its occupants crying out in heart crippling, soul tearing fashion, that buried Timmy under a mountain of guilt. Mere seconds passed as he thought of who to save first, who deserved to be rescued more.

How could such a question be asked? He thought to himself as he pulled at his hair. Debilitated, over encumbered by the decisions he could make. His survivor's guilt had plagued him once again and this time it festered to a boiling calamitous high. Nothing could quite take his breath away such as the shackling imprisonment of his guilt. Clinching his chest tightly he sucked in the smothering smoke and dust that filled the air.

Wheezing in barely uttered breath. "No..." He muttered defiantly. "I won't let you scare me... not this time. You won't stop me from saving these people!" Timmy shouted, tightening his fists as he fought off his guilt and fear. Arching his feet as he steadied his breathing, before the flowing waters of the Styx rushed beside him. Casting him away as he broke forward into a full force sprint. Rushing back into the city center. People ran past, carrying what they could as they avoided their torched homes.

Timmy snatched them best he could and vanished with them before reappearing in a wild blitz as he took crowds of families and individuals to the tunnel entrance. The groups gasped with strained eyes as they exited the choking air and blistering heat as Raph waved them to safety. Running through the blazing city Timmy skid along the harsh brick pavement, the soles of his shoes began to buckle and tear beneath the stress of every extraordinary bound of his blurry, swerving, burst of speed. Matched with equally discombobulating concussive blasts of sound during every imminent stop as he scooped up two more into his arms. Holding them firmly as he ducked and cracked across the pavement back to the tunnel's entrance.

Buildings began to deteriorate crumbling from the explosions. Broken glass from shattered windows, littered the streets. Which scratched and sliced at Timmy's now exposed feet, and yet still he muscled through. Gritting his teeth as he endured, not for himself but for all those in Sanctuary who needed him. Even though he was compiled with such pressure, he pushed on adamant on only one thing. Saving as many lives as he could and no matter the cost. Support beams that nearly trampled running pedestrians, were blown back as Timmy slammed into them, burning his own body in the process to protect the fleeting innocent.

A child nearly crushed by a burning lamp post that had begun to fall, saved just barely in time as Timmy slid over top them. Using his back to carry most of the fall. He winced from the pain and the boiling heat of the metal light post as he slowly pushed the young child away with all his might. Once seeing the child safely swept away by passerby's he rolled himself out from under the scorched post rising intently to his feet. "Biscuit!" He shouted, remembering his creature that had been so loyally stationary, hardly moving from where he had been placed on his back.

"Are you OK?" He asked it, slowly rubbing the creature on his back. To which it affectionately hummed in response. "I almost forgot you were back there." He smiled softly, wiping dust and ash from his face. "I'm glad I'm not alone in this." He said, looking back slightly as he patted the creature. Suddenly snatching Timmy's attention, a lone desperate scream drove him back to his current situation. "Hello?" Timmy called out. Intensively he stared his eyes, hoping to see anyone in the sickeningly hazy air. Yet nothing, nothing could be heard in the now desolate city. Aside from the crumbling infrastructure, and the fire that raged across the residential side of the cityscape.

"Help!" Again, he heard that feminine hapless screech that pleaded in A carrying echo.

"Where are you! Keep screaming, keep making noise so I can find you!" Timmy yelled back franticly as he held his breath and listened tentatively Relying on a great deal of effort to not let the burning city drown out the stranger's helpless call. But it had fallen silent, sent into a panick, Timmy tried several homes where he believed he heard the cry for help. Trying locked doors, banging on walls, and attempting to open entrances buried in rubble only to be met with more of the same. Emptiness. Until reaching single house already taken nearly completely by the fire.

The entire roof charred black under the fanning flames. Timmy ran to it hoping more than anything that he was not too late. Billows of smoke rolled upwards from the open windows. And his heart sank as he attempted the door, the handle scolding his hand which flashed his mind to that fateful day. He froze, staring at his slightly marred hand and for a brief second in that sweltering underground city he swore he could feel a cold drizzle of rain. Hacking coughs snapped his attention to the left side of the building. "Hello !?" He screamed once again. Running over, he squinted his eyes trying to peer into the cloudy house through an open window. Coughing a bit himself as he pushed himself closer into the smoke.

Without warning jutting through the smoke were extended arms that nearly swiped across Timmy face with him ducking narrowly avoid it.

"Please take her... take my baby!" The voice pleaded. Too stunned to speak, little could prepare Timmy for what was at the end of those arms, a small barely breathing infant child. Reactively his hands stretched outward for the baby, and as his mind rattled with countless questions. His empathic heart knew better of what to do.

Making his body react necessarily in securing the child. "Thank you! thank you! Oh God thank you" The mother cried.

"Is it just you in there?" Timmy managed to utter.

"My husband he's in here too, but he got hit by a falling light fixture! I thank God he's still breathing though." The woman spoke through heavy coughs. "The front door is blocked... Please just get my baby out of here!" She whimpered. Timmy swaddled the infant holding it closely to his Chest. It pained him to hear such desperate acceptance.

A mother fully realizing her situation, and already condemning herself to this fate. Solely caring for the betterment of her child, and nothing more; thoughtlessly without a moment's notice. Timmy called for the mother saying

"I will be back! I will come back for the both of you!" Before vacating to the tunnel. His pace was significantly slower pacing his steps more carefully. His feet finally beginning to sting from their exposure to the strewn about debris.

He however held a smile after finally hearing the baby's coughing stop and turn to a soft cry. He had known that she was at least stable from that. Loud heavy slow steps slammed on the ground as he braked himself just before Raph.

"Oh Christ... is that a baby!" Raph exasperatedly said with outstretched arms, taking the child from Timmy and checking it over. With a nearby female offering her aid handling the infant.

In a frantic rush Timmy's body snapped back to the burning city.

"It's parents! I... there's no time! I gotta go back!" Timmy said, rushing off hardly hearing Raph's call to join him. Returning to the home, Timmy noticed its roof had now collapsed inward. Peeling back around to the open window he called out for the woman. This time she had managed to break out the window glass, but the opening was still too small for her, let alone her unconscious husband, to fit through. "Miss are you in there!" Timmy called out.

Coughing surged through the opening as the lady came to the window and looked through, covering her mouth her shirt.

"Your back? How did you get back so fast? Is my baby safe?" She asked through shortened breath.

"She is, but I gotta get you two. Let me try and get the window." He said grabbing an edge and yanking as best he could, attempting to pry off the framing.

Each pull was met with little to no give. Every inch of leverage and angle tried was futile. The clouds of smoke mockingly growing with the flames crashing louder beside them.

"Honey please look at me... What is your name?" The woman asked and yet Timmy ignored her dedicated only to freeing them. "Honey please... Look at me." She pleaded and in Timmys frustration sliced the palm of his hand on a broken shard of glass from the window.

He growled as he held his hand shaking it around as he winced. Gently reaching through, the woman grabbed Timmy's hand. Holding it softly and in such a lovingly motherly tone, called again for him to speak his name. With watery eyes, he looked back at the woman who he now noticed had strikingly resembled his late mother. And in a moment of weakness and self-contempt, he responded with the last thing he ever heard his own mother speak.

"Timothy." He choked through gushing tears.

The woman smiled.

"Oh, bless you Timothy, you're just a boy, and yet you're here. What a hero. Please Timothy, forget us. Please... save yourself." It dug. Crawling into a festering black pot of demolished dreams. Dreams of happiness, love, or family. And it scorched it to ashes. Burning the roots of his heart until all that could be felt were the flames. He crumbled to the ground.

Screaming out he tearfully grit his teeth and with reckless abandon slipped free of the woman's grasp. Like a force of nature, he enveloped the house in a spiraling gust of wind as he slashed and pushed and kicked every inch that he could connect with. The door. He thought it had to have been his best chance. Looking at the handle he aggressively stomped at it repeatedly snapping it off its placement.

Pushing against the ember engulfed door, he winced. The charred splintering pieces burning his hands and arms. Ignoring the blistering heat, he continued. Smashing himself feverishly into the door, budging it ever so slightly. Reaching deep within his will to continue. Once again, he glowed that angelic gold and porcelain white, and as he stepped back, he drove himself rapidly into the door. Pieces of burning paint branding his skin as he defiantly chanted.

"I... will ... save you!" He screamed at the top of his lungs.

Winding back one final time before bursting through, launching himself across their homestead and bashing across a wall indenting himself into it. It cracked crumbling as he fell limply to the ground. The mother screaming from the loud blast of speed Timmy had produced. Running into the room she gasped through heavy coughing as she looked on at Timmy's smothered-in-ashes face, tied with his deeply scarred feet and arms. Pushing weakly up from the ground, Timmy could only manage to slightly raise his body. Still slumped on his hands and knees, he weakly pointed to the door. "Go, go quickly it's open n-now" He mumbled through exasperated pants, before falling limp and fainting.

Shaking violently, he forced his eyes open, scanning around to notice he was now amidst the other survivors. In a panicked jolt he shot up looking about at his sudden change. "The family! The mom and dad!" Timmy shouted. Rushing to his side, Raph dropped beside Timmy on his knees.

"Whoa kiddo, slow... slow. They're safe. Everyone here is, thanks to you." He said calming Timmy as he helped him sit up.

Pushing past the crowd, a man walked up to Timmy. Cautiously Timmy eyed him, noticing he wore a bled through bandage on his head as the man reached out and shook his hand. 'The father!' Timmy thought to himself. Noticing in his other arm his now sleeping baby girl, with the mother now walking up beside him.

"Thank you, son. I don't know how you did that. But you saved my family's life." The father said with a smile, as he wrapped his arm around the mother. "Words can't say how grateful I am...What's your name son?" The father happily asked.

Bashfully Timmy smiled back at a loss for words, having never expected words of gratitude for his actions.

"Uh it's..." He tried to mutter his name but stammered in his mixture of emotions.

"It's Timothy honey. His name is Timothy." The mother said with a smile, as she ran over to Timmy. Kissing him repeatedly on the cheek as she thanked him profusely.

Warmly she hugged him, looking gratefully into his eyes. "Your parents must be so proud to have such a brave young man, they raised a hero!" She spoke. Tears filled his eyes as a shiver crossed his body.

"I ..." Timmy stammered for a second. "Thank you. I would hope that I'm making them proud." He smiled, with prideful tears, streaking down his cheeks. Thanking him once again the family then followed the others leaving Sanctuary for Last Salvation Plaza.

Looking about the tunnel, he saw the shambling and aching people. Weeping for their loss of homes and loved ones. Timmy growled at this, cursing Escalero's name.

"You really think that one guy did all this?" Raph asked.

"Not alone...but he's the one in charge." Timmy said, looking at Raph. "That's why me and the others ... Captain Rivers!" The entire time Timmy had been saving the city residents, he had distracted himself from the whereabouts of Nomadic 5.

Pulling his earpiece to his ear he called out over his communication device. "Rivers? Team One? Are you there?" Timmy said. Static was all that met him. Stepping back and forth in a rising panic he called again. "Captain Rivers! is anyone there?" He shouted over the radio.

"Copy, go for Team Two is that you Timmy? This is Nimitz. What's your status?" She replied, her voice sounding quick and tense.

"I'm okay I saved as many as I could." Timmy said, with a heavy heart. Still happy to hear Nimitz's voice.

"Thank God, I thought you were dead. Hold your position there." Nimitz said, shots audibly cracking over the radio.

"What? Why here don't we need to get to Escalero and the Final Crusade? Where's Rivers?" Timmy worriedly asked.

"We tried to regroup around the city center, but we've been ambushed. We have Final Crusade and Escalero's mercenaries engaging on multiple fronts." Nimitz said frustratedly. The gunfire sounding increasingly louder as she continued. "The plan is to retreat and wait for Omega 1 to help bolster our offensive, then regroup with Team One." Nimitz said as she yelled for her squad members to take cover.

"They could die before Jason even gets here!" Timmy yelled back.

"This is our only choice, Timmy. Hold your position and wait for us to retreat." Nimitz ordered explosions echoing through the radio and in the distance as Timmy looked to the city center beneath the moon.

Taking a deep breath Timmy sat down on the tunnel floor. Slowly working on removing his tattered shoes. Getting back to his feet, he held his amateurish running stance. Visualizing his route back to where he left Team One until, in a blinding flurry, he rocketed across the city scape once again. Reaching about a mile away he could see the slightest outline of Team Two. More importantly noticing two cladded in armor Crusaders, flanking them readying their swings before two members of Team Two.

Forcing himself to move faster and bracing his calf muscles he leaned his body forward and giving one last sturdy step forward he lunged. Spiraling his body and cracking himself like a whip using Astrapi as an extension of his body. In a fraction of a second, he spun clockwise connecting his foot with one of The Crusaders and Astrapi against the other. Both men flying back from the residual energy of speed, as Timmy stood before one of the members of team two.

"Deshawn lookout!" Queenie had shouted to X-ray before comprehending that Timmy had secured their flank.

"Jesus! Blink and you fuckin miss him! Good shit kid!" X-ray said swapping his gun to his other hand, as he offered a fist bump to Timmy, who excitedly replied with a fist bump of his own. Cheerful tones however were quickly hidden as Nimitz marched over to Timmy with Xray rearming himself and joining the rest of Team Two holding position a few feet away.

Nervously Timmy forced himself to keep eye contact with the equal in stature yet tremendously more imposing woman.

"I gave you fucking orders!" She snapped. Readying himself to defend his action. He was instead met with a gentle hand on his shoulder however with Nimitz saying. "But...good work. Team One's location isn't too far away...but you can make that time in seconds." Nimitz said pulling Timmy down to her eye level as she pointed at the path ahead. "Run ahead, past the soldiers down there, and regroup with them." She said, a look of hesitance holding her words for a moment before adding in. "There are at least five Nobles between us and Team One." She said gravely as she looked over Timmy's face.

To her surprise Timmy still seemed determined. Weather ignorance or confidence she couldn't tell. Regardless of the reason she finally began to acknowledge the potential of Betas High Value assets, of the crew he plans to create. "Hmm...well kid, if you got it in you, try and use that sonic boom that you did at the base. That might take care of them. Or knock them down long enough for us to take care of them." She said.

"What about the other enemies?" Timmy asked noticing a much larger group of Escalero's mercenaries.

"They're no issue. The Nobles are the only thing to worry about." She redirected, pointing a finger into his chest.

Giving a quick stretch Timmy nodded his head to Nimitz.

"Okay, Got it. Get the guys with the shiny red and white gear." He said giving Nimitz a smile.

"On your go Timmy... Team Two be ready for covering fire." She said, returning to the front with her team. Guns drawn down the city street with the mercenaries now firing back. Taking a deep breath, he held his stance. Vanishing in a spectacular blur, as he tore through the streets. Mercenaries and Crusaders alike seeming in slow motion. Even the bullets that were soaring past Timmy, were visible and even slow to him.

The more he looked at them, the slower they got. And for a brief second, he became entranced by it all. The waves of the Styx crashing wildly across the buildings in Sanctuary, with the world itself seemingly phased between a fusion of the golden branches of the Styx, and the battlefield that raged before him. His mind felt folded, strained, and constricted. As it tried to make sense of both realities at the same time. He felt almost at home, but still not himself. Almost as if he was another person entirely. Braising across his arm, a bullet still having its kinetic energy, managed to slowly peel back on Timmy's flesh.

Wincing harshly, he jerked away from the bullet. Realizing that his mind was shifting between both realities. He shook his head, forcing it to focus on only the world he had his feet firmly planted in, as he rushed forward. Yet still he could hear the loud ambiance of the Styx and the creatures in their flowing waters. He strained his mind, focusing all that he could to not be swept away in its loud boisterous melody.

And indeed, although it had felt like minutes passed only a few seconds had transpired as he reappeared before the marching fortuitous Nobles. Ranting and raving a number of things as they instantly unsheathed their swords, startled by Timmy's sudden appearance.

"Heresy!" One Noble shouted.

"Demonic bewitchment!" Screamed another.

"Further proof that this world needs a cleansing fire of blood!" They all chanted, as one lunged outward swiping at Timmy with their sword.

Timmy evaded, vanishing before them and in a tremendous, advantageous, blast of energy, he recreated a sonic boom once again. Blasting back two of the Nobles that stood behind the other three. The two flung back, smashing into nearby buildings, and through windows. One of the Nobles which held a type of crossbow weapon in hand, shot at Timmy. With its scolding red hot iron rods setting fire to the surroundings that it had plunged into.

As Timmy dodged them each in rapid succession, he slid over to the last three Nobles, as he took Astrapi from his belt and wrapped it around the crossbow wielding Noble. Flinging them as hard as he could using his speed to send the much larger man flailing across the street. Spinning back, he tore into another burst of speed, launching the last two Nobles into the building behind them. Their swords flying from their hands as they crashed through the brick style buildings.

Taking a quick breath Timmy radioed back to team two. "Nimitz?" An annoying sigh suddenly came over the radio.

"I have got to teach you proper protocol because it's getting to me now." She said, holding her tongue, as she continued. "Report in. How's dealing with the nobles?" She asked, with Timmy looking around at all the winded and unconscious Nobles half smashed into nearby buildings.

"They're all knocked out from what I can tell." He said sheepishly wincing at their pain.

"Good work, keep moving to Team One. We'll regroup when we can." She replied.

"On it!" Timmy shouted through the radio before turning to face the city center.

He could hear the fierce gun fight in the distance. And as he took off in its direction, he hoped the others had managed well. Slipping down the street toward Team One, Timmy was shocked to notice a cavalcade of bodies gunned down. Men holding the branding of the Final Crusade and countless mercenaries.

Distracted by the massacre at his feet, he barely had time in his swift advance, to narrowly avoid a barrage of bullets. The street cracking, as the brick lined pavement uprooted from the ground, as Timmy turned himself and dodged its lethal connection. Slamming himself into a building he was faced by the barrel of a gun. Freezing up time slowed to an almost complete stop as he noticed holding the gun was none other than Shining.

"Cazzo kid! I thought they had a tank rolling down! I was about to lob this explosive at your feet, get over here." He said through winded breath as he helped Timmy to his feet. "I'm glad you managed to stop...any further in those landmines we planted in the streets would have blasted your ass into little meat chunks." Timmy simply gulped as he fallowed Shining through a storage room that had a whole in it that lead to an office room.

A dead Noble draped across the improvised entrance to the office a large gaping wound clearly visible in his back.

"Shining is that you I didn't hear the explosion. Do you need another charge?" Rook worriedly yelled before noticing Timmy being walked in beside Shining. "Timmy? wait did you breakdown the tank?" Rook exclaimed, shocked to see him back so soon.

"No, he was the tank!" Shining said pointing back to Timmy.

"I don't think any man is strong enough to take down a tank with his hands." Doc said from the corner of the room as he sorted supplies.

"It could be possible; Timmy shredded that gun with his hands from what Rivers said." Rook retorted. "Well...he said that Timmy said he disassembled the gun, but I still think it's possible." Rook added in. Clinging her gun on the ground Reaper pulled all their attention.

Standing in the doorway behind Doc and Rook she signed to the group, making it clear that another envoy of mercenaries and Crusade we're making their way through the office corridors.

"Fuck! They must have noticed us planning out those mines after all." Shining growled under his breath. Looking beside him, he wrapped an arm around Timmy as the too made their way next to Reaper.

"Well, I suppose you showed up on a good timing." Shining said with a sigh. "We were trying to hold position here, long enough for Team Two to regroup, and help us get over to Beta" Shining said with Timmy shocked by the sudden realization that Beta was not with them. Timmy looked around in vain as he worried for Beta. "They separated us in the beginning, was a big old ambush... it's as if they knew that they needed to separate him." Shining snarled as he clenched his fist.

Looking over to Reaper, Shining unclenched his fist as she ushered for him to calm himself. "Carolina did send a drone out, and they can't find him luckily." Shining said exhaling heavily. "With you here now, we might get a good window... or you could at least get to him and make it so the two of you can retreat back to us." Shining said, as Timmy nodded his head and cracked his neck loosening his body as he readied himself for another sprint into combat.

"That sounds easy enough." Timmy replied with a smile.

"Should be, but we have soldiers constantly coming from where Captain Rivers was moving... If you can help us handle this little scout right here, we should be able to move up together actually." He replied, lifting his mask and scratching his scarred chin.

"Are you sure Captain Rivers is still, okay? ...what if they got to him?" Timmy worriedly asked.

"Oh no, we'd be hearing a lot of their screaming before they took out our Captain." Shining said, a heavy smirk grinning through his skull mask. Echoing across the city shots started rapidly popping off. "Aw those poor fuckers, they found him." Shining said raising his rifle as he shook his head.

"Well...looks like we're gonna jump to the first plan. Reaper we're gonna need you to clear him a path! The rest of us get ready to clean up Reaper's mess!" Shining ordered, as he motioned for the rest of Team One to get back and line the walls of the office room. "Once you get over to him you be ready for a fight. You have to stick it in till you drop, or you drag your asses back." Shining said to Timmy. standing in the center of the office room Timmy shook his body as he prepared himself. "Are you ready Mr. green?" Shining asked.

"I'm ready!" Timmy shouted back and reply.

"Fuckin right you are! Alright then, ladies first!" Shining said. Tilting down the corridor of the building Reaper move forward pistol in hand before switching to her much larger sniper rifle.

A 50 caliber BMG, to which she angled out in the doorway. Holding a firm stance, she unloaded multiple rounds, rapidly scattering the walls, as a rushing horde of Crusaders suddenly turned into a blender of flesh and blood. A hallway from hell was what she left behind as she then laid flat in the corridor propping up her bipod. Waiting about a minute before two more mercenaries peaked from doorways, with her quickly firing on either side of the corridor and effortlessly shooting both in the head. The high caliber vaporizing their heads instantaneously.

"Now!" Shining shouted and with an even louder and more ferocious shockwave, Timmy ripped down the corridor and out the office building. Leaping into a neighboring building running down its warehouse scaffolding and zig-zagging around the resounding enemy numbers. Timmy left the building as he slipped in a tip toe fashion across the city street and into a nearby alleyway. Perking his ears, he stopped for a minute, hiding behind a trashcan. Listening deeply as he tried to pinpoint the exact location of Beta. Popping bursts of sound rattled again in the distance, echoing off across the city. *"Left... behind me... he doesn't seem to be getting farther..."* He thought to himself, as he opened his now shining golden eyes, springing around and running down the rest of the alley.

Turning left down a similar back alley until, with wide eyes, he was met with twenty Crusaders cladded in a dirtier silver armor looking much more medieval to their clean and glistening counter parts of the Nobles. Unable to stop in time, Timmy collided into them tumbling along with several of the men. All of which groaned and barked angrily. Front members even drawing their swords and crossbows. Spotting him one of the crossbow welding men shouted for him as Timmy slipped back over top a guard, marginally avoiding a bolt that in turn impaled their comrade. Leaving Timmy panicked and surrounded completely, as the men reached for him.

Pulling out Astrapi in his frantic push back, Timmy inadvertently pressed down a button on the tool, extending it from its hilt causing it to hold stationary into the two brick walls that made up the back alley. Consequentially knocking out two men who had been on either side of him. pulling himself up onto Astrapi just as a Crusader dove for his legs. Timmy balanced himself kicking at the charging men. Out maneuvering their swinging swords with his burred speed. Managing to space himself from the others for just a second.

He crouched down on Astrapi pressing the same button he used to extend it. Luckily, it began retracting as opposed to needing to be compressed manually. Thinking fast and spotting a small catwalk connecting the second floor of the two back-alley walls, Timmy spun Astrapi tossing it up onto the catwalk grappling himself quickly up to it as the Crusaders chased after him. Vaulting the railing of the catwalk Timmy rushed ahead as red-hot metal rods struck through the catwalk just behind him.

Gunshots suddenly rang more clearly as he now jumped over smaller building rooftops the edge of the city clear in view. And there a mile away holding ground amidst a scrap heap of a junkyard was Beta mountains of bodies at his side wrestled with more charging Crusaders. The red eyes dancing as his body swayed around them. A perfect killing machine absolute in every designated shot he made.

All of which being headshots, leaving no missed rounds, no margin for error. Timmy ran as fast as he could but even as he almost reached his compatriot he wondered if he even needed his assistance. That is when from the shadows a Noble emerged unnoticed by Betas methodical onslaught.

"No!" Timmy screamed, and like a rushing tsunami crashing across a shoreline, he bolted into the Noble his concussive speed blasting him into the junkyard building at Betas back. Turning back, he was met with Betas handgun pointed squarely at his face.

"Interesting you have gotten faster already...Where are your shoes?" Beta said lowering his gun to a crawling mercenary, before shooting him. Timmy jerked from the sound giving a sheepish smile to Beta.

"Long story... looks like you didn't need me." Timmy shrugged.

"Help is always welcomed, especially from a ... decent fighter." Giving glorious war cries, more Crusaders entered the junkyard. "I trust you are ready for a fight?" Beta said, reloading his rifle.

"I hope you can keep up!" Timmy replied with a wink.

Whipping around Beta, Timmy hurled himself bashing Astrapi into the rows of Crusaders that charge forward. rhythm building between the two warriors. One worn but experienced and the other amateurish but nuanced. Betas precise and methodical actions mixed with Timmys brash and spontaneous movements. The two forging a hyper lethal effectiveness completely unbeknownst to one another. The two molded into a motion of harsh and unforgiving combat that was both concise and unified.

Separated from blood each fallen foe gave the other an inkling of respect for their counterpart morphing their infant collaboration into a solidified bond as brothers. A bond about to be severed as quickly as it formed. Like a predator stalking its prey. A snake with disgusting yellow eyes grossly licked its lips. Slithering sinisterly as to divide the ferocious duo, Escalero's metallic tendril like fingers raked down the building that met the backs of the two men.

Decrepitly coiling around Timmy's neck hoisting him from the ground and pulling him on top of the buildings shambled metal roof. Beta turned in a panic as he cried out for Timmy pointing his gun at Escalero only to be slashed down his back by a charging Crusader. Beta recoiled grunting as the blade tore through flesh, causing the Captain to grit his teeth. Beta then gripped the stock of his gun before bashing it into the Crusaders face knocking him to the ground with a bloody broken nose. Stepping onto his chest Beta then laid two rounds into the man's body.

Swiftly followed by him backing in his previous corner as he engaged with other enemies. Jerking about on the roof Timmy flailed his arms and legs is he tried to scramble free from Escalero's clutch. Escalero cackled at Timmy's struggle as he licked his slimy lips.

"I think it's time for a bit of takeout" his gravelly voice cooed. Flipping himself around Timmy shuffled his body to a standing position.

And anger flashed in his veins as once again he locked eyes with Escalero. Timmy gripped Astrapi's chain tightly as he spun his wrist. Using Astrapi to tear at the loose metal roofing causing pieces to fly at Escalero. Hissing animalistically he made his metallic tendril teeth lash out covering what parts of his body they could. The roofing sliced across his abdomen and shoulder. Screaming out in pain he released Timmy.

Free from his grip Timmy bolted towards Escalero however as he got behind Escalero, he was suddenly torn away from his speed, as he burst into a quick fit of coughing. Failing to give himself enough time to recover from being choked by Escalero's hold. In this brief moment of hesitation, Escalero turned his head to see Timmy was now behind him. Lunging at Timmy, Escalero extended his metallic tendril like teeth, thrashing them at Timmy as if they were spears. Nearly serrating his hands, as Timmy pushed back on the rooftop sliding away.

Winding Astrapí, he rocketed the Goliathan made weaponry at Escalero. With him dropping heavily to the ground as to avoid Astrapí's swipe, before sending his now retracted tendril fingers straight on at Timmy. Pulling back on Astrapí, Timmy used the heftiness of it to smash down on the worming tendrils as they inched closer. Realizing Timmy's lacking numbers of defensive weaponry Escalero extended individual tips of his fingers in a more sporadic unpredictable barrage.

Timmy knowing he could not in fact defend against so many swipes he then chose to whip Astrapí in the X like fashion forming a Semi practical barrier. Sending back each attempted strike from Escalero's tendrils. Again, the mad cannibal thought past Timmy's stratagem realizing that the pattern Timmy had made was very simple. Abusing his untrained adversaries blind spot Escalero secretively snaked one of his tendrils along the roof before striking upwards across Timmy's back.

Timmy screamed in pain and in a lapse of judgment swung back with Astrapí to deter the singular tendril. His barrier now faded Escalero struck again, digging into both of Timmy's shoulders. Screaming in pain Timmy grit his teeth as he dashed away, attempting to move behind Escalero. Not giving himself enough time to breathe with his wounds. His speed abruptly stopped as he had just made himself behind the wicked man.

And in the fraction of a second that Timmy paused to take a breath, Escalero had noticed him vanish retracting his tendrils and digging them straight down at his feet before extending them upwards in a 5-pointed direction as to cover multiple possible approaches from Timmy. Lunging back at Escalero Timmy had mere milliseconds to react as a sudden burst of tendrils nearly struck Timmy in his neck with him sliding back just in time as to only leave a minor scratch but across his Adam's apple.

Grabbing at his slightly scratched and bleeding neck, Timmy took Astrapí tightly winding it up again, before flinging it in an overhand toss yanking it downwards directly onto Escalero's position. His speed slightly fading from his worn nature however allowed the slower approach to be noticed, with Escalero quickly retracting his fingers and evaded backwards as Astrapí caved down into the roof.

Looking at the other end of Astrapí Timmy used the vine like chain as a whip, snapping it at Escalero's feet before his tendrils could deflect, sending him sliding down the roof. Running to pick up the rest of Astrapí, Timmy chased Escalero as he slid down the building stopping himself momentarily with his fingertips until Timmy rush up to him kicking him in the face causing him to flip off the roof and onto a lower floor. Before Timmy could move again though Escalero yanked him down after sending his finger tendrils back up and latching onto his leg.

Timmy slammed hard onto the concrete floor knocking the wind out of him as he instinctively shot up gasping for air. "Audacious little meal you are... So many chances to tuck tail and run back to your herd, and yet still you chuff and scamper about with me." Escalero said as he creepily grinned, as he sat up to face Timmy whilst wiping blood from his lip. "What an odd catch indeed." He said happily, as he disgustingly licked his blood off his hand. "I must thank you. For saving so much of my cattle... As I said before I hate burning my food." He said with a wicked smiled as he clashed and whipped his metallic tendrils.

Blood boiled through Timmy's aching body that pulsed in waves of pain. Taking a deep anger filled breath, he spoke not a word to Escalero instead sending Astrapi like a screaming head on at Escalero. At the same time Escalero had dug his tendrils into a nearby cinderblock tossing it upwards, the force just barely enough to alter Astrapí's trajectory upwards. Causing it to lodging itself into the roof they had just slid off. Timmy's eyes widened, and in a quick jolt of panic wound the chain around his hands desperately trying to pull Astrapí down off the roof and on to Escalero.

Astrapí however wouldn't budge. Stuck in the hole it had created when clashing on into the roof. Panic growing with every second Timmy did not have Astrapi by his side he began to feverishly pull on the chain with it still barely budging. Escalero mockingly laughed as playfully sidestepped out from under Astrapí. Making sure not to give Escalero a chance to retaliate, Timmy spun the back half of Astrapí striking the chain across the gap between himself and Escalero. With Escalero continuing to sidestep away as he deflected Astrapí's chain with his tendrils. Retreating enough for Timmy to gain the leverage needed in order to break Astrapí from the roof. Taking note of Escalero's ability to read and recall Timmy's prior moves. Timmy devised an idea of chaotic offense.

Swinging Astrapí counterclockwise Timmy then swung the tool up into an overhead toss. Slowing time as he did, focusing intently on Escalero. Watching every reactive queue that was sent across his body. Sure enough, Escalero followed Astrapi's movement upward. Falling for the bait Timmy then yanked Astrapí back down. Mustering all of the speed he could to swing Astrapi back, before sending it flying straight on at Escalero. The aim being slightly off however, which caused Astrapí to careen between Escalero's legs.

"Shoot." Timmy grunted. Yet, instead of pulling Astrapí back, he instead allowed with the sheer momentum of it to drag him forward sliding his own body between Escalero's legs as Timmy extended out an arm sweeping Escalero off his feet, causing his face to slam to the ground. Slowly picking himself up Escalero smiled, licking his lips once again, tasting the blood that dripped from his mouth and his nose savoring its taste as he turned to Timmy ready to taunt him again.

Only to be met with a downward drafting vortex from a cyclone of surging energy. As Timmy began twirling Astrapí over his head In such a quick succession that it mirrored helicopter blades. Without a moment of hesitation Timmy planted his feet firmly and swiped Astrapí into Escalero's back sending him flying through a neighboring building beside them. Escalero's body falling through the warehouse styled building. Loudly clingang metal and broken glass echoing in the building and yet after a brief and subtle grunt of pain, it suddenly became quiet.

Stepping up to the hole and looking down at the perpetual darkness, Timmy looked back wondering if he should wait. Taking a deep sigh, he instead faced the darkness, as he stepped inside. Watching his step as he made his way down a rickety metal scaffolding on the edge of the building. He became entrenched in the warehouse's darkness. With only one source of light that barely dimmed the area, being that of the hole Timmy had created when slamming Escalero into the building. Thinking about his surroundings Timmy instantly regretted his decision. He felt as if he was a young rabbit who had ventured into a snake hole.

Understanding far too late that he blinded himself willingly while Escolero given his aura sensing abilities was now at the peak of his advantage. Trying to step away and to possibly retreat up the scaffolding Timmy was suddenly reminded again of his current lack of preparedness and equipment, as he stepped back into a shard of glass. "Ah!" He yelped as he grabbed the foot that had the piece of glass embedded in. Biting his tongue, he tried desperately to muffle his wince but was sure more than anything that Escalero was already mockingly watching. Timmy knew he handed himself so easily to Escalero on a variety of occasions.

Timmy understood this, but what he couldn't make out was why. *"Why he hadn't taken advantage of this fact. Did he truly see himself as a predator taunting his prey?"* Timmy questioned to himself. Sitting down he pulled his knife from its sheath and with his fingers pressing against his heel he slowly popped the glass shard from his foot. A tear slipping from his eye as Timmy gnashed his teeth together tossing the shard aside. Putting back his knife he stumbled for the button he accidentally pressed earlier on Astrapí. Extending it once again as he used the tool to help himself up. Hobbling over to a barely visible support beam beside him he then activated a flashlight on his vest. Hoping to illuminate a bit more of the big warehouse. Yet it could barely cut through even the thinnest parts of this shadowy premise.

Anxiously Timmy hobbled forward using Astrapí to hold himself up. Each step focused on being both deliberate and intrepid. Stepping into the darker areas of the warehouse Timmy could not help but be overly alert to every creek, or electronic buzz. To the fact that Escalero was nowhere to be seen, and once again he felt like he did on that fateful day where his family was murdered, ***hunted***. Sparks suddenly traced along one of the walls of the warehouse. Jolting Timmy's heart whipping around only for the light to illuminate nothing but the scratch marks on the metal warehouse walls.

Swiping past, one of Escalero's tendrils sliced at Timmy's light now allowing for the both of them to be enveloped in darkness.

"How very interesting..." Escalero's said, his echoing haunting voice gutting Timmy as he froze in place. Timmy scrambling to retract Astrapí to its smaller size. "I've started to spot something... peculiar... about you boy." His voice berating Timmy from all directions as he continued to scrape along the warehouse walls. "You cut your foot mere moments ago... and yet it appears that 6 feet away from us is where the bleeding stopped." He said curiously.

Timmy tried to focus in, to gather from what direction Escalero had been talking but he could not through the echoing and the loud reactive activation of the Styx which shook in waves around him. "And when I struck you in the shoulder and slashed at your back. Those two have healed have they not?" Escalero asked, the question confusing Timmy as he frantically looked for Escalero. "Don't say a word I can taste your aura. Mmm. What is it I have found?" Escalero said an unsettling cheerfulness exuding from his tone. "The Holy Grail? The Ark of the Covenant? The Garden of Eden? Oh, I could not tell what the Lord our new Messiah had told on to me!" Escalero chanted a crazed fever shaking his voice as he quickly spoke.

"Truly I thought him taking me from that countryside was a blessing enough! Truly I did not understand the words he spoke when he told me I would never grow hungry again! Truly he must have seen what would come to be!" Escalero began to shout, hardly allowing for a breath of air as he ranted. "That I would be gifted a most wonderful blessing! No longer shall I worry about cattle, for with you! I have an endless bounty of food!" He maniacally cackled before bursting into a fit of sheer insane uncontrollable laughter.

Chills struck like icicles that pierced into Timmy's flesh as he could feel the damp vile cloud of breath from Escalero breathing down his neck. With golden eyes and a mixture of fury and fear. Timmy spun back with all that he could muster and swung Astrapí straight on. ***Clang!*** Was all that could be heard before that of a loud thud with Astrapí dropping to the ground. The clang reverberated hammering on either side of Timmy's head making him wince from the audio overload. Suddenly from the direction where Timmy had swung Astrapí, came the sound of loud mechanical motors that stretched and whirled, compressing and decompressing. The lights of a particular cockpit flashing over the entire warehouse. Standing before it, Timmy couldn't help but feel like a man with a slingshot going up against a giant. Timmy had found it, what both Nomadic 5 and Omega 1 had been looking for.

The thing they were worried would be in the wrong hands. Something primarily used against the Titans that fought in the Galaxy wide war. And here it stood like a mountainous avalanche primed to bury Timmy alive. Dragging Astrapí back to his side Timmy hooked it onto his belt loop turning to the entrance that he had come through and ran to it. Charging up to the scaffolding he was impeded by a laser that shot out from project David. Slicing across the roofing of the warehouse causing it to collapse in on the hole he had entered from, cutting off his best chance to escape the warehouse.

From the outside looking in lasers and loud blasts rocketed across the shaking building. The beam slicing through nearby buildings and hitting even the foundation of Sanctuary. Using his speed Timmy was fairly effective in keeping a distance from project David. Though with the sporadic firing of its grenade launcher attachment it had boxed Timmy in, with nowhere left to go Timmy unhooked Astrapí swinging it through a garage bay door of the warehouse. The hole just barely open enough for Timmy to leap through.

Now in a new environment Timmy scoped the scene. Surprising himself that he was at one of the back entrances of Sanctuary. Around him was an entire construction yard with support beams littering the area. It was the tunnel system, specifically the one meant to connect Sanctuary directly to the city above, and sure enough, as Timmy looked farther down the tunnel. He could see light peeking into Sanctuary from an existing highway. One of which had been closed off for many years. Timmy had no time however to devise a plan as project David stormed through the garage bay door as it barreled down on him. Quickly winding up Astrapí Timmy grappled himself away. Hooking it around nearby scaffolding as to pull himself farther beyond the behemoth's outreach.

Lasers and grenades again started to fly across the highway system, with dirt and debris from the roof of the tunnel starting to fall on top of Timmy with him hurtling out of the way. Flipping, vaulting, and swerving over and under the loose concrete, scattered rebar, and vacant machinery. A blast from a grenade snapping against a nearby support beam causing it to buckle and bend just out of place as to hit Timmy in the shoulder knocking him to the ground. His arm falling numb instantly as Timmy stumbled stifling the pain best he could as he began to panic.

He could not take on such threats alone. He was a fool to continue taking on Escalero. He felt like a fool to even be here, and now he would die alone in a forgotten tunnel system under a forgotten city. Blasting at Timmy's feet a sudden shockwave propelled him forward. Sending him flying into a nearby support beam and out into the broadness of daylight. His eyes burning from the sudden exposure, as he gasped for air.

Managing what little speed he could he rolled away from a single strike of project David's laser, as the pilot had maneuvered his Mech to hovering just over Timmy. Looking beside himself Timmy panted heavily as he saw the scorched ground from where the laser had nearly sliced off his head. Timmy barely having regained and regulated his breathing, as a foot from the Mech stomped down onto his chest. His body locking in place as pain encompassed his body. The air being exerted from his lungs, being compressed in his chest as Timmy spat up blood.

Tears filled his eyes and yet he could no longer cry. Standing up Timmy began to move away from the Mech. His bones feeling shattered, ribs being cracked, his body now covered in bruises. The Noble that piloted the Mech now laughing through his cockpit, as he questioned out loud at how Timmy was still alive let alone how he could continue to stand. Saying this, the pilot then used project David to kick Timmy down sending him face first. Timmy could not move again laying there soaked in blood and tears he wondered why he was still alive years after his family's death. Wondering why he lived this long only to die like this. Wondering if he would at least see his family again.

And as the Mech once again raised his foot Timmy felt a shaking tremble in the ground, as the weight of project David had begun to destabilize the decade old tunnel with the highway dipping in, beginning to collapse. The pilot quickly backed away, nearly falling into the hole it had created. Dust and rubble filled the air from being kicked up. Looking into the hole the pilot looked around for Timmy. Digging his gun into the ground pushing aside the rubble to find a body.

That is until he felt a tapping on the side of his canopy. Beside him stood Escalero who ushered him to look down the highway. About a mile down was Timmy who had ran down a catwalk that led under the highway for inspections. During the minor sinkhole in the highway Timmy had managed to navigate away from project David. Slipping down nearly the entire length of the highway and using Astrapi pulled himself back over top the highway and off the catwalk.

Once on the other end he looked back at both Escalero and project David standing by the tunnel entrance. Escalero mockingly smiling at Timmy as he waved his metalic fingers at him. Defeated, feeling more than anything that he could not take on these insurmountable odds, he pulled his slightly damaged X board off his belt clip and tossed it in front of himself unfolding it. Beginning to attach his arm control device, he fumbled with it, causing it to pinch his hand.

Again, he winced in pain, but with tears in his eyes he dialed to 7 and started to flee. As he began to reach the end of the highway, He wondered where he would go, what he would do, what the others would say. Could he really be this close to finishing Escalero and run away? Could he look at Beta, could he look at Sapphire, could he look at anyone else after running like he is. 'Maybe' He thought to himself. 'You should just run away from everything.'

Booms clashed in the sky as Thunder rolled In. The morning skies suddenly growing dark and heavy, as rain pelted Timmy. The storm having blocked the morning dawn so quickly it could give a person whiplash. Bare to the elements Timmy started to shiver as lightning webbed across the sky. He could not help but think back of that night. Of his poor brother, of his taken mother, of his defeated father. Had he known what he was up against? Could his father Andrew possibly understand the weight of what Timmy was dealing with? Would he understand why he is running? That he could not take on such odds. That he could not endure such struggles.

What would he say? *"Do you know what makes someone overcome their fear?"* Timmy heard warmly spoken to him. *"Some might say it is bravery, other's strength. But do you want to know what I believe? I believe it is hope... its hope that gives people the bravery to face their fears head on."* He swore he could hear it plain as day. But it didn't stop. It continued and it spoke to his heart, and it spoke to his mind. *"That everlasting natural desire that resides within all of humanity. The desire to seek happiness, safety, and a better tomorrow. It's our hope in those things that drives us forward."* And like a hand guiding him he stopped then in his tracks. Slowing the X-board to a steady hover as he stood in the rain and listened to his father. *"So do you know what you need to do Timothy?"* It echoed in his mind as he stared at himself in a reflecting puddle and saw his father staring back.

Turning around, Timmy dialed the acceleration back to seven, the fear washing away in the rain as a new wave crashed along. His eyes flourished with a golden divine determination. As his father's spirit cheered him on from the heavens. *"You need to find that hope. Use it to build your own strength, and bravery to stand up to any of your fears. Use it so that you never run away from what you fear, but to run at it, to overcome it!"* And with one final turn of the dial to a level of 11 Timmy drove into a new ravenous limit breaking surge of speed as he bulleted across the bridge. Back at all his hate, and all his fear. At what had taken his family from him. Back at Escalero! And for a brief moment as lightning stretched across the sky and raced Timmy along that fateful bridge.

Timmy blisteringly careened past it. Exiting from the storming side of the city he was embraced by the warming morning glow. With which his newly freed spirit cast Astrapí around one of the drawn-out arms of project David. Angling the X-board, he launched himself to the mechanized unit wrapping the entirety of Astrapí's chain along the arm before yanking it. The chain acting like blades of a saw that tore through the laser gun, sparks flying as Timmy mounted the window of the cockpit and bashed Astrapí over and over in an unrelenting momentum that pushed back the two-ton single manned tank like unit.

Even its bullet resistant cockpit window beginning to crack and splinter under Timmy's consistent barrage. With the unit eventually bending back and caving in to the highway. From behind two of Escalero's tendrils lashed out to Timmy stopping his assault and redirecting him to his true target. Hearing the mechanized movement from Escalero's fingers Timmy vanishing before they could even reach the Mech. Seeing this Escalero withdrew his tendrils, digging them again at his feet and creating his fortification.

Anticipating this attack, Timmy timed the precise moment at which Escalero would extend his tendrils holding off until after he had extended them, then using said openings within the tendrils to swiftly strike at Escalero. Swinging his bare fist across Escalero's face. Enraged, Escalero turned to where Timmy had swung extending out his teeth tendrils as to slice at Timmy's hand, but again Timmy vanished. This time behind Escalero swinging Astrapí down onto his heel, knocking the old man to his knees.

This time in a more obvious fit of pain Escalero swung back after retracting his fingers. Only to miss yet again. Another hit from Astrapí striking his stomach causing Escalero to lurch forward. Frothing at the mouth Escalero roared in pain, as his tendrils now lashed out in all directions trying desperately to swipe at his untouchable opponent. ***Clang!*** Whipping his head to the loud clang of metal to the left of him Escalero swung with all his energy sending this tendril skewering into whatever was in the distance.

"You worthless piece of meat!" Escalero screamed.

Seeing that Timmy had purposefully swung Astrapí at a metal support beam to divert Escalero's attention to the left. Where Timmy had been right beneath Escalero, and as his sickly yellow eyes gazed on to the boy who got away, he voraciously screamed sending down his tendrils. Only to be struck upwards with every fiber in Timmy's being. As Astrapí smashed into Escalero's jaw, knocking it clean from his face. Falling back onto the railing of the highway half choking, as he struggled and began to force himself to breathe through his nose.

Restrained from his claws digging too deeply into the support beams he tried to retract the motors in his back mechanism smoking as he tried amplifying his effort all for nothing. And in his frustration, swung out his nonlethal hand, not even it being able to reach Timmy anymore. And as he stood over Escalero, Timmy triumphantly declared, through panting shaky breath.

"I have... Overcome you!"

Timmy took deep breaths as he looked up and thanked the heavens and his family, with a tear drifting down his eye. Extending Astrapí, Timmy leaned on to it resting his brittle body, until rubble shifted from behind him and Timmy turned quickly winding up Astrapí as the Noble piloting project David lifted the Mech upright aiming it's still functioning grenade launcher on the boy. ***Kaboom!*** Loud blast of shrapnel and debris came flying from the machines back side. And as the machine turned, Beta rushed out of the tunnel slicing across its supports causing the leg mechanisms to buckle.

Stepping around the mechanism Beta then pointed his gun into the cockpits window and rattled 10 rounds into the Noble piloting the machine causing the Mech to drop back onto the road. Beta faced Timmy asking.

"Are you okay?"

"I am." Timmy replied happily through deep pants. "I got him." He said with a heavy smile as he pointed to Escalero.

"I see that... You did good work Timmy." Beta said as he began to speak into his communication device. "Omega 1, this is Nomadic 5, I'm transmitting my location. We're on the west side of the city near the outskirts. Targets have been secured, awaiting retrieval." After a few minutes Omega 1 began to land near them on the highway with the rest of Nomadic 5 having already secured Escalero more effectively as they loaded him into Omega 1's Scorpion. Looking off in the distance Timmy rubbed his hands together.

He had done what he had set out for, avenging his family, bringing their killer to justice. And yet there was more. So much more beyond just him, and his family. Beyond earth, wars raged, and he had the ability to possibly sway the odds for the better. "I told you before." Beta started as he stood beside Timmy, who now leaned over the highway railing. "Escalero is just a part of the Final Crusades command, and you have seen yourself how interwoven this insurrectionist group is, and how willing to fight for their cause their men are." Thoughts of the battle that had transpired flashed across Timmy's mind.

And as he mourned those lost in Sanctuary, he could not help but feel drawn to those not yet hurt or influenced by the Crusades' reach. "You have seen firsthand the damage they can bring. You did what you needed to, did what you wanted. But I will ask, and I will give you a choice once more." Beta said softly as Timmy gently patted Biscuit who still remained suctioned to his back. "With that I will bring a bit of honesty." Beta said. "This was not a sanctioned mission... I was not given permission to be here. Nor does the Alliance or the U.M.E. believe the Final Crusade is a big enough threat to indulge themselves in." All of which stunned Timmy, angered him.

Timmy, however, was overall unsurprised with the lack of attention given to the Crusade. After all it was the lack in taking his families death seriously that caused him to look for answers on his own. "Although this is a right step in showing them how serious of a threat, they can be...I need off the books help." Beta said, with Timmy feeling somewhat comforted that he was not the only one who struggled with the Crusade. "I need help I can rely on, help that can take on the big threats that the Alliance and that the U.M.E refuse to handle... as you know, I'm putting together a crew. I've done my research, and you are a piece of a much larger puzzle." Beta said, waiting for a response.

Hesitant at first Timmy nodded his head willing to at least listen to what else Beta had to say. "I am already looking into two brothers out in the states of Michigan and Illinois, I have also been hearing whispers about a man traveling along Europe saving many lives." Beta said as his red eyes flashed with him sending Timmy the full files of the other high value assets, aside from himself. "All of which having surprising abilities possibly similar to your own." The statement shocking Timmy leaving more questions than answers. What abilities did these men have? Had Beta known that he had these abilities? "I would like you to help recruit them too ...the crew. Making the only question left be... will you join me?" Beta asked, as his red eyes faded, and his stiff robotic nature melted away.

Now more than ever he seemed her Timmy had felt all those years ago when he had his family wrongfully ripped away from him. when he had no one to help him. how could he refuse?

"If there are more Escalero's out there... if there are worse out there. Then I owe it to every kid just like me, to protect them. To give them hope that someone will stand up for them. That they don't need to run away." Timmy said clenching his fist as he stood up straight, and in his head, he promised to every kid who he had not known. To every possible victim of the Final Crusade. to those troubled by the war that spanned across the Galaxy. he would do everything in his power to save them or die trying.

Looking back to Beta, with hope in his eyes, Timmy asked one final question. "I just gotta ask... what's next?" Beta leaned onto the railing and with a deep sigh. Smiled, truly and happily with this being the first step to forming his crew. He wasn't sure himself what would come in the future. And even though Timmy had such abilities and was as promising as he was. Beta still struggled too fully open up. To trust that he would not turn tail and run like he nearly did facing off against Escalero on the bridge.

Indeed, Beta had watched the entire thing, and was able to rescue Timmy at a moment's notice, but instead tested the boy. To see how truly capable, how truly ready he was. Although he performed well, Beta still chose not to delve into the much darker roots, the more hidden in the shadow's parts of the Final Crusade, of darker parts of the Galaxy spanning war. Of the emerald green and heavily armored Knight, that had been standing off in the distance. Watching intensively, learning, scouting, hunting.

Socials & Other works

www.youtube.com/@Placeholder_AoS[1]
www.instagram.com/aosofficial2023
www.tiktok.com/@placeholder_aos[2]
www.reddit.com/u/AoSOfficial

...Coming soon,
Age of Shadows: The Beta Initiative

1. **http://www.youtube.com/@Placeholder_AoS**
2. **http://www.tiktok.com/@placeholder_aos**

www.ingramcontent.com/pod-product-compliance
Lightning Source LLC
Chambersburg PA
CBHW032019140726
47988CB00017BA/136
9798227960603